SHELTER

SHELTER

Wesley Gibson

HARMONY BOOKS / NEW YORK

Published by Harmony Books, 201 East 50th Street, New York, New
York 10022. Member of the Crown Publishing Group.

Harmony and colophon are trademarks of Crown Publishers, Inc.

Manufactured in the United States of America

Library of Congress Cataloging-in-Publication Data
Gibson, Wesley.
Shelter / Wesley Gibson.—1st ed.
I. Title
PS3557.I2263S48   1992   91-43723
813'.54—dc20   CIP
ISBN 0-517-58582-0

1   3   5   7   9   10   8   6   4   2

First Edition

In memory of Janet Hobhouse—
brilliant, generous, passionate, beautiful

ACKNOWLEDGMENTS

would like to thank my mother, my sisters, Debbie and Karen, my brother, Michael, Virginia Gibson, Marti, the two Ralphs, Anne McGinnis, Karl, David, Gloria, and Tom Wingfield for their love and generosity during a lean, mean decade. I would also like to thank Edward Hower, Melanie Jackson, and Michael Pietsch for their necessary enthusiasm and intelligent advice. Finally, I would like to thank the Corporation of Yaddo, the Virginia Center for the Creative Arts, and the Cummington Community of the Arts for the luxurious gift of time.

1976

Joan went out to the porch of her new house. The neighborhood was what she had in mind when she dreamed of neighborhoods, of herself living in neighborhoods. It was a place of large silences, of trees, where smoke from cookouts would stitch the summer skies and winter snows would bleach it into a kind of perfection. Their last house, a rental, had been near the airport. Planes had rattled the windows and jerked Joan and her family awake from catnaps and the seven-layered sleeps of night. Here, roads dead-ended. The city, with its drunks scouring dumpsters for food, and its alleys, and its casual murders, was fifteen minutes away by interstate, but it seemed as far away as lands in fairy tales. On Dogwood Street the neighbors would get to know your name or what kind of gardener you were, but they wouldn't know that your father had killed himself with ten thousand bottles of whiskey in a loitering suicide of alcoholism or remember, with the tenacity of people who have nothing better to do, the day you had gotten your period and cried and thought you were dying.

The front porch was not ideal. It was poured concrete the size of a washer-dryer. A couple couldn't sit comfortably drinking iced tea on it. It wasn't for listening to crickets or guessing the neighbors' lives. Joan couldn't imagine herself waving from this porch. To anyone. Her porch was a flat rock and temporary harbor for cockeyed pamphleteers.

The porch in her mind was wooden, spacious, screened-in, painted green, lit and cooled by a ceiling fan-lamp bright enough to play canasta under, but hushed enough not to dispel the seeming mystery of night. The ideal porch was edged by a shaved row of hedge with tiny leaves and sprays of red berries. There would be metal chairs, identically green, their backs shaped like fans, and, resting in them, old friends would sip coolers while the kids played Red Light, Green Light until it was too dark to play.

Most important, and this was the whole reason for the porch, there could be a swing. Joan could mark the seasons of her life from her mother's porch swing. She'd spent a childhood listening through late-night summer storms, imagining the creak of the swing's chains as ghosts. She'd sat with dates, clandestinely holding hands while Hilly, clumsily hidden behind lace curtains, knitted in the dark. When she'd come home to introduce her husband, Kyle, and her baby, Melissa, to her mother, there had been that one moment of peace when Melissa had been inadvertently rocked to sleep on the newlywed laps, her improbably small shoes pressed into Joan's stomach, the huge black country sky shattered by stars.

Joan wanted a small-town porch without the small town. She'd thought about hanging a swing from the upstairs deck off the kitchen, but it wouldn't be the same. The view would be gloomy: her yard casually drifting into the kudzu-glazed woods and the tool shed whose door wouldn't shut because the humid summer had fattened it with moisture.

She and Kyle had bought the house because of the fireplace, because of the incense of burnt wood, because cushions could be pulled down from a couch and dragged in front of the ragged, dancing light. If a porch swing was amazing for its intimations of flight, a fireplace was hypnotizing as chaos cornered. Flames could be stared into.

4

She went back inside.

Puddled milk, dyed pale pinks and frail oranges by bright hoops of cereal, littered the table in mismatched bowls. There was the green plastic mixing bowl left over from the set won at the grocery store drawing. There was another, antique and ceramic, that had made its way from Hilly's. There was the wooden salad bowl, one of two left though Joan hadn't seen the other in she didn't know how long. Coffee cups cracked and soup spoons migrated to the large piles of dirt children had an instinct for finding, but her dishes seemed to evaporate. One day she'd have a full set of new dinner plates and one arbitrary day later she'd notice that two were missing and she was using one from the previous set and one from the set before.

Kevin drank his cereal from a large mixing cup, using his four-year-old hands to get at the last stubborn fragments. He'd snare one, mouth it from his fingers as milk trickled down his arm onto the tray of the high chair he refused to give up. Joan wasn't sure she approved.

"Do you think you could use a spoon?" she asked.

"They swim away from the spoon," he said.

She frowned. "O.K. But don't do it in front of anyone except Mommy."

He nodded, his fingers in his mouth.

Joan swirled coffee with her finger. She studied the healthy pools of milk left in the mismatched bowls strewn around the table. She'd bet she poured out a quart a week. She had considered pouring the pastel milk back into the carton—but that smacked of crazy Hilly's tactics.

Kevin slid under the tray (the yellow strap that had separated his infant legs long since broken) and sped wordlessly out of the room in search of "Sesame Street." Joan wondered briefly if television influenced the quality of childhood, but was too tired for anything more than a vague, flickering concern. Her finger was wet and cool and limp. It was eight o'clock. There was a whole day. She knew what she would find. Kyle's rumpled socks would be near the end of their bed. Melissa, fifteen and surly, would have her room in its usual state of emergency. Joan would simply close the door on the disaster. She worried that Daryl would undergo a similar transformation in a couple of years when adolescence charged through his body. In nine-year-old Brenda's room Joan would find combs neatly arranged into a sunburst on the dresser, the bed severely made, the stuffed animals a strict regiment of clean lines. Brenda was frighteningly fastidious.

Joan stuck her tongue out at the dirty bowls. Self-cleaning ovens; self-defrosting refrigerators: these were her idea of an invention.

■　　■　　■

The guinea pig's fleshy tail flicked again. That was all you could see. The rest was encased in the python's mouth. The python actually looked deader than the guinea pig. At least Daryl hoped the guinea pig was dead. He'd seen decapitated chickens run on his Aunt Lanie's farm, fresh blood matting their neck feathers, and he hoped that was the deal with the tail, that the rodent did not know it was in the snake's dark, damp, suffocating mouth. In his science book, Daryl had read about the juices the stomach squeezed out to melt down food and for weeks afterwards he'd looked at his shit and thought, I made that out of pizza . . . French fries . . . Brussels sprouts.

The pink tail flicked again. Normally, he would have found it sort of weird, but kind of great, like the chickens, their necks a bloody nub, scampering left and right, swerving here and there, like a soldier outmaneuvering bullets in a movie, as if they could outsmart death by pretending to be alive. But Daryl had owned a guinea pig named Weasel and he didn't like the idea of Weasel being digested to

death. A horrible way to go. Daryl was almost twelve, and
he didn't cry; but he could hear a sound like putting a conch
shell to your ear and his nose was stuffing up and his lips
were trembling and his face was flushing and, yes, those
were big, hot tears wetting his cheeks and splashing on the
hands gripping the cold metal bannister that kept you from
tapping on the glass. In front of his dad, too. How baby. If
you could embarrass to death, he was going to.

Kyle heard the sniffles. He hoped Daryl wasn't crying.
Kyle was bad with words and grief. Joan had wanted them
to bond, a word he was sure she'd picked up from one of
the magazines she was always reading. When Kyle was a
boy you didn't worry about bonding. You loved your father
and that was that. He didn't have to earn it. It was best to
leave him alone on weeknights, but on weekends he was
available for fun. If he wasn't drunk.

But this was the Modern Age, as Joan was quick to remind
him, and in the Modern Age you took your son by yourself
to the zoo, where pythons made meals of household pets.
Kyle knew this was about Weasel. Daryl was definitely crying. A snack seemed like an inappropriate suggestion but
Kyle couldn't think of anything else.

"What would you say to a hot dog?" he asked.

Daryl nodded yes.

"Here," Kyle said. He pulled his rumpled handkerchief
from his equally rumpled work pants and closed it over
Daryl's fist. "And keep it," he said. "A man needs a
handkerchief."

■   ■   ■

Halfway through the monthly column "Can This Marriage
Be Saved?" Joan realized there'd never been one that
couldn't be. The drama was gone for her. She drifted over
to an ad for Midol. The menstruating model looked so

doped with contented femininity that Joan decided to try some, though impatience was her only problem during menstruation. Lines irritated her especially.

The master bedroom of the new house seemed too large for her old furniture. She thought she could hear the crackle of her magazine pages echo. The walls still smelled of off-white latex and sometimes it made her dizzy or made her imagine that she was dizzy. She'd wanted to paint the room where she lived her deepest, most secret life an exotic color, but Forest Green and Sky Blue weren't that color. The color she'd wanted hadn't been invented yet. White was a compromise. It went with everything.

Kyle laughed from the living room. When he came to bed he'd retell the stories of sitcoms and miniseries, which were actually more interesting than the plots he brought home from work. But since the characters in the job anecdotes were real—paid mortgages and near-misses being the miracles of their lives—she felt obligated to care. It was self-interest, really. She hated to think someone would be bored by her life.

She tried *Cosmo*, wandered toward an article called "Pleasing Your Man (and Yourself)." After sixteen years, sex with Kyle was good, if infrequent. There was the occasional hot fuck, unnerving in its ferocity: when they had a few drinks in them; the unexpected Sunday afternoon; on a picnic table in a rest area shelter as Daryl and Brenda lay in a tangled sleep in the back of the station wagon. Still, a few pointers, new positions, unexamined erogenous zones: it couldn't hurt.

She was surprised by the number of tips that included food and disappointed that she had tried all of them except the ones she'd already dismissed as too silly, messy, or unsanitary even for an orgasm. She considered approaching Kyle, herself undulate and naked, and without a word, throwing open his robe and blowing him. His shock and gratitude would pleasure her. But Melissa would be home any second now from her date and the prospect drained the fantasy of its pleasure. It wasn't simply the interruption, the potential for embarrassment; enforced spontaneity seemed like the drab ruins of a ritual one had ceased to believe in.

She mentally scanned the refrigerator. There was leftover meat loaf. She imagined slabs of it arranged artfully across her body, but a catsup bottle in one hand and an oven mitt on the other spoiled the image. Olives? She could push out the pimentos and stuff the green casings with her nipples; bury the salty baubles in her cunt to be fished out by Kyle's large but awkwardly effective tongue. She could slip on fishnets, if only she had fishnets, but as she saw herself casting them over her legs in hopes of snaring some lost appeal, she was distracted by her real body, the one four children had passed through.

"Kyle," she called.

"What?"

"Come here."

"What for?"

"Just come here."

" 'Ironside' is on."

Could this marriage be saved?

The chair creaked under his rising body. The television clicked off. She fluffed her hair and curved herself across the bed into what she hoped was a sleek S of sexual healing.

When he entered, his robe was hanging from his hard-on.

"Yeah?" he said, pretending boredom.

She laughed.

He bobbed the robe.

"Be serious," she said, laughing again. "You are the night clerk in a motel who sneaks into my room with a pass key because he finds me irresistible. You are forceful, yet tender."

"Forceful and tender coming right up."

He turned off the light and eased his familiar weight onto the bed. He grabbed her forcefully by the hips and bit her tenderly on the neck. Even in the dark he was Kyle. She knew where the moles were, the calluses, the stray hairs. It was all there.

■   ■   ■

Melissa lay the smoldering joint on the cold windowsill and picked up her jacket. Balled-up hose, a Neil Young T-shirt, and an earring she'd given up for lost fell from it.

Melissa got through her family high. Dinner was the worst. Her father ate with concentration, as if each mouthful were a puzzle he was chewing toward solution. Her mother babbled. Daryl battled his plate, hurtling great glops into his mouth; food a dandruff in his hair, a pattern on the wall, an inadvertent arsenal. Brenda babbled. To Kevin, catsup was a paint, mashed potatoes a putty, the high chair tray a canvas or a potter's wheel. Melissa wanted her tubes tied into unbreakable knots. She was fifteen.

Her locked door rattled.

"There's such a thing as knocking," she said, rubbing the joint out on the side of the house outside the window.

"The clothes are dry," Brenda called.

"So what?"

"So Mamma says it's your turn to fold them."

"Blow me."

"What's that mean?" Brenda asked, her ignorance in its ninth year.

"Nothing."

"Mamma," Brenda yelled downstairs, "Melissa says 'Blow me.' "

"Melissa," Joan yelled back.

"I'm coming," Melissa hollered.

She opened the door brusquely, knocking Brenda to the floor.

"Bull's-eye," she said.

"MAMMA," Brenda wailed, her bottom lip smeared and bloody and beginning to swell.

"MELISSA," Joan screamed.

"It was an accident," Melissa said in her put-upon voice.

■　　■　　■

Brenda rearranged the circle of Wise Men into a straight row.

"I don't think they would like waiting in line to see Jesus," Joan said.

"That's how they do it in the Bible," Brenda said.

"It says 'They waiteth in line'?"

"In the pictures," Brenda said to her brain-dead mother.

Joan knew her daughter meant the glossy colored illustrations of this pivotal birth, but what she saw was Joseph with an Instamatic: "Come on, honey, one with you and the Wise Men"; a postnatal Mary smiling wanly from the hay; the imperial faces bleached out by the flash bouncing from their crowns.

"You win," Joan said.

"Do we have any Easter basket grass?"

"In the attic."

Melissa had picked out the manger almost a decade ago. Joan didn't go to church. She believed in God, but He was more like a distant cousin you remembered on holidays than an all-powerful Father. She didn't see much of His touted mysterious presence in her life. It wasn't that she thought Creation a complete failure; but she couldn't fathom why if you could create a thing as subtle as, say, sound, an invisible vibration in the air that could be organized into music and implied the wondrous perfect completion of the ear, the same imagination would be engaged by the pointless savagery of, say, cancer. These two examples were linked in her mind because she'd recently read of a nine-year-old Japanese prodigy who had played Mozart in the morning and died that afternoon of leukemia.

Still, God seemed as sensible an explanation as some gigantic accident. She could not place the cosmos on a par with runs in hose, overbaked cookies, traffic fatalities. So twice a year she trotted the kids to church to see what they made of it. She half-prayed that the Word of God writ large on their minds clean with innocence would perhaps startle her into firmer faith, forgetting that no mind is innocent, least of all a child's, and their belief, while it lasted, differed from hers only in the childishness of its misunderstanding.

Melissa had declined this year's spiritual field trip, howling. You would have thought she'd been asked to mount the cross in Christ's place. Brenda had pronounced her sister's eternal damnation to the preacher gleefully.

Brenda returned from the attic with a spongy ball of tangled plastic grass that was a translucent green. She hoped to add luster to the dingy manger figurines. Mary's clothes had chipped. The halos were a stubble of gold. The myrrh had been broken and improperly glued back, and there was now a jagged crevice between the black Wise Man's hand and the intricate box. The only bonus of their long use was that the ceramic seams from the molds they'd been formed in had worn away and they seemed less like ornaments, more sacred.

The grass so overwhelmed the small figures that they appeared to be hiding in a swirling bluster of tropical foliage. Press and tear as she might, Brenda could not shape the grass into cooperation and wound up crying in frustration, wrinkled green tresses clinging to her nightgown and hair.

■ ■ ■

Kevin rocked back and forth on his new tricycle, wearing the gun and holster, Raggedy Andy under one arm, Brenda's Barbie under the other. Christmas bows were scattered around Joan like a tribute. She kept saying, sensing Melissa's groggy disappointment, "We can take that back. I kept the tags." Kyle unexpectedly tickled Brenda, and her laugh was startlingly clear, like a series of perfectly shaped crystal bells ringing. Daryl did not look up from his electric football game.

■   ■   ■

Joan, menstruating, pulled another blouse from the rack. She had tried Midol. It had chased away the irritation and replaced it with depression. She'd never felt so much like a woman bleeding.

"What about this?" she asked.

"I don't like this store," Melissa said.

"You don't like anything."

"I like the Clothes Horse."

"The place with the flashing lights?"

"Wendy got the coolest jacket there. It had like this butterfly on the back made out of studs."

"You don't need butterflies; you need clothes."

"You want me to look like I teach vacation Bible school or something."

"Fine, it's your Christmas present. If you want to look like biker trash, it's your wardrobe's funeral."

"Are you calling me a slut?"

Six women spraying perfume on their wrists looked up.

"No," Joan said.

"Maybe I'll just be one since that's what you think I am anyway."

Joan grabbed her arm. "You're not too old to slap, young lady."

Melissa jerked her arm back. "Just try it."

"As long as you . . ." but Joan stopped because she heard Hilly in her voice. Melissa's eyes were glassy with rage. Joan said, "It's your present. You can have whatever you want."

Melissa seemed slightly disappointed by the oddly serene back road the argument had turned onto.

"Oh," she said.

■   ■   ■

Bulldozers had demolished a chunk of the woods. There weren't even stumps. At the edge of the new moonscape there was an enormous nest of trees and brush. Daryl made his way towards it. His fort was in there: pictures torn from the water-warped pages of *Playboy;* an unopened can of Bud, found in a ditch, waiting for Daryl's courage to pop it open; hedge clippers stolen from the tool shed to carve his fort from the thick cushion of bramble. It was more a rabbit warren than a fort as other boys built and imagined them. His was a crisscross of tunnels that led to rooms large enough for sitting and little else, except for the one spacious alcove, the leader's room, his room. The completion of his kingdom had required a whole fall of Saturdays. Unlike other inferior forts in the vicinity, you could stand beside Daryl's and not know it was there. It was perfect for hiding in after raids.

He was the only member of his fort. He couldn't risk the commonplace defections, the traitors trading secrets they'd promised with their blood not to divulge. Daryl was his own and only initiate. Puncturing the flesh below both thumbs with a burned needle and mingling his blood with his blood.

The upheaval of dead forest was taller than when it had been trees. His fort had been leveled. He pushed through the wreck, scratched by branches, tripped by roots that seemed frozen in the act of writhing. It was like being inside of cat's cradle gone wrong. He found the smile of a Bunny he had liked and a rusted saucepan he recognized from a fort he had betrayed just before he built his own. That was all.

■   ■   ■

When Joan considered it, Dr. Frankenstein hadn't done much worse than the great genes lottery. It was the same principle: a pinch of great-grandmother, a dash of Uncle Ernest, two heaping spoonfuls of parent. People were soups, sloshing around in their designer genes, desperate to make other soups. Melissa said she didn't want children. In Joan's day, wanting had nothing to do with it.

Daryl was trying to stare his spelling words into his head. Children retreated into themselves as they got older. Maturation was the process of becoming private. She did not know this son who was training letters in their correct order into his mind. The Daryl she knew was a sediment of memory: the infant who had been a thoughtful and fastidious eater; the toddler whose curls Kyle had cut after one too many strangers gushed, "Isn't she adorable?"; the boy who tied his shoes on the first try but took a year to potty-train, preferring to shit in the toy box.

"Daryl?" Joan said.

"Huh?" he said, not looking up.

"What do you want to be when you get older?"

He looked slowly and sarcastically towards her. "Grow up, Mom."

■   ■   ■

Melissa was warm and woozy from the beer, but kept her coat on to keep up her breasts' first line of defense. Case played the same fucking Led Zeppelin tape every time they went out. He scratched the shoulder of her butterfly jacket. She supposed the slow, crawling fingers were meant to be erotic. His legs were spread, boy-style, which implied a hard-on, but his long-haired head was leaned against the driver's window, which suggested drunkenness.

"Can we listen to Blue Oyster Cult?" she asked.

"Whatever," he said, upping the tempo of his fingers.

She fumbled through the tape box she'd given him for

Christmas. She wanted to lean towards the green glow of the dashboard for light, but Case might get the wrong idea. The tape her blind hands settled for turned out to be Humble Pie. At least it wasn't one of his two thousand Led Zeppelin tapes.

His hand moved to the back of her neck, which he squeezed. She was going to have to touch his dick soon. He'd given her a ring for Christmas. She'd wanted to refuse the gift but they'd been going out for five months. Wendy was already blowing Jumper and they'd only been together for three; but he had given her his class ring immediately. Wendy said going down on a guy was like scarfing down a Big Mac late at night when you were totally fucked up: it was fun while you were doing it, but afterwards you wanted to puke puppies. She said Jumper's come, which she'd recently learned to swallow, was salty, and she'd started buying him boxes of Twinkies to see if that would influence matters.

Melissa wasn't swallowing nothing. No way. No how. Wendy said you could tell when they were going to shoot and pull it out in time, but she had ruined three of Jumper's T-shirts that way, including one that couldn't be replaced from the Peter Frampton tour. Wendy'd determined to swallow when she'd seen the shirt recycled as a car-waxing rag.

Case would have to stock up on T-shirts. Melissa wished she liked him more. He had the two C's, cool and cute, and she didn't mind kissing, and she didn't mind breast-squeezes. The night of the ring she'd let him lick her nipples. That had been unpleasant, but she guessed she would get used to it. Wendy didn't have to get used to anything. She'd already picked out the names and sexes of her children. She'd come the first time Jumper had fingered her. She was in love. You'd have to be to do what she did. The thought of Case's fingers, currently twirling her hair, inside of her, panicked Melissa.

"Any more beer?" she asked.

"I've got something better than that," he said, pulling her to him. She tried to ready herself by thinking of the purple mole under his moustache, her favorite part of him.

"Vodka?" she said, the steering wheel lodged in her back.

"Better than vodka."

He kissed her. It was not better than vodka. She knew he'd be licking her breasts soon. Privileges couldn't be withdrawn once they'd been extended. She moved her tongue and pretended ecstasy, but not much. She thought the most sensible tactic might be to beat him off at the start of their dates so that she wouldn't spend the whole evening dreading this end-of-date car cat-and-mouse.

■ ■ ■

More than Pop Tarts, which he would steal if he could reach them, more than riding his tricycle in a fast circle around the front yard tree, more than Big Bird—unless he could meet him really live—Kevin loved his mother. Waking up from naps, he cried to hear the mother's voice she saved for him, and cried for her to pick him up (he wanted to know she would still do it), and cried until she kissed him and asked what a big boy like him was crying for.

He was not interested in other children. They wouldn't play his games, which were better than theirs, and that was all they were good for. Their yards were too far away. When mothers visited with their children Kevin pushed the other child down unless it was bigger, and then it pushed Kevin down for not playing its own stupid way. Kevin wished the world gone except for his mother, especially dumb Brenda, who twisted his ear into a big pain and made him play her way. He wanted to kill her off the whole planet.

■ ■ ■

It was Brenda's tool shed and she was older so the role of M.D. fell to her. She'd borrowed her father's one white dinner jacket and wore it over her winter coat. They moved the lawn mower up on the patio to enlarge the office. Sherry, who lived across the street and was seven, alternated between nurse and patient, but dolls were mostly their victims. One poor dear suffered such terrible migraines, just like Sherry's mother, that they'd had to saw her aching head off.

Sherry couldn't see very well because the Easter basket hat covered her eyes and made her half-blind, which was perfect: she was playing an old lady. Brenda wasn't sure what was wrong with Drusilla, Sherry's pretend-name, but it was awful. She was old enough to be dead and not know it. Crayons had colored her skin a peculiar orange. This was serious.

"Take off your hat," Brenda ordered.

"Yes, Dr. Boner," Sherry said in a creaky voice she made up on the spot. She was an excellent player for her age. Dr. Boner conked her on the head with her fist.

"Ow," Sherry said, forgetting her voice.

"It's worse than I thought."

She ordered her to remove her coat. She poked her with a hammer. It was a difficult case. It required more investigation. Their breath clouded around them like cartoon balloons with the words erased.

"Take off your coat," Dr. Boner commanded and Drusilla did. "The shirt too."

"But it's cold."

"Doctor's orders," Boner barked.

It proved to be an exceptionally tricky illness, requiring the patient, and eventually the good doctor herself, to strip naked and attach clothespins to their flesh. Sherry, being younger, could withstand more pain, and had them drooping from her butt, her nipples, her coochalolly. They sang "Sugar, Sugar" using a rake as a microphone. The cure was working splendidly when Melissa, the big spy, pushed her ugly face to the window. Brenda could tell from the satisfied smile on her sister's face that this meant trouble. Big Trouble. It was the smile Brenda used when she was about to turn someone in. She wondered if she had anything on Melissa. Could her older sister be bribed? Given Melissa's smile, it didn't look promising.

■ ■ ■

Kyle couldn't remember how much champagne he'd had, but he loved everybody, even Herb, who'd stolen part of his route. The other day he'd heard Melissa say, "He fills cigarette machines. Can you believe it?" He'd wanted to hurt her.

The office looked like a real dance hall. A banner exclaimed HAPPY NEW YEAR and swoops of silver tinsel from the company Christmas tree draped the filing cabinets and desks, which were all pushed against the wall. Joan wore a long red velveteen skirt, a matching bow in her hair, and— nesting in the frill of her white blouse—a Santa broach whose electric nose was operated by a small string with a bell on its end. She was the best-looking wife there, other than Trish, who wasn't a wife and who was young. He tried to imagine Trish naked, but the cup of red punch in her hand and her high heel tapping out the music's beat jammed his imagination. He wished she'd put down the cup and stay still for thirty seconds. He ambled casually towards Trish, lifting his drink to colleagues across the room, lighting a cigarette, and feigning absorption with a flaw in his shoe. His nose felt as electric as Santa's.

"How you doing, Trish," he said, leaning against the food table and reaching for a celery stick. Some ash fell in the cauliflower.

"Great," she said. "You seem to be having a pretty good time."

"Yeah, great party. The decorations look nice."

"Nice? We worked really hard to get this place looking halfway festive."

"They look great, better than great, the greatest."

"That's better."

They both faked interest in the dancing for a few seconds.

"Do you mind if I ask you a question?" he said.

"Depends on what it is."

"It's not dirty."

She snapped her fingers. "Shucks."

"But it could be," he said, winking.

"Ask your question, stud."

"Are you happy?"

She gave him a look. "How much champagne have you had?"

"No, I mean it."

"Well, sure, I guess. Are you?"

"Yeah, fine, no complaints."

"Have some coffee, Kyle."

The next morning he remembered only one person answering negatively to his informal poll: Herb's wife, Nancy. She cashiered in a discount dairy store, had stopped eating cheese, was obsessed with smelling like spoiled milk. She said she'd tried to strangle Herb on Christmas Eve, but wasn't strong enough, and he had laughed. She said she hated her life. Three times. She apologized for repeating herself. She cried. She threw up in the punch.

He wondered if you could be unhappy and not know it. He'd never wanted to be a fireman or a cowboy or any of the other men boys wanted to be and usually didn't become. He'd never wanted to be anything. He'd assumed he'd get a job and marry and have a couple of kids. That's what you did. When he thought of heaven he saw angels with golden wings. When he thought of war he saw John Wayne in a beret. When he thought of other lives he saw replicas of his own with slight variations in hair color and car model and the manner of death, like corridors of cracked mirrors reflecting one another into infinity.

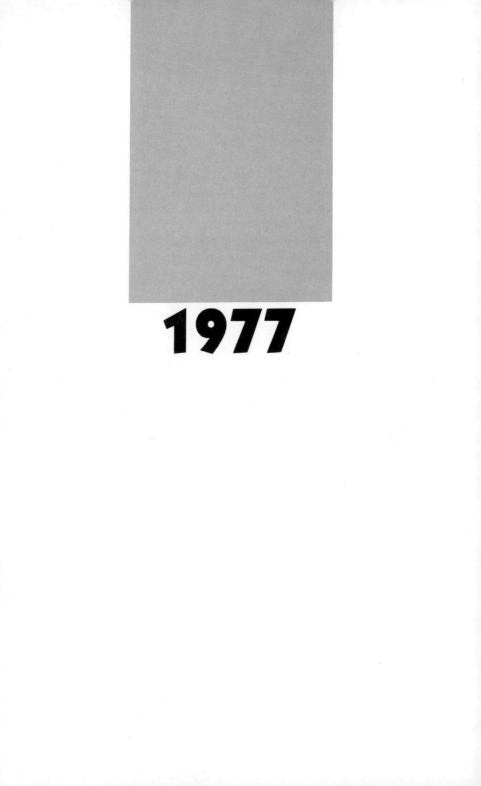

1977

Joan could not get the rusted mailbox flag down. She stood in the mist, her housecoat dampening, the rain on the grass bleeding into her slippers. She wrestled the flag with one hand and held an unforgiving stack of bills with the other. The sky was smudgy and bleak.

She gave up and turned to head back inside. Her house seemed shorter.

She hopped and leaped across the sodden yard, hoping to protect her feet from further saturation. Halfway to the door, she stopped and looked up. From this angle, the house seemed house-sized, but she could not shake the perception that it had shrunk. Her gaze skimmed it to the brick base, scudding over the imperfections detectable to an owner's eye. She idly counted the cinder blocks of the foundation, not even realizing she knew how many should be there: eighteen. There were seventeen. She recounted and came up with the same figure. She pushed through her hedge sideways, holding the bills above her head as the branches sling-shot water. She kicked the pine bark mulch that might be concealing the bottom row of blocks but her foot bounced on hard dirt, brown with rain. Two inches of her home were concealed beneath it, along with the bulbs she'd planted last spring.

She stepped up onto the porch and stood there, her mail now limp and wet. She opened the door and stood some more, wondering if her weight would send the whole structure plummeting to the center of the earth. She stepped in cautiously. It seemed stable enough: firm and flat and heavy. The neighborhood silence was unsettling. They'd forgotten to turn off the porch light last night and she left it on. She wondered if she was crazy. She wondered if Kevin—this was his first day of kindergarten—had been a support she hadn't known she needed, shoring up her defenses against anxiety and solitude, which in her off-kilter state seemed like the same thing. Could it be a revelation: that change was subtle but immutable, that you found yourself there before you knew where you were going.

One morning alone. She wandered her past in search of another such morning, or any instant that wasn't crowded with others' needs, and she could not find one. It embarrassed her. She'd imagined herself as bright, though she'd never been to college, and as capable. She was capable. She had raised children, taught them words that became phrases that became sentences that became questions and answers and demands and declarations and dares. You were born almost dead, the senses nearly numb, intelligence dumb except to its cravings. She'd taught them to walk, their small fists clutching her fingers. Agility. She'd taught them hot, cold, on, off, spoon, spin, knob, nest, table, turn, return. But in her vague terror, the whole enterprise of family seemed suspect. It wasn't the conscious wrongs that filled her suddenly with regret—they could be named, listed, apologized for. It was the forgotten moment of temper, the unknowing neglect, the minute psychic deaths that did not announce their passing but showed up years later (like insane guests who had gotten the decade of their arrival wrong) in baffling acts of cruelty, rumors of themselves. Hate-filled

Melissa wearing ripped jeans riding around in cars with Case. They were not collecting alms for the poor.

Joan slapped the bills on the stereo. She was freezing. She put on a pot of tea and ran a hot bath that she hoped would steam away her fears. In two hours she'd pick Kevin up and treat him to Burger King. She pictured him finger-painting at a long table with other messy-handed post-toddlers and it soothed her. Private failure, public disgrace, missed chances, shortcuts that proved to be dead ends, all the loud and soundless tragedies that damaged and mangled the heart: it was all possible. But children painting implied hope.

Maybe the house hadn't sunk. She could have imagined it. When Kyle got home she would ask him. They would have a discussion. He would know.

■　　■　　■

Unsurprisingly, surprisingly, Hilly died. She was a bed-ridden seventy-six. She had lived with Joan's sister, Lanie, and Bert, Lanie's husband. They were seven years older than Joan, a strange childless couple who seemed to view life as a grim task to be gotten over with. They tended invalids. Before Hilly there had been Bert's mother, and before her, Joan and Lanie's adored brother, Larry. Cancer had eaten him with the slow stupid patience of a cow chewing cud. He had been forty at the time of his death and fifteen years Joan's senior all of his life.

Larry's death had given Joan access to the odd, pointless, mechanical, infuriating nature of her life. Staining white bread yellow with mustard, she'd think, Now I am making Melissa's lunch, as if these unadorned declarations were a simple science that would add heft to the weightlessness of gestures and objects.

One afternoon, exhausted by despair, she'd fallen asleep on the couch. Larry had appeared to her as a point of light.

He'd said he was fine. That was the word he'd used: *fine*.
And you would have thought it a word so worn-out as to be
powerless; but she had woken refreshed, the transparency
of things banished, their meanings restored.

Joan felt none of the gulping anger she'd felt at Larry's
death when Lanie called to tell her of Hilly's, but a long
letter of grief unfolded within her. She had not liked Hilly.
Their love, if that's what it was, had been a bloody ravine
that had snaked off from the family, and Joan felt that Hilly
had abandoned her post at its mouth, leading to incalculable
damage at Joan's end, where she stacked slippery stones for
an unknowable purpose.

The hour-long drive to Lanie and Bert's was almost unen-
durable. She did not want to see her mother dead. She
nattered on about Kitty Wells, campfires, and a Coppertone
billboard they passed. Kyle was interesting on hand lotion
and bad haircuts, but she lost him during an extended harangue about cake mix. Melissa burst into tears when Joan
could not decide if she liked Paul Harvey or not. Joan tried
to comfort her daughter but the seat belt held her back as
Melissa banged her head rhythmically against the window.
Daryl remained silent. Kevin asked if he could be dead too
and Brenda slapped him savagely, which led to arbitration,
presided over by Kyle, as to which part of the backseat
belonged to whom. John wanted to crawl into the glove
compartment with the maps and the car registration and the
bag of Branch's butterscotch candy she suddenly remembered was there. What she'd forgotten probably added up
to more than the total of her memory and it made her bitter.

It wasn't until the car was in park and the wheels had
stopped spinning and the speedometer read zero that she
realized she couldn't get out of the car. She shooed in the
family with their suitcases and the bucket of fried chicken,
saying she'd be along shortly. She could not be in the house
where it had happened. She would suffocate. Lanie and
Bert's had always been a place of censored voices, censored

light. They had once been Church of God but had seceded into an obscure, severe order unto themselves.

She sat in the car sucking butterscotch and studying a three-year-old map of Florida, a vacation leftover. Brenda carried out a paper plate bent with ham and butter beans and potato salad. Kyle, Kevin on his hip, stopped by to inform her that Great-Aunt Lucy, a favorite, was asking for her, but he did not suggest that she come in. Cars pulled in, gussied up with wax for the funeral procession. Strangers waved. Cousin Sally, who Joan saw at Christmas, which mercifully came only once a year, paused to say how much Hilly had meant to her. Sally's hand-held eight-year-old, Billy, made funny chewing noises and Joan blamed Sally for it. The loud squishes seemed to hint at a general unpleasantness that Sally's practiced ebullience, temporarily subdued, seemed at pains to hide.

Two maps later, Lanie visited, her hands red and her apron splotched from washing dishes. At forty-three she was already an old woman though she'd probably live to ninety—there was a sturdiness to her. Her stockings were bunched around her big, pragmatic, black shoes. Frivolity fled from her.

She leaned one arm on the car's roof and said, "Mamma wouldn't like this."

"Mamma never liked anything I did," Joan said.

"Well, she really wouldn't like this."

"Mamma's dead."

Lanie looked out over the deserted tobacco rows for several seconds before saying, "You can't sit out in the car forever."

It seemed like the most practical advice Joan had received in a very long time. You couldn't stay in a car forever. It was a simple but irrefutable fact. She picked up her cosmetics bag and found the hair dryer under the seat. Lanie opened the car door. Kevin would get cranky for his nap. Melissa would need help with her hair. Daryl would have

to be talked into his Sunday shoes and Brenda talked out of
changing ten times in two days.

■　　■　　■

Daryl was halfway out the door when his mother said,
"Where are you going?"

All day had sucked. He'd had to do a problem on the
blackboard and had gotten it wrong. His pencil wouldn't
stay sharp. Joan had packed a bologna sandwich, vanilla wa-
fers, and an apple, again, effectively barring him from all
lunchtime trading. He'd faked a stomachache and the school
nurse hadn't bought it. Ruthie had called him a turd on the
bus home and you couldn't tell and you couldn't hit her,
because it was sissy. He'd said, "Same to you but more of
it." Real bright.

Now this where-are-you-going crap.

"Africa," he said, smart ass as possible.

"Good," Joan said from the couch where she watched
"Matchgame" every weekday afternoon. "You can take your
sister."

"Brenda?" He couldn't believe it.

"She's been whining ever since she got home. Africa
might cheer her up."

"Mom."

"I know you kids really love each other deep down under
the name-calling and the charley horses."

"Mom. I'm almost a teenager."

"Maybe you'd rather clean up your room."

Brenda sang the "Daryl has to take me" song all the
way down the street. He had to push her down. She had
to cry.

"I'm telling," she said, rubbing her hip.

"Fine. Tell. Run home to Mommy, you little baby."

"No, turd-knees."

Daryl pulled her up by the hair. "You say that again and I'll cream you right into the pavement."

Brenda bit him. By the time he'd checked to see if the little cannibal had drawn blood, she was almost to the woods. She turned around long enough to stick out her tongue and disappeared. That did it. She really was in for it now. Daryl hated having tongues stuck out at him. He was going to pull hers out and make her eat it.

After an hour, he started to worry. He remembered Brenda wasn't allowed in the woods by herself. A little girl three streets over had disappeared last year and been found in the creek a week later. She'd been molested.

"Brenda," he yelled again. "We have to go home. It's time for supper."

Nothing.

His parents would blame him. He knew how their minds worked. They would use some form of the word *Responsible*. It was the word of choice for lecturing the teenaged, which he almost was. Melissa heard it at least once a week. If they found Brenda facedown in a creek with horrible things done to her, he'd be Responsible. An awful word, big as a mansion, with long, dark corridors that echoed. He'd be grounded for life.

"BRENDA."

Dusk made the trees seem denser and played tricks with distance. Very near could be very far. A cold dew was settling. Brenda hadn't worn a sweater. Panic played in his guts. He hated Brenda and if she was killed, he wanted to be the one to do it, not some stranger.

"Brenda, please."

It was no use. The night the dusk had suggested was suddenly everywhere you looked. You couldn't tell a tree from a child molester. Branches swatted him. Bramble tugged at his clothes. The air had been sucked of warmth, of fragrance. The crickets were blasting. He knew where he was and how to get home, but if he stayed much longer he wouldn't. He hoped Brenda wasn't cold or wet. He felt like he'd swallowed something large and heavy and glass. An empty fishbowl.

When he hit the front yard he saw her, she, it sitting on the front porch. The smell of dinner was spread thick as peanut butter through the neighborhood. His stomach finally allowed itself to be hungry with a giant squish. The fishbowl in his middle disintegrated. He was lightheaded—happy with relief. He would have a life. He would not be sent to reform school. His parents would still like him. Except he was late.

"Boy, are you in trouble," Brenda said.

"Wait till I tell them you said 'turd' and went off into the woods by yourself," he said. He thought about cuffing her upside the head, but she was just a little girl, even if she'd never seemed like one before.

"Hold on," she said, grabbing the hem of his jeans as he opened the storm door. "I think I can get us out of this."

■   ■   ■

Kyle heaved another case of cigarettes onto the loading dock, then cupped his hand over a sting on his neck.

"Haven't you ever been hit by a rubber band before?" Trish laughed. She was wearing the white she favored. Clothes fit her better than they did most people.

"You're quite a shot," he said.

"I was aiming for your butt."

"My wife might say you come pretty close."

She laughed again. "Conducted any more surveys lately?"

"Yeah, I been asking people why women who wear white are such a pain in the neck."

"Their rubber bands are stronger."

Herb pulled up late again. Kyle hoped the son of a bitch would choke on the piece of Kyle's route he'd bitten off.

"Could you go for a guy in uniform?" Herb asked Trish.

At McGee the men wore brown shirts with their names stitched in red over the breast pocket. It wasn't exactly a uniform. Trish got Herb on the cheek with one of her rubber bands.

"That's the only crack a married guy like you is going to get," she said.

Kyle picked up the rubber band she'd stung him with and wrapped it around his thumb.

"Does this mean we're steadies?" he asked.

■   ■   ■

Joan stared at the ceiling, Kyle asleep at her side. He was wearing a T-shirt, nothing else. At the beginning of their marriage she'd asked him about this strange habit and he'd said, "It's something I picked up from the army." It wasn't until years later that she'd realized the explanation wasn't one.

He didn't snore. She was grateful for that. They slept well together, not in one another's arms, but who did? Hands fell asleep; legs cramped; sweat glued the separate bodies in sticky patches of unpleasant alliance.

There had been one other man, Jimmy. Fucking and writing had been the only activities he'd excelled in. Not writing a story you could read, but the physical act of printing words on a page: the baroque script of a Bible's frontispiece, the dictionary's boxy type, the spindly line of letters crammed into fat books. He could not read but he could copy print. To him, they were pictures, not ideas. She still had his letters from boot camp stored in a recipe box tucked away under the discarded Christmas frippery in a corner of Lanie's attic. Jimmy had dictated the letters to other recruits who were delighted to oblige him, as the communiques were horny, blunt, unashamed. Jimmy would recopy their dictation, dressing up his unabashed desire in ornamental flourishes of curlicues and the other frou-frous of penmanship he was the unversed master of. They were covered with gorgeous markings, but at the time had made Joan blush to think an entire barracks knew every shadow, each contour, the various textures of her body. Kyle had been one of the young soldiers lucky enough to be there. Jimmy had gone AWOL after being assigned to Alaska—he had a morbid fear of the cold. Kyle had called Joan and they had married on his second leave. It had taken the first year of their marriage to assure him that he was the superior lovemaker, a harmless lie. Joan thought Kyle should be grateful for her liberation from Hilly's unspoken—and all-the-more forceful for it— maxim that sex was what other people did. It had taken the unremitting thoroughness of Jimmy's inventive exuberance to shuck Joan of her inhibitions. Kyle assumed the letters had been destroyed.

Joan licked behind Kyle's ear, a sure-shot, and trickled her fingers over his dick just so.

"Wake up, honey," she whispered. "You need me."

■   ■   ■

There was never anything to do. Joan was reading. Kyle was helping Daryl patch a flat. Melissa was out shopping with Wendy, a euphemism, Brenda was sure, for shoplifting, pot smoking, and other juvenile delinquency.

Boredom sent Brenda barging into Kevin and Daryl's room, where two styles of interior decoration clashed. Daryl's side was all pennants and photographs of trucks ripped from magazines. Kevin's, decorated by Joan, was centered around a polka-dotted animal motif.

Creepy Kevin was on the floor under a bedspread with a flashlight on. It looked like science fiction. His nursery school had branded him "anti-social," Brenda's latest favorite insult. She could drive Melissa crazy with it.

"What are you doing?" Brenda asked Kevin.

"Playing."

"Playing what?"

"A game."

"What kind of game?" Brenda was getting impatient.

"A game."

"I bet you're not playing anything."

"Am too."

"Are not."

"Am too."

"Prove it."

"I can't."

"See." Brenda wondered if "anti-social" was a fancy word for retarded.

"It is too a game," he said.

"Well? What is it?"

"I can't tell."

"Says who?"

"Somebody."

"Who?" Brenda was going to be forced to punch him if this kept up.

"Promise you won't tell?"

"Cross my heart and hope to die," she said, crossing her fingers.

"Mr. Tartar."

"Come again, Sambo," a phrase lifted from a saucy, teen-aged vixen in a late Saturday night movie.

"My friend."

"Well, he's not here now."

"Is too."

"Is not."

"Is too."

"Where, retardo?"

"He's bigger than the whole house, and bigger than our whole family put together, and bigger than fifty billion, zillion, jillion."

"Oh, brother."

"You better not tell or he'll kill your head off."

"Geezy-peezy," Brenda said, a dismissive word that bordered the forbidden, not that Kevin's five-year-old pea brain would notice. "Who would want to tell about a strango like you?"

"You just better not ever, ever."

Kevin was hopeless. Brenda threw a pillow at him. "I hope you smother under there," she said.

"Mr. Tartar wouldn't let me, stupid breath."

Brenda slid her feet down the hall, which tugged her socks down past her ankles and formed wrinkled rabbit ears of white cotton cloth in front of her toes. Maybe she'd pick Melissa's new lock. The last one had been depressingly easy, requiring no finesse, only a bobby pin.

■　　■　　■

Joan had a friend who had a cousin who worked at the construction site nearby who said a shy boy came every afternoon to watch them work. They'd shown him how the concrete mixer and pourer whirled the dust and water into a paste that made buildings. Joan figured it was Daryl, who came to dinner dusty.

The last Melissa-battle had been over an orange tube top borrowed from Wendy that Melissa had thought she was wearing to school in mid-February. Joan wished she could freeze-dry Melissa until the possession was over. *The Exorcist* wasn't a horror movie, it was a documentary about adolescence.

Joan had hoped that nursery school would bring Kevin out of his shell, but last week he had bitten Miss Tracy rather than play ring-around-the-rosy. She worried he'd have to see a psychiatrist. She didn't want her children rehashing their childhoods with a stranger licensed to crucify mothers who weren't there to defend themselves. For reasons she couldn't quite muddle through, she thought taking him to the park on a regular basis might help.

Brenda walked into the dining room wearing all of her barrettes. She wasn't the normal one after all.

"Very glamorous," Joan said.

"I'm choosing for school pictures tomorrow."

"What about the cherries?"

"Too babyfied."

"The simple pink ones are nice," Joan said, wiping crumbs into her cupped hand.

"You're boring me out."

"What about a ribbon?"

"This girl Clara at school always wears a ribbon and she'll think I'm a copycat."

"Braids?"

"Dorko."

"We could shave one side of your head."

"So funny I forgot to laugh."

Joan stuck out her tongue.

Brenda said, "You aren't very mature for a mother."

■   ■   ■

Boys' come was like warm snot. Melissa had it in her hand, on her wrist. That first time had taught her to roll up her sleeve, as if she were a nurse or a patient, though there were close encounters when sleeve-rolling couldn't help her. If she hadn't done him in a few days, he went off like a Roman candle. On the toy dog bobbing in the rear window. In her hair. An expensive, shoplifted blouse she'd almost done time for had been ruined. This stuff stained. Like toxic waste. A drop that had landed close to her fragile, blinking eye had brought on vows of celibacy—Case's, since hers wasn't at issue. But when the anticipated disfiguration hadn't occurred, he'd worn her down and she was back at it by the weekend. When he was drunk she thought her arm would fall off and made him finish himself.

When Melissa masturbated at home she didn't spew like an uncapped fire hydrant. It was gradual, it moved in waves, not that it was gentle. Her orgasms shuddered through her worse than Case's seemed to, though he was louder, gasping as if she were stabbing him repeatedly, the only worthwhile aspect of the ordeal. His eyes clenched shut, his body rigid; the violent contractions of his body fascinated her. Once, she nibbled his ear at the precise moment—a Wendy tip— and he'd kicked the eight track from its metal clamp. When he bruised her with an unconscious knee or bit her with his helpless mouth, she felt she'd called up a coded secret, compelling in its implications, but useless in that it couldn't be passed along.

She diddled herself at home to prepare for his inevitable fingers. Wendy and Jumper were fucking. Half the school was. Melissa had constructed a serviceable Case—unmoustached, softer, understanding—to fantasize by, but other disturbing, unbidden faces interfered: her father, Wendy, strangers. The perfected Case was a channel that came in only when the weather was untroubled.

She wiped off her hand on a McDonald's bag. Case panted, his half-hard cock arced over his bunched-up underwear. Dicks were ugly. Odd. She didn't see what the big deal was. Any woman's body was more interesting.

He took her by the chin and kissed her eyes with a gentleness startling in its mimicry of her dreams.

"I want to do something for you," he said.

Jumper, probably, had wised Case up by suggesting this strategy for finger intrusion.

"You already have," she countered, whispering. A boy's ego was a gift to the girl who knew how to use it.

■   ■   ■

"Sweet Sixteen." They needed new songs for the teen-agers. None of the adolescents Joan knew were sweet and most were downright menacing. Take Case, please, as the joke went. Two short beeps were his mating call. Through her picture window Joan had deciphered long hair, a moustache, and denim worn with the strict regular-ity of a uniform, all of it further obstructed by his Mach 1, a sleek, sexy, blue machine, the back jacked up where she surmised he was jacked off. Joan's station wagon plod-ded. Case's hot rod prowled. The one time she'd waved to him, he'd pointed back at her as if his finger were a gun, herself the hapless midnight clerk at the convenience store.

Brenda was at a safety patrol meeting. Daryl was at his construction site, she hoped, in his winter coat, the good one. Kevin was growling in his room like a dog or a cave-man or the engine of Case's sexed-up car. Melissa blew in, late from school, and was halfway downstairs before Joan could call her name. Joan could have identified any member of her family solely on the basis of the way they entered the house or left the house or creaked across floors. There were rhythms; there was cadence. Human movement was its own idiosyncratic music, clumsy and divine. Kevin was a garage band transistorized—tinny, small, rambunctious. Brenda was a delicate string quartet. Daryl was syncopated jazz. Kyle was a small tribe of tubas—heavy, basso profunda. Melissa was an orchestra falling from their seats in mid-note. Her entrances seemed to drag in whatever path she traveled—each tree, every mailbox, stray dogs—and she had given up trying to sneak in past curfew.

"Yeah?" her noisy daughter said.

"Come here," Joan said.

"Why?"

"Do I have to have a reason to see my favorite daughter?"

You could hear the inconvenience in Melissa's ascent. She looked cheap and tired in a tinselly way that put Joan in mind of movie-of-the-week runaway teenaged prostitutes.

"What?" Melissa said in a perfect imitation of annoyed despair.

"Happy Birthday."

"Thanks."

"Would you like to open your present?"

"I guess."

Joan nodded towards the fussily wrapped pink package sitting on the stereo. Melissa nervously and cautiously untaped it as if it contained the exact hour of her death. She held the sweater up by its shoulders.

"This is sort of cool," she said, mistrustfully.

"Shock, shock."

"Wendy won't believe it."

"I'm not such an old fogey."

"Wow," Melissa said, hugging the garment against her for a tentative size check.

Joan wished there was a list of words or a collection of signs known to women, but not men, that exposed potential boyfriends and husbands as the frauds, emotional cheapskates, and wanton destroyers, which their courting manners sometimes disguised. She wished there were a recipe or a brand of soap or a manual diagramming the various acrobatic feats required to land on your feet after disaster or disappointment or a particularly bad day. She wanted advice she could dispense like a preventive medicine, some injection of good sense or character that would protect Melissa as much as protection could. But the concept of dignity as a kind of armor presupposed a world where all the morals were scrubbed and stacked neatly in place, and as far as Joan could tell, somebody had torn through and played havoc with the shelves.

"I made lasagna," she said. It was Melissa's favorite.

"Case is taking me out for pizza."

"Pizza?" she said, as if the concept were new to her.

"With Wendy and Jumper."

"Jumper," she said, as if she were still at the stage when repetition was a form of learning.

"The one who burned his eyebrows in the Harley wreck."

"He always looks surprised."

"That's Jumper."

Joan wondered how Kyle saw his TV shows through the thick layer of dust obscuring the screen. She pushed her slippers from her hot, sweaty feet.

"You could invite them over here," she said.

"I could."

"We don't bite, except for Kevin, but only if you make him play ring-around-the-rosy."

Melissa rattled the wrapping paper at Joan. "Do you want me to save this?"

If that bit of training had taken, there was hope.

■　　■　　■

Joan wasn't sure why she was reading an article about the Pill. She'd had her tubes tied after Kevin, who this week had entered a Silent Phase. Kyle was bowling. He thought it was sport. Joan thought any sport you drank beer before, during, and after didn't deserve its name. Melissa was out with Case, who'd rung the doorbell. They must be getting serious. Joan felt like her daughter was a sullen bait they were using to gradually woo some wild beast from the cave of its Mach 1. Fifth-grader Brenda had wrested control of the safety patrols from a sixth-grader. She polished and re-polished her badge as if it were a heirloom. She'd initiated a series of seminars on the hazards of childhood. Joan tried to remain calm as her daughter rehearsed each week's subject, but the statistics were alarming. Between streets crossed without looking, abandoned refrigerators, and tonight's topic, "Strangers and Their Cars," she was surprised any of them made it to adolescence.

Daryl, it turned out, was late, not drowned. Joan yelled for him.

"I'm sorry," he yelled back up the stairs, detecting the you're-in-for-it tone of voice.

"Come up here right now."

He was skinny and tall for his age. Visions of basketballs danced in Kyle's head.

"What?" he said sullenly, so perfectly like Melissa that she wondered if he'd been taking lessons.

"Do you know what time it is?" she recited from the Mother's Book of Practiced Responses, chapter four, Tardiness.

"No, ma'am."

"Seven o'clock."

"I said I was sorry."

"This is the second time this week."

"I was playing and stuff and I forgot."

Joan shut her eyes, reopened them. It wasn't a trick of vision. He was glowing.

"Come here," she said.

He dragged over, expecting to get whaled. She ran an index finger down his cheek. A patina of fine, blue dust powdered him.

"What's this?" she asked.

"I don't know. They're pouring it into the concrete mixer thing to make like a big round thing under the buildings."

"March right in there and take a shower and then throw those dirty clothes in the wash. I don't want you getting this stuff all over the house."

"Yes, ma'am." He trudged towards the bedroom as if it were an abandoned refrigerator.

"And," she added as he closed the door, "I don't want you over at that construction site anymore."

He didn't answer.

"Did you hear me?"

He blasted on the water. She was going to ground him

when he emerged, unblue. One Melissa a lifetime was sufficient, thank you.

■   ■   ■

Kevin picked the large, fat red crayon from the pack he'd stolen from nursery school. He kept them under the very middle of his mattress where his mother wouldn't find them. The mattress was heavy and he had to lift it with both arms and hold it up with his head so he could get to them.

He did not like coloring books. The things drawn by the fat black lines did not look the way they were supposed to. They were flat and the faces were goofy. He tried to color in a way that made them more walking-around, sometimes barely touching the crayon to the page, and sometimes mashing it down with both fists even if the page ripped and color got on the cow or car or cricket behind it.

He used red because it was Mr. Tartar's favorite color. Mr. Tartar liked lots of red and sometimes yellow and a little bit of orange, and he had shown Kevin how to make orange with the two other colors. You could make more colors too, but Mr. Tartar wouldn't show him until he'd learned about red. Red wasn't one color: it was Mamma's lips, a streak in the sky, spaghetti sauce. They were not the same as each other but they were all red.

Mr. Tartar talked in Kevin with a deep voice. He came when he wanted but could be called from under a sleeping bag or a sheet with Daryl's flashlight. Kevin was careful to put the flashlight back so Daryl wouldn't know.

■   ■   ■

Melissa and Wendy were riding around. Joan's dull station wagon had been exchanged for the impressive Mach 1 at the gas station where Case worked Monday, Wednesday, and alternate Friday nights. Jumper had dropped out of high school last week to make a killing as a roofer, but he was at a bachelor party with his new buddies tonight. Wendy pounded a coughing fit from her chest, swigged a beer to celebrate her recovery, and handed the joint back to Melissa.

Leaning back and shutting her eyes, Wendy said, "They better not have a fucking stripper at that party."

"I'm so fucked up," Melissa said, hitting Wendy's shoulder with the fist that held the joint.

"No, man, I'm blown away."

Melissa tamped it out in an ashtray already crowded with roaches. Below the gear shift, in the hollow where they kept toll change, was a Quaalude folded into an empty cigarette pack. Somewhere was the hit of acid they had lost one night while laughing into the Jack-in-the-Box speaker they'd eventually driven away from without ordering. That was the night Melissa had given in beside the Mach 1 in her family's driveway. It had started as an innocent good-bye kiss. They were leaning against the car. It had not been unpleasant, though the metal was cold on her back and ass. In the role of jerk-off queen, Melissa had been more intrigued spectator than participant, but peculiarly, she still felt an unastonished distance even as her hands encouraged his bare, hairy ass. While he fucked, her glazed attention had drifted from her parents' bedroom window to the splinters of splinters of light the stars seemed to be in the black, cloudless sky. By the time he came, a door handle had almost been pushed into the small of her back. She had developed a sneeze from the winter air their systems were too blasted to sense. No big deal, she'd thought when it was over until she'd felt his heart pounding over hers as if it were trying to synchronize their pulses. She pushed him off to escape. When he said he loved her she felt it was a medal she'd earned for a long, bewildering battle over territory whose strategic importance was still questionable.

"I've got to have some fries before I die," Wendy said.

Melissa looked at her eyes in the rearview mirror. "Do you have any Visine?" she asked.

"If I find out Jumper's been looking at some other chick's tits, I'm cutting him off for a month." She paused as possibility became probability. "Maybe a week." That seemed more realistic.

■   ■   ■

The basketball hoop drooped from a pine tree. The net was a bedraggled bunch of red, white, and blue string that had come untied. Kyle's brother, Gary, had given it to him. Gary had a small court neatly painted on the driveway in front of his new garage. The Demerest family court was the undrawn space around a pine tree. Out-of-bounds was past the several convenient roots thrashing up from the ground like frozen tentacles. The foul line had been worn in by their sneakers and Joan complained about it every time she thought to. They couldn't slam the ball, and it was the one aspect of their court that Daryl regretted.

Kyle looped the ball over his head and missed. Daryl, ready for the rebound, tapped it off the tree trunk into the hoop.

"Take five," Kyle said, clapping.

Daryl sat leaned against the tree, the ball held between his knees. Kyle bent for a rock marring the field of play and hummed it into the woods.

"No wonder I haven't hit anything today," he said.

Daryl laughed.

■   ■   ■

Kyle played with the stapler. His work shirt was stained under the arms, as he'd known it would be, but a change of clothes would have been suspicious. This morning, Joan had nodded and turned another page of the newspaper after he'd said he'd be late. He didn't know why he felt guilty. He and Trish were going to have a friendly drink; a man and a woman could be friends; there didn't have to be anything more to it.

Trish came out of the ladies room. He wished she hadn't touched up her eyes and fluffed her hair. Friends shouldn't primp for each other. She was too young for him, but her spunk attracted him. If you told one of the other women in the office an off-color joke, they blushed, tittered, averted their eyes, like movie geishas practicing a dead art. Trish came back with one filthier. She clipped funny headlines from the newspaper—"Man Mistakes Mother-in-Law for Raccoon"—and taped them to the sides of her desk. She had a framed ad cut from a Sears catalog featuring a blond family she claimed as her own, replete with ordering numbers and breezy descriptions of their outfits. People thought she was weird and Kyle guessed she was.

"O.K., sport," she said, "let's hit the road."

They took her car, a cinnamon-colored Camaro with mags and fluffy white headrests. In the back window a pink plastic ostrich plumed in every color of feather bobbed crazily. There were two bumper stickers, one from Six Flags Over Georgia, and one that seemed like a threat disguised as a command—Love Me, Love My Camaro.

When they pulled into the Holiday Inn parking lot she pulled out the Z.Z. Top eight track that had rendered conversation pointless, and said, "This O.K.?"

"I don't know if I'm dressed for it."

"Oh, bullshit. The Pirate's Cove isn't nothing but a damn bar."

She got out, assuming the matter settled, and as he followed, it was.

They sat at the bar on swivel chairs. Nets loaded with shells and leering pirate portraits decorated the walls. Waitresses in short skirts, anchor earrings, and blouses tied at the belly button set out steaming buffet trays of cut-up hot dog in barbecue sauce and plates of cheese cubes speared by frilly, whored-up toothpicks. There were goldfish crackers on the bar. It was early but the restaurant was dark as dusk. Kyle wondered what Joan had made for dinner.

The bartender, a man Kyle's age with deeply black hair but a salt-and-pepper moustache, high-fived Trish. Kyle had a gin and tonic instead of the unsophisticated beer he wanted. Trish ordered a Long, Slow Screw Between the Sheets, which seemed to consist of every liquor behind the bar, but was deceptively pink, like her ostrich. The elaborate drink made Kyle feel pudgy, old, near death.

He called Joan twice from the pay phone by the bathroom, once to assure her that he would be home. The second time her "Hello" had struck him dumb and he'd hung up.

"You got a bladder like a peanut," Trish said when he returned.

■   ■   ■

Joan held the film canister under the end table lamp and swished the pot around. She hated being played for a fool. Melissa was late—it was past midnight—but she wouldn't be late again because you had to be somewhere—the movies, a dance, a dope deal—to be late from, and Melissa was, from this day forward, grounded. Joan hoped her daughter was enjoying her last night as a free, if drugged, young woman.

Joan wondered if the canister's contents constituted a nickel bag or a dime, an ounce or a pound. She headed for the kitchen. She flicked on the light, pulled the kitchen scales from under the sink, and placed the pot on the top, which was faded and dusty. She squinted. A quarter ounce . . . If it were sage it wouldn't have seasoned a good-sized chicken. But you never knew. Size was no test of a drug's power. Look at penicillin. The faintly registered sample before her might be enough to destroy the minds of a family, a neighborhood, a nation. She'd read somewhere that drugs were a communist plot. Melissa could be Big Time. How else was she getting the money?

Joan switched on the "Tonight Show" on her way back to the couch. The San Diego Zoo guy was on, but she couldn't enjoy it for Melissa's ruined life.

Unfortunately, Brenda, safety patrol at large, had been the dope's discoverer. She claimed that Melissa's door had been open, but Joan doubted it. Melissa kept her room locked up like death row, another privilege whose time had come and gone. Privacy was one issue, concealing contraband another. Brenda had been innocently searching for a pencil when she'd found the drugs in a boot in a box in the closet. She'd been confined to her room for that whopper. She'd been wrong to snoop, but Joan was glad she had. Brenda, not naturally disposed to forgive and forget (especially when the crime was Melissa's to be forgiven and forgotten), had suggested that the police be called.

The police. Melissa had deteriorated from insupportably rude teenager to potential felon. Jail was a real place where bad people went. You had conversations through thick windows while prison matrons looked on. You came out hardened. If the cops burst in, the family—Kevin in nursery school—might be carted off in handcuffs, whirling red lights announcing their shame to the neighbors in shades of hot scarlet. Melissa had endangered them all. Worse than felonious, she was inconsiderate.

A car crunched into the driveway. Was it the fuzz, pigs, coppers? Joan hid the stuff between the cushions. A door slammed. Case beeped his mating call. She'd planned to confront him as well, but a disturbingly vivid image of herself mangled in the grill of his drug-crazed car had tempered her.

As the front door opened, Joan said, "Melissa."

"Uh-oh."

"That's right, young lady. 'Uh-oh.' "

Joan pulled the pot from its hiding place, intending to place it as Exhibit A on the couch's arm. Instead she hurled it when her daughter came into view. Melissa caught it with one hand, infuriating Joan, who'd wanted to be the calm one.

"What the hell is that?" she asked.

"Film?"

"Guess again."

"I'm not Kreskin."

"It was found in your room."

"What was Brenda doing in my room?"

"Jigsaw puzzles. Answer the goddamned question."

Melissa looked at the canister, rolling it over and over in her hand, as if she were a jeweler considering a diamond's flaws. "It's pot," she said, looking up.

"How can you say that?"

"You asked me what it was."

"You have a very smart mouth, young lady."

"I don't know what you want from me."

"I want you to wear nice clothes and date someone who doesn't look and act like a hood. I want you to try at school, just try. That's all I expect. I'd like you to be civil for once in your life. I'd like you to clean your room. I want you not to be a FUCKING DRUG ADDICT."

"AND I WANT YOU TO STOP HOUNDING ME LIKE A FUCKING CRIMINAL."

"YOU ACT LIKE A CRIMINAL."

"YOU HATE ME."

"I USED TO LOVE YOU."

A tactical error. It was and wasn't what Joan meant. She didn't know if she could express the tangled nest of emotions she felt for her daughter. It had been like this with Hilly, who had died, which had resolved nothing.

"See," Melissa said. She sat the pot on the stereo and went downstairs to her room.

Joan, foolishly, had expected Melissa to be changed forever by this confrontation; but Melissa had won the battle, maybe the whole war, and, horrible to admit, Joan was too tired to care. It was two in the morning. There was a weather map on TV.

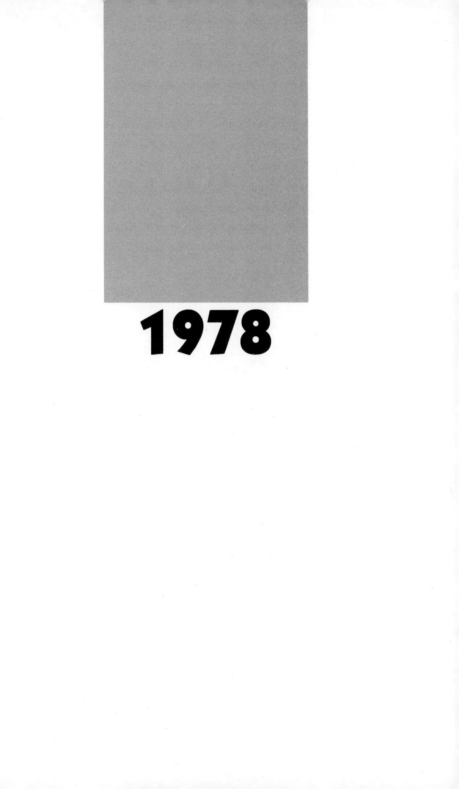

1978

bout fifteen blocks of the foundation were visible above the earth. The bottom step of the porch was level with the ground. Joan had stopped studying, through the sliding doors, the meaningless map of hairline cracks that had shattered over the patio. She worried for the upstairs deck off the kitchen. She had warned Kyle. He had ignored her.

This was the fifth or sixth time they'd circled the house with the county inspector, Mr. Belmont. It was freezing. She and Kyle were wearing coats. Mr. Belmont wasn't. He was scrawny and old and unperturbed by the weather. Joan didn't trust him.

"Yep," Mr. Belmont said for the umpteenth time, "you definitely got yourself a problem here."

"We know," Joan said, congratulating herself on her calm, "but what is the problem exactly?"

"Oh, it wouldn't be right for me to speculate without all the necessary information."

"When will you have that?" she asked.

"I'll have to get some of my boys down here to sniff around and see what they come up with."

"What *might* it be?" she asked. Kyle was toeing a hole in the yard like a three-year-old. She ordered him to quit.

"Could be anything," Belmont said. "We had one fall clean through. Turned out it was built over a cave."

"This happens a lot?" she asked.

"Occasionally."

"Why don't we ever hear about it?"

"I'm a county planner, ma'am, not a newspaper man."

Kyle made hot chocolate and massaged Joan's numbed toes back to life. Blood seemed to pour into them and they throbbed. She had almost forgiven him his intimidation by Belmont. Ties bullied Kyle.

"It's only a couple of inches in two years," he said.

She instantly withdrew her absolution and her feet. "If we live to seventy, God willing"—she knocked the dining room table—"we'll have to use the chimney like Santa Claus."

"The guy said he'd take care of it."

"The guy said he'd send his *boys* over as soon as he could, which might not be for another month."

"That's not so long."

"You really are an idiot, aren't you?"

He looked over her head as if he'd spied a distant figure making its way towards them. She crossed her feet under her as if they were the symbol of her and Kyle's intimacy and by concealing them she could drain intimacy of its humiliating power.

Kevin, in first grade, left her alone much of the day. She'd accumulated more than a dozen magazine subscriptions, including one to *Bird's Life,* ordered from a door-to-door old lady. The funds were for the protection of parakeets. Joan hadn't realized that they were an endangered species. She'd later read, surprised by her surprise, that it was a scam organized by widows who couldn't live on their husbands' pensions, though the nature of the scam was obscure to Joan as she received her copy with neurotic punctuality and was considering renewing. The bird pics were inexpressibly suggestive, almost pornographic, and Joan felt she needed another year to figure them out.

She didn't watch television but studied *TV Guide* ferociously, as if the secret meaning of her life were hidden in the guest-star lists for variety shows, in the two-page vistas hawking smokes. She could reel off air dates and filming dates of morning, midday, and late-night movies. She could recite the terse plot synopses of reruns.

"I said," she repeated, "you're an idiot."

"I heard you," he said, peeling the label from the jelly jar Daryl had left out.

He smacked her, hard, scalding her cheek with the print of his hand. He pushed his chair backwards and it bumped across the kitchen floor, halting beside the garbage can that awaited emptying. As he reached the staircase her thrown cup tumbled through the air, hot chocolate dispersing, spinning, then recombining: a damp fern across his shirt; pearls clinging to the wall; clusters of stains, like unnamed islands, sprayed over the folded, laundered clothes waiting on the couch to be stacked in drawers. She got him in the small of his back. She couldn't have planned a better shot. He had back problems and wanted to spend their tax return on a new mattress. He paused. She wondered if he could kill her and decided "Of course" so quickly that the answer and the question seemed like the same thought.

"I'm getting a job," she said.

He rubbed his hand back and forth across the bannister, as if to test its reality. The cup was lost in shadow under an armchair. She could just make out its handle.

"We could use the money," he said.

They sat in the driveway for a few minutes more. The radio station was topping off its Aerosmith hour with "Dream

On," one of Melissa's favorite songs. Normally, she and Wendy would be blasting it and screaming along, passing a joint, and not in Melissa's driveway, but the higher Steve Tyler sang, the worse she felt.

"Could we turn that off?" she asked.

Wendy did.

The transparent model of the uterus, the counselor's voice practiced into a warm syrup, the businesswoman sitting beside Melissa who reeked of Ivory soap and efficiency and thumbed through *People* magazines at breakneck speed, the loose hospital gown, the nurse's bony hand, the roaring wind of the vacuum, the doctor's minted breath, the startling pain, the lingering bitterness of the Valium: the cubism of memory.

"How ya feeling?" Wendy asked, her voice small.

"Like I'm having the worst period in the history of the world."

Wendy lit a cigarette and it turned Melissa's stomach.

"Could you not do that?" she asked.

"Sorry."

"I'm a little queasy."

Daryl skidded up on his bike, spraying the car with gravel.

"Hey," Wendy said, "watch it."

Melissa opened an eye and said, "Hey, bro." She never called him that. She guessed it was the Valium.

"What's wrong with you?" he asked.

"She's sick," Wendy said.

"She better be," Daryl said.

"Do I look that bad?" Melissa asked, smiling. It was hard to tell how much of her relief was genuine, how much was Valium, and how intricately it was veined with regret.

"You guys are busted," he said.

"For which thing?" Wendy asked.

"Skipping."

"Fuck," Melissa said.

"School called," he said, "and Mom's on a rampage."

"Great," Melissa said. "Just what I needed."

"You better hurry up if you want to get to your room and lock the door. She went to the grocery store, like, forty-five minutes ago."

"We better get our stories straight now," Wendy said.

Melissa opened her other eye and turned to Wendy. "I don't have the energy to lie."

Wendy thought for a second. "That's cool."

"It's too late anyway," Daryl said. "Here comes Mom."

■　　■　　■

The uniforms were the color of stale cream, their aprons dingy, and the lacy triangular paper caps would have been hideously ugly if they hadn't been monstrously silly. Joan had learned to blind herself to her reflection in the long, wide aluminum pans, temporary barracks to the regiments of doughnuts awaiting orders. It was no consolation, but Jenny, who was retiring next year, looked worse than Joan. There should be a law against degrading old women, thought Joan, though in Jenny's case it was hard to remember why. Jenny fed her epic coughing fits with packs of Pall Mall Gold 100s that she kept stashed—Joan couldn't get over it—between her arid breasts by means of the elastic of her ancient bras. You had to admire her cunning; no one bummed from her.

A customer left and Jenny hauled herself over to clean up after him. People annoyed her. They smudged the glass counters shielding her doughnuts with their oily human skin. She went through two rolls of paper towels and a bottle of Windex a week.

"Have you changed the coffee lately?" she asked Joan.

"About an hour ago."

"I'll get it," Queen Doughnut sighed, which provoked another explosive plea from her lungs.

Used to doing the work of two, she had the fresh coffee

going in just under twenty seconds. She returned to her end of the counter, where the regulars sat, and said, "Did you hear about them UFOs that landed in Yugoslavia?" Extraterrestrials were her favorite subject after communism and disease.

Joan checked in on Sammy, who came in after school to help with the doughnuts: encrusting them with peanuts; punching out their holes; puffing them up with apple, raspberry, and kreme fillings squeezed through pastry tubes. Joan could discern Sammy's artistry from that of Belinda, the girl who worked nights. The chocolate glazing of Belinda's eclairs was stingily applied; her powdereds were patchy. Jenny didn't like either of them, but Jenny didn't like anyone except Jeanne Dixon, a vicarious friendship conducted through prophecy. Jenny had a grandson, Rider, who lived with her and who had been between jobs for two years while he struggled towards an elusive GED, and Jenny thought Rider would make a dandy doughnut merchant.

"Are the Choc-O-Nuts ready?" Joan asked.

"Just about," he said.

"They smell great."

"Zat's because zhey are, how you say, cooked, by zee great Sammee." He put his finger over his lip for a French moustache.

Joan giggled.

Joan had tried to interest Melissa in Sammy, who played intramural volleyball, was shy, and had the thickest, blondest hair in the History of Thick Blond Hair. A year ago Joan wouldn't have bothered. Sammy wouldn't have been degenerate enough for her daughter. But the new, Case-less Melissa was an enigma who might go for the safe charms of the Sammys of this world. Since the abortion, Melissa had transformed herself. She made honor roll, pierced ears for money on a Formica island at a nearby mall, visited the drop-out, Wendy, when Wendy wasn't busy being married to Jumper, and watched TV silently with Kyle while eating caramel popcorn by the fistful. She'd put on weight. Only her earlobes hinted at her old self. There were three earrings stamped into one, the other was naked. Her newly acquired docility made Joan as nervous as the former cloak of hostility.

"If you don't mind," Jenny said, poking her head in, "we have some customers."

Joan couldn't bring herself to wish Jenny dead, but she could imagine the harridan up to her eyebrows in doughnut batter. Or someplace far away. Antarctica. The Congo. Mars.

■   ■   ■

Daryl listened uneasily as Mike strutted around the locker room, a hard-on bobbing from a fistful of pubic hair, and bragged about the girls lined up flexing their hands excitedly in anticipation of beating him off. He was supposed to be in ninth grade and had been kicked off the team last year for smoking during halftime. His ass-slapping and dirty jokes after practice were an ordeal Daryl had to get through five afternoons a week.

It had taken a few lousy games to get used to the shining wooden floors, the Plexiglas backboards, but the boot camp of Daryl's backyard court had proved good training. He didn't have time for the construction site anymore, which was just as well. Its guts had become the building it hinted at. There were fences hung with red, threatening signs and a guard house staffed by one old man who sat reading the paper and drinking from a Thermos when he wasn't sleeping, mouth open, or dully waving past trucks seriously heaped with supplies. It was a huge place that hummed and it was easier to imagine it had landed there than that it had been built.

Mike snapped his wet towel at Daryl and missed. Daryl jumped away, his dick flopping awkwardly.

"Great shot today," Mike called out as Daryl escaped into the shower.

Daryl had hit a doozy from across the court. "Thanks," he said, lifting his underarm to the warm pelting water. He hoped the massaging water might stimulate hair growth. He used deodorant for the same reason. Hairier, he might feel less naked, might snap wet towels, might wink at the cute cheerleader with braces who Mike claimed had blown him. Mike had gathered the guys around to witness the tooth marks. Daryl bet Mike had caught his dick in his zipper.

■   ■   ■

Kyle finished his route early and decided he'd treat Trish to lunch. As he wheeled into the yard he noticed that Herb, the bastard, had finished early too, despite the latest piece of Kyle's territory he'd gobbled up. Kyle couldn't understand how Herb did it. Kyle could barely get the job done, even with Herb's encroachments. There were other reasons to hate Herb: he knew the latest music though he was Kyle's age; he wore big rings; he didn't sweat; he never brought his lunch and his truck was littered with fast-food trash despite strict company policy about vehicular cleanliness. Women liked him. He kept a sleeping bag rolled up under the driver's seat for tossing off afternoon fucks in the back of his van.

Nobody knew where Trish was, but Kyle found her Saran-wrapped salad in the break-room fridge so he didn't think she'd gone to lunch. Kyle and Trish met for lunch casually, frequently. They'd found they both liked George Jones and were suspicious of Jimmy Carter. They liked complaining. They'd developed a taste for Chinese food and tried new dishes each time they ordered it. She hadn't convinced him that moo goo gai pan was best, but had come around to hot-and-sour soup, his favorite appetizer.

Joan didn't know. He felt like he was having an affair with none of the benefits and all of the hassles. He and Trish had kissed, to be done with it, one Friday afternoon over mai-tais and fried rice. For a week afterwards they had avoided one another, the friendship not rekindling until Trish, a bag of take-out in her hand, ran into Kyle hidden in the warehouse on a box of Kools polishing off an egg roll. They had laughed until they hurt. They were friends. That was better.

Kyle decided to catch a burger. Trish was probably running errands. He was about to jump down from the loading dock when he saw Herb. The back window of Herb's truck was cereal box–sized and filthy and he must have assumed that no one could see in through it. But in the intense midday light he was foggily visible from the waist up. He was naked. He was fucking some broad for all he was worth, his head thrown back. His mouth formed words and Kyle knew, without hearing, exactly what Herb was saying. He had her by the waist, dog-style. Kyle had to hand it to him, screwing a chick on company property for lunch: the guy had balls. Kyle had a hard-on.

It was odd to watch a man come, and stranger still since Kyle couldn't hear him. Herb's mouth dropped open and his eyes went wide, like a man being hung by the neck. When his orgasm was over, he pushed away and hurried into his uniform. While he struggled into his pants, the woman seemed to be lying naked on the truck's floor. His shirt buttoned, he pulled her up by the hair and kissed her brutally, one of her large nipples scissored between his fingers. He kissed her eyes, her nose, her chin, her mouth. It was Trish.

■   ■   ■

"Kevin's not like other children," Joan said.
"He's a kid," Kyle said.

"Harriet is afraid of him and she's been babysitting for thirty years."

"Harriet's an old fart."

"He almost bit Mrs. Tate's finger off. He's in the first grade and he's already been suspended twice."

"High spirits."

"High spirits my ass. That little girl's mother had to be talked out of a lawsuit. We could have lost the *Titanic*." Her pet name for their sinking house. Mr. Belmont's "boys" hadn't shown up yet and Joan was calling again tomorrow. His secretary knew Joan's voice and had developed this heavy, oh-you-again tone that Joan hoped the girl would choke on.

"He's curious," Kyle said.

"He glued her eyes shut during rest period because she was looking at him funny."

"O.K. O.K."

He took Kevin to Shoney's. They sat in a booth. When the waitress, a pert girl about Melissa's age, bent down into Kevin's face, Kyle said nervously, "Don't do that." Kevin had bitten enough people to form a club rivaling the Jaycees in membership. He ordered a hot fudge cake. Kyle ordered one too, to establish solidarity. Kevin called him a copycat. What Kevin needed was a good whipping, Kyle thought, but they had tried that. Kevin wouldn't cry no matter how hard or how many times you hit him. The old fart was right: Kevin was scary.

"How's school, sport?" Kyle asked.

"Yucky," Kevin said, wrinkling his face.

"Yucky?"

"Yeah. They make you do stuff all the time."

"There are a lot of things in this world that we have to do that we don't like. You're just going to have to get used to that."

"Why?"

The waitress set their desserts down.

"Anything else, sir?" she asked, careful to stand away from Kevin.

"No thanks," Kyle said.

"Some French fries, please," Kevin said.

The waitress looked at Kyle tentatively. "I don't think we need any fries," he said.

"Why do we have to do all that stupid stuff we don't want to?" Kevin asked again.

"Because that's the way things are, that's why. You're just going to have to trust me on this one."

"I don't think that's a very good answer." He didn't say it smart-alecky. Still, Kyle wanted to whop him one.

Kyle said, "If people only did what they wanted to, they wouldn't do anything." Unsettled, he wondered what he would do if he weren't compelled to work.

"I would," Kevin said, chocolate around his mouth, whipped cream on his nose, like other little boys. It was a relief.

"All right," Kyle said, "what would you do?"

"Draw pictures of everything."

"Are you a good drawer?"

Kevin shook his head yes. Kyle wanted some water. Sugar made him thirsty. Their waitress was busy pouring coffee at another booth.

"Will you draw me a picture when we get home?" Kyle asked.

"I can do it right now."

"I don't have a pen on me."

"I can draw with anything."

"Oh yeah?" Kyle said, humoring him.

Kevin unfolded his napkin. "Mr. Tartar showed me."

"At school?"

Kevin dipped his finger in the chocolate sauce.

Kyle said, "Why do you think you have a fork?"

"Let me show you this one thing and I promise not to ever do it again, not even in fifty drillion trillion."

Kyle looked around. People seemed too busy to notice. "O.K.," he said.

"I'll be real fast," Kevin said.

He dipped and drew, drew and dipped, now carefully, now quickly. He used the maraschino cherry. It was over in a couple of minutes. It didn't look like much upside down. Kyle felt taken advantage of.

"You just wanted to play in your food," he said.

Kevin turned the napkin around. It was a remarkable likeness of their waitress, except Kevin had drawn another mouth on her neck and stained it pink with maraschino cherry.

"How did you do that?" Kyle asked.

"Mr. Tartar showed me."

"Is he your teacher?"

"Kind of."

It was spooky anyone so young could draw so well. Kyle dimly remembered an aunt who'd drawn depressing flowers and who had shot herself in a motel room in Tucson.

"You should play more," he said.

"This is playing," Kevin said.

"I mean outside, with other boys."

"I don't like outside. I don't like other boys."

"I'll teach you how to play ball this spring. We'll go to a couple of Daryl's games."

"I don't like balls."

"You'll learn to."

Kevin pulled the drawing in two with chocolatey, splayed-out hands.

"I won't," he said.

■　　■　　■

Kyle was drunk again. He sang over the top of the band and roamed his hands over Joan's backside. He'd already spilled two drinks. At least he hadn't pissed on himself and passed out in the bathroom like three weeks ago. Yet. Joan would have given up Saturday nights but the doughnut shop made her crave them.

She was wearing her Eva Gabor wig. She had two others and a fall pinned to the Styrofoam heads on her dresser. Wigs weren't as popular as they once had been. Used to be every other woman had one. Tonight she'd noticed only a couple of others unless some exceptionally naturalistic ones were floating around. She was a wig master. Hers were expertly camouflaged. Half in the bag, she'd shocked the crowd one night by tossing the hair helmet into the air after an especially good song. Other wig-wearers followed suit. Joan had known the glamour of trendsetting for an evening. At the Moose Lodge, it became known as the Hair-Raising Night.

Kyle tongued her ear.

She pushed him away.

"Don't you love me, baby?" he asked, falling back on her.

"Not when you're like this."

He walked two fingers up her thigh. "You still turn me on, wifey."

Joan blocked the toy hand when it got to her panty line. She was not going to let those fingers do the walking.

"Later," she said, "if you behave."

He pressed her hand against his erection. "Remember this?" he whispered.

She took her hand back. "Would you please stop acting like a goddamned fourteen-year-old who's never been laid?"

"You should be damn glad I still want to fuck you," he said loud enough to turn heads.

There were so many ways to humiliate him at that moment that she didn't know where to start. He was a drunk. He'd put on a few more pounds. He'd never been a fantastic fuck. He was losing his route, not to a younger man, but to one with more spunk. He was not bright. She had to face that. He didn't even read the funny pages. She tried to remember a single comment he'd made in eighteen years and nothing came to mind. His eyes were unfocused. He chose that moment to belch. She gave the marriage another two years, maybe less. She felt like a runner who had rounded a long curve that brought the finish line unexpectedly into view.

"What are you looking at?" he asked.

"You," she said, kissing his forehead and leaving behind the pink shadow of her lips. He grinned. He wasn't a bad man. Bad had nothing to do with it.

■　　■　　■

Buddy, Kristy McNichol's character on "Family," was speechifying about friendship. Melissa hoped that Wendy, the traitor, was listening from her married apartment. Melissa picked another kernel from between her teeth, caramel popcorn's only flaw. She wished she could meet a guy like Kristy, but nothing doing, not in her lifetime, not on this planet.

Kyle was asleep. Unless it was basketball, he never made it through the ten o'clock shows, but she enjoyed his silent company. She still hated her mother, not actively; it was more like a habit she couldn't break. It seemed a form of protection, but from what she didn't know.

Case and Melissa said hi when they passed one another in the halls. He had a new girlfriend, Taffy, a ninth-grader who actually wore high heels to school and hung all over Case in the smoking area. She had "babymaker" written all over her, the kind who would get oven mitts to match the stove. He was welcome to her.

People thought Melissa had broken up with him because he wouldn't acknowledge the baby, but he was the one who'd wanted to elope and find an apartment near Wendy and Jumper. Melissa had gotten the abortion behind his back. He'd taken it hard, crying, asking whether it had been a girl or a boy. "An egg," she'd said. "It wasn't fucking anything." He'd literally kicked her out of the car onto the school parking lot, frantically reaching over her to open the passenger door and shouting, "Bitch, bitch, bitch," as if it were a spell, deadly in its simplicity. In spite of her pavement-bloodied elbow and her bruised thigh, she'd been relieved. She didn't know what she wanted to become, but it didn't include a gas station attendant grinding on top of her for the rest of her life. She was thinking about college, though her guidance counselor had told her she'd be lucky to get into beauty school with her grades. She responded by making honor roll. Joan seemed to resent the change in her daughter, sensing she had nothing to do with it.

"It's almost over," she said, bouncing a nugget of caramel popcorn off Kyle's red nose, shiny with TV light.

"I'm awake," he said, not stirring. "I'm just resting my eyes." He said that every night. It moved Melissa that he disliked going to bed, like a child, or a person who was dying.

■   ■   ■

The eighth valentine Brenda made looked as queer as the other seven. She could not get it like it was in her head.

"Daddy," she said. He was watching a game with Melissa, who'd grown as strange and silent as Kevin. Brenda hoped weirdness wasn't a hereditary trait that reached out and grabbed you unexpectedly one day. It would disqualify her for cheerleaderdom. She'd have to join the science club or the debate team or some other nerd organization for quiet dorks.

"What, sugar?" Kyle asked.

"I can't make this work right."

"Give him one of the bought ones."

"It's for Louis, though."

She was going to be a cheerleader and Louis was going
to be her sports-boyfriend. Louis had dimples and a Dennis
the Menace cowlick that begged to be patted down when
he passed to sharpen a pencil or turn in a test. She was
determined that this wouldn't be just another sixth-grade
romance that petered out in junior high. She wanted his
babies. Not that they'd talked except for hi on the blacktop;
but he had chosen her first for kickball after the good boy
players had been picked over. She hoped he didn't think
she was boyfied.

"Get Kevin to do it." Kyle popped another beer from the
cooler by his TV chair.

"He's a first-grader."

"He draws like nobody's business."

"Kevin who bites?"

"The very one."

"You're tricking me."

"I'll prove it. Hey, Kev, come help your sister with her
valentine."

"No," he called from his room.

"She doesn't think you can do it."

"Can too."

"So show her."

Giant pause. "O.K. But it won't be for her."

He came into the dining room dragging his blanket and
wearing his baggy Spaceghost pajamas. His face was red and
sleepy. On the table were the tools of love's trade: glue,
glitter, tinsel, crayons, scissors, construction paper, cardboard from Kyle's dry-cleaned uniform shirts, watercolors—
a Surprise Inside from Captain Crunch—that wrinkled the
paper more than painted it. Brenda had glitter on her elbow,
glue on her cheek, a Band-Aid on her pinky. Now she understood why they were called pinky shears.

"What?" Kevin said, sleepy-blinking.

"Do you really draw good?" Brenda asked.

Kevin nodded yes.

"O.K. If you make me the coolest valentine, I promise to give you all my Valentine's Day candy."

"Promise-swear?"

"Cross my heart and hope to die."

"Even the chocolate marshmallow hearts?"

"Everything."

"O.K. But go in with Daddy 'cause you can't see or it'll mess up."

"Deal."

She sat on the arm of Kyle's chair, circled her arms around his neck, and rested her cheek on his. He was old and wore greasy kid's stuff. His beer smelled awful. Ripping sounded from the dining room. Kevin might be destroying her supplies. He would do that.

"What's going on in there?" she asked.

"Daddy," Kevin yelled, stopping.

"Leave him alone," Kyle said. "He's a genuine artist or something."

Kevin took a million weeks. Brenda could have made a store full of valentines. The tearing drove her crazy. If he was ripping everything up, she was going to cut off his fingers. The pinky shears seemed sturdy enough. Then they'd see how well he drew.

"O.K.," he said.

Brenda made it into the dining room in three leaps, a Demerest record. The valentine was more beautiful than a dollar with lace. It was the size of Kevin's shirt and glued from the scraps of Brenda's failed valentines. It was all colors but looked like one whole thing. She couldn't figure it out. Coolest, though she didn't like it personally, were the tiny eyes and knives he'd drawn over it. Louis would love that. The other cards would look like toilet paper.

"Amazing," she said.

"I want my candy first thing after school or else."

"I'll give it to you on the bus. Don't worry, I'll get a lot."

"You just better. This was hard. I didn't like it."

"Can I touch it?"

"The glue has to dry, stupid."

■　　■　　■

Joan was nervous. She'd invited Sammy over for dinner without telling Melissa. He was following her in his nice, green, unsexy Maverick. He jumped Joan's car when it rained. She hoped he wouldn't be as disappointed with Melissa as she was. Not that she'd told him this was a set-up. She supposed she had lied, not lied exactly, but played up Melissa's good parts. "Melissa has beautiful skin," when it wasn't hidden under a slab of makeup. "Melissa is such a sweet girl," when she wasn't locked up silently within herself. "Oh, Melissa likes that too," Joan would say when she saw Sammy bopping his head to the transistor radio he kept on top of the freezer.

Joan turned into the driveway and Sammy pulled up in front of the mailbox. She hoped he wouldn't notice her house was sinking. They were still running tests to figure out why. She hadn't noticed any drops lately, but it was a gradual thing you could fool yourself about until another layer of cinder blocks had disappeared. She sometimes feared the whole shebang would plunge into the earth when she stepped on the porch. She had nightmares about it.

Sammy had made a large glazed doughnut for dessert. Thank God Brenda was practicing cheers at Fiona's. She'd gotten testy about Joan's working in a doughnut shop. Joan had explained to Sammy that her youngest, Kevin, was still in his biting phase and to steer clear. Kevin's latest suspension had been over a realistic rendering on the chalkboard of his first-grade teacher. He'd given her enormous breasts and a dog's tail. He'd entitled it "Uglyhead."

Kyle was home early again. Soon his route would consist of street corners where he loaned cigarettes to bums. Daryl was at practice. Joan never saw her son anymore unless she went to a basketball court. She wished life had a speed button so you could fast forward through the unpleasantness—Kyle's drunken humpings that felt like rape immediately sprang to mind—or slow down, maybe even back up, when she'd missed something like her son not being a child anymore. At what moment had it happened?

Melissa and Kyle were sitting in the dark, the TV light shimmering over them. They looked long dead. It was gruesome. She turned on a light.

"Welcome back to the land of the living," she said.

Sammy stood behind her, smiling, the doughnut in a box in his hands.

"Who's he?" Kyle asked.

"Sammy, this is my husband, Mr. Demerest, and my daughter, Melissa."

"Nice to meet you," Sammy said.

"You're the perfect one Mom works with, right?" Melissa asked.

Joan wanted to throw herself between him and Melissa's sarcasm.

"I try," Sammy said. He was too pleasant for this family.

"You're too much, Mom," Melissa said, leaning back to stare at the television. She was already onto Joan's plot.

Sammy leaned forward to see what they were watching. " 'Bewitched' is my favorite show," he said. He smelled like sugar.

Joan allowed herself to breathe. It was Melissa's favorite show too. Maybe this could work.

"Did my mother tell you to say that?" Melissa asked, goring him through the center with her smile.

"Huh?" Sammy said.

"Maybe I should just take you down to my room and blow you to get it over with so we can eat in peace."

Sammy turned to Joan, who was weak with embarrassment. Kyle jumped Melissa, slapped her two, three, four times. Joan lost count. She shut her eyes.

"I won't have that kind of slutty talk in my house," he screamed, crying.

When Joan dared to open her eyes again, Kyle was leaning against his chair, his shirt tail half in, half out. Melissa stared at him, dry-eyed. She reached into her pocket, pulled out a cigarette, and lit it, something she had never done before in their presence.

"Relax, Dad," she said, turning back to the TV, "it was a joke. Have another beer."

■　　■　　■

Now that she and Louis officially liked each other, Brenda needed a bra. Joan had objected, but a tantrum unlike anything Brenda had ever mustered before had convinced Joan of the essential nature of this purchase. Even Kevin, King Tantrum, had been impressed by Brenda's sobs and shrieks and stamping feet.

Brenda loved the girls' lingerie section, the clean cotton smell of it. She would never wear simple underwear again, and certainly nothing with pictures on it. From here on out it was going to be lace and pastels. A silly crone with glasses around her neck was helping them. She asked where the young miss was who needed the training bra, though Brenda was standing right in front of her blind eyes. Joan shrugged, thinking herself very funny.

Brenda narrowed it down to three. They hadn't even measured her because her mother, funny as a heart attack, had said "the smallest" when Helen Keller had asked what size.

Brenda went into the dressing room. She did have breasts and she didn't care what they said. Joan hadn't seen Brenda with her shirt off since last summer at Buckroe Beach when Brenda had still been tomboyish, so what did she know?

Brenda put her coat on the bench and unbuttoned her

blouse. She looked at her chest in the mirror. She pulled
on her nipples and hunched her shoulders together. There
they were; she knew she hadn't been imagining them. They
weren't as large as she remembered but they were there.
She put on the pink one first. She fluffed it up a bit. It still
looked empty. Maybe it was the wrong size. She hunched
her shoulders again but that bunched and wrinkled the bra
something awful and made her chest look bony. She had to
have breasts if she was going to be a cheerleader and the
future Mrs. Louis Taylor. Where were they? She'd just seen
them a second ago. Oh wait, there they were. When she
was kind of sideways you could see them. She'd just have
to stand that way all the time. She wondered how you got
boys to know you had one on so you could hate them for
snapping it.

Her mother knocked on the door and said, "What are you
doing in there, having implants?"

"MOTHER," Brenda whispered as loud as a yell.

"Brenda, I have ten thousand things to do today. I'm sure
the bras are fine. Just put your breasts back so we can get
to the grocery store before it closes."

Brenda said, "You're not a real mother."

"I'm sorry. It's just that I've been working all week and
. . . tell you what, you can have all three. How about that?"

"And can I pick out the cereal at the grocery store?"

"Sure."

"I do have breasts. You just can't see them yet."

"Whatever you say, Raquel Welch."

Brenda understood how Melissa could hate a mother like
Joan, who didn't care about anything but her stupid new job
selling doughnuts, an embarrassing to the max thing to do
if there ever was one. If Brenda saw one more box of stale
misshapen doughnuts laying around the house, she was
going to spit blood. Nice mothers listened when their daughters said they had breasts. They didn't call them big-boob
women names like Raquel Welch.

"You're the queerest of the queer," Brenda said back.
"I think we're back down to two bras."
Brenda hoped she wouldn't have to cry to get her way.

■   ■   ■

She'd had to tug at her bra until after lunch before some
idiot boy had noticed and chanted, "Brenda's got a bra."
Louis was proud. He'd pushed Reggie down for saying she
was flat and now held her hand every day at lunch. She
didn't mind eating with one hand, though Salisbury steak
was hard to cut that way. She would have eaten with no
hands for their love.

She spent a good part of the next week going to the
bathroom with various girls. The pink one was everybody's
favorite. She really wanted a bra and she guessed it was time
now that she and Louis were so deeply in love. Their favorite song was "The Way of Love" by Cher. Cher was so
beautiful Brenda could cry.

Melissa was babysitting tonight while their queero parents
were out dancing. It was a total insult. People who wore
bras didn't need babysitters and, to drive the point home,
Brenda was lying around with her wet hair up in a towel
and the yellow bra, her least favorite, under her nightgown.
Kevin was being punished for drawing an Indian head in
green Magic Marker on the bathtub. It wasn't very good,
but Brenda hadn't seen it until after Joan had already taken
the Comet to it. Brenda was nicer to Kevin now that she
realized he was useful. He still hated her, but that was
youth. Daryl was out roller skating with the team. He'd
been a big hero at the last game and Brenda had been proud
to be his sister. Also, Louis was impressed by her brother,
the basketball star, though she'd accidentally said that Daryl
had been on TV and Louis had not stopped bugging her
about it: when was he going to be on again? Louis was
gullible.

Brenda had decided that she and Melissa should be friends. Brenda was the trailblazer in boy-girl relationships at her school. A couple of other people liked each other but no one else was going together. Brenda needed information she was sure Melissa had, though Melissa was into this Kristy McNichol thing and had her room plastered with fanzine pictures.

Melissa stuffed another wad of caramel popcorn in her mouth. They were watching "Carol Burnett." It was the boring part where everybody sang. Girls at school were asking Brenda questions now that she was practically married, and she couldn't keep making things up. Last week she'd told them that not every woman bled every month (that couldn't be true), only the clumsy ones who bumped into things a lot. She half-believed her own theories and moved with greater caution and grace, lest she trip some blood lever inside her.

"Melissa?"

"Huh?" she said through a mouthful of caramel popcorn.

"What's a sixty-nine?" Brenda sounded as matter-of-fact as possible.

"It's when a man and a woman lick each other's toes."

"Liar."

"No, really. It's called a seventy when they bite."

"Gross out."

"You have to do it after you're married. I hope Louis has nice, clean toes."

"Have to?"

"Ask Mom and Dad." Carol Burnett pulled on her ear as a sign to her grandmother. Brenda thought it was sweet. She bet Carol didn't go around licking things.

"They don't do that," she said.

"All married people do."

"Why?"

"Why do people do anything?"

"You're a big, fat liar."

"Suit yourself."

"Did you and Casey do it?"

"We weren't married."

Brenda couldn't tell this at school. It was too embarrassing. She'd have to make something up. She realized she was wriggling her toes and stopped. She'd have to get Louis to take off his shoes to see what she was in for.

■   ■   ■

Kyle walked down the hall the boxes of cigarettes formed. The warehouse was dusky and cool and the air was sweetened by the scent of cured tobacco. He had a service report to turn in. It had not been a bad week. Herb had the flu and Kyle had gotten back some of his old route, which he'd worked overtime to finish. A hand turned him around by the shoulder of his shirt. It was Trish, in baby blue, unusual for her.

"O.K.," she said, "what's going on here?"

"I don't know what you're talking about," Kyle said, gently removing her hand from him.

"I've sat there and listened to your whole life—I know your mother's maiden name, for Christ's sake—and you have the nerve to say 'I don't know.' " She said this last part simperingly.

"I've been busy."

"You're a fucking coward."

Even angry, her face had a kind of perfection, and she had let a slob like Herb near it. She shook her head in disgust and turned away from him. She'd gone about ten steps when he said, "Besides, I don't think it's a good idea for me to be seen eating lunch with a whore."

She stopped and stood for what seemed like long enough to consider her whole life, but it was probably no more than ten seconds. She turned around and spit. It sprayed across his right cheek.

"You're a goddamned hypocrite."

He wiped his cheek on his shirtsleeve and said, "Back where I come from, that's what we call girls who get fucked in trucks on their lunch hour."

The change in her expression was subtle, the way earthquakes are said to register a hundred miles from the center of the collapse and ruin, but it made the month he'd spent hating her worth it. She stood as if poured and solidified to that one spot. She kept blinking. She said, "You were too nice to screw," and shrugged and laughed. The laugh was more like a cough.

He could not discern the exact moment when she disappeared into the warehouse's darkness. The blue of her dress seemed to flicker for long seconds after it should have vanished, like a streak of sky that rejects the idea of night.

■　　■　　■

Melissa wished Leon Russell would play rock and roll, and quit talking about it. The magic mushrooms weren't helping. She couldn't remember disliking a concert so much. The flashing lights widened her eyes until she thought they would split. She wondered if she was remembering to blink. If gravel were music it would sound like this. She could feel it in her heart. It seemed to be taking over her body. The smell of pot was thick as syrup, nauseating. Her mouth was dry. It seemed to be flaking away.

She remembered thinking her date handsome, but currently his bearded face looked like a stuffed toy. He was twenty-three and worked with Jumper. She liked his earring, a simple gold ball. He'd pierced it himself, using an ice cube, an ice pick, and a pint of Jack Daniels. He'd tried a needle but the hole wasn't big enough. From a professional's point of view, Melissa thought he'd done a workmanlike job, vulgar but effective. Wendy wanted her daughter's ears pierced and only by godmother Melissa, but Melissa had convinced her to wait until the child was at least a year old. Rochelle was with her grandmother tonight. It was the first time they'd been out in months. It was starting to freak Melissa out that she punched holes in people's ears for a living. It seemed too dark and primitive for $7.95.

"Let's go to the bathroom," she whispered to Wendy.

They bumped along the row of knees. The floor was sticky. Melissa felt like she was in a used condom. The corridor outside the collseum was bright and yellow. The edges of objects were too sharply defined. Everything seemed on the verge of moving. Melissa concentrated fiercely to keep the world from flying apart. The bathroom was empty and quiet, the fluorescent light gray and calm. She could spend the rest of the concert here.

"What are we doing?" Wendy asked.

"I had to pee," Melissa lied.

"Oh."

"But now I can't."

They laughed for ten minutes, then Melissa noticed the mirror.

"Look at us," she said.

"Our skin's glow-y," Wendy said, rubbing her arms.

Melissa touched Wendy's skin also. It was smooth. There was light in it. Her hand moved to Wendy's neck. She felt the astonishing beat of Wendy's heart there. Her own heart seemed to scoop up Wendy's rhythm. Wendy's hair was luminescent and seemed the embodiment of some truth. She kissed her the way she'd always wanted Case to kiss. Wendy wiped her mouth and pushed Melissa away. Melissa bruised her hip on the sink.

"What the fuck is wrong with you?" Wendy asked.

"I don't know," Melissa said, whirling inside. "I thought you were like Case or something. I must be totally tripping my brains out."

"Are you a dyke or something?"

"I had a fucking abortion."

"Why didn't you marry Case?"

"I didn't love him."

"Why?"

"I don't know." Her answer seemed like a trick.

"I think you're a fucking dyke."

"I like . . ." Melissa began, but no phrase seemed to fit the end of the sentence. The bathroom was horrible and long. There were hundreds of Melissas and Wendys in the mirrors. Time seemed stuck in its effort to hurry so many selves to the next second. Any instant now, it was going to resume. Melissa willed the present not to start. It was like trying to stop traffic with your bare hands. She'd read about mothers stopping cars to save their children, but she couldn't stop this; and suddenly, drowning in Wendy's disgust, she quit wanting motionlessness. She felt as if, for the past year, she'd been saving herself from saving herself, and she didn't have the will for it any longer. She decided to murder her life. Relief and fear poured through her like ice water. Three words.

"Yes," she said, "I am."

■   ■   ■

There were games when cheering fans were adrenaline, when you knew where your opponent would move before he did, when tired was what happened to other players, when footwork was a sly form of dance, when the hoop was the gravitational center of a universe only you inhabited. Then there were games when you were half a second off, when your feet were as clumsy as animals due for extinction, when the ball was everybody's friend but yours. Practice helped. The games that were like a form of intuition came more easily, but still weren't guaranteed.

Daryl was beginning to wish his father would stay home. Kyle yelled at umpires. He'd been caught sneaking in beer. His clothes were old and rumpled. He brought caramel popcorn, an addiction he'd picked up from Melissa, who'd abandoned the TV club of two. Kyle got worked up. He got sloppy. Daryl hated himself for his embarrassment.

Daryl struggled for the Cs you had to make to stay on the team. Reading tired him. He couldn't talk to girls. Only the court forgave him, transfigured imperfection, gave his body an eloquence it lacked in classrooms and other earthly realms. It was a form of grace.

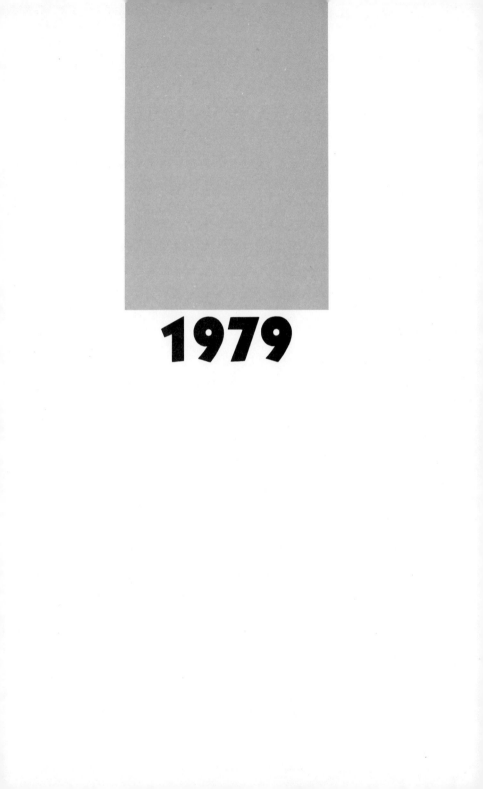

1979

Joan tried to ignore the house: the first step of the front porch completely submerged in dirt, cracks in the backyard patio wide enough to stick your finger in, the bottom foot of the foundation missing. It was on its way to becoming a furnished cave. The other houses on her block sat placidly atop the earth. Families glided in and out of them, swathed in the silken assumption that terra was firma. Joan was touched by their ignorance. It moved her to nostalgia. She had been that way once. Now only her terror was firmer. She prepared for moledom.

"They" still didn't know what the problem was. She didn't think they ever would. There was talk of "girderizing," that is, attaching large steel Ls to the walls and securing them to more stable soil. She had to understand that this was an experimental method of support. In fact, she had to sign a contract absolving the county of any and all responsibility. Mr. Belmont had shown her tentative, desolate drawings: her house in spidery, black lines, an abandoned oil rig in a sea of normality, the unsinkable houses surrounding hers sketched in pale greens and pinks, like mints.

Her yard still blossomed. The rose bushes and crepe myrtle had buds. The hedges were green and healthy. The marigolds bordering the patio were vibrant, as if decayed concrete were a flower elixir. The tomatoes she'd planted on either side of the chimney had grown to the size of succulent softballs and had attracted prehistoric-looking bugs that snapped off leaves with their large claws and stuffed them whole into their ugly bug mouths. She'd gone through a case of Raid. When she mentioned the odd creatures to her neighbors, no one else seemed to have noticed them.

■ ■ ■

Sandy Rhodes had hoped the spontaneity of teaching children would reinspire her. This past year, though she'd gone to her father's river place on weekdays, when it was silent of family squabbles and family card games (these were often one and the same), she hadn't done more than a dozen sketches, all of them stilted. Instead of drawing, she had canned vegetables. She was still giving away mason jars of string beans. She knew her paintings were intelligent, well-crafted, but she was beginning to suspect those very qualities as her enemies. Her surfaces were exacting but they were dull. They took flight but lacked altitude.

Each of the thirty-two elementary classes took a turn to come and bake ashtrays and fingerpaint and weave macrame belts and it was not inspiring. It was babysitting. She didn't hate them, but there were too many and they bled together like a watercolor left out in the rain. They liked art because it was messy and they could make their mothers birthday presents. The other teachers horrified her. Rudeness, rebels, and 'rithmatic had burned them into cynical crisps.

Then there was Kevin. At first, he'd been one more smudge in the blur, but in the third quarter of the school year, when she'd tried vainly to interest second-graders in color theory, she'd noticed him listening. Then she'd noticed him applying everything she'd said to his sheet of newsprint. When she'd asked him what he was doing, he'd said, "Trying to make the color more walking around when it isn't on stuff." That sounded like a reasonable definition of nonobjective art to her.

Why did he want to do that?

Because, he said, still drawing, if the colors could make people be walking around on paper, why couldn't it be walking around by itself?

Her heart had punched.

His drawing was at least junior high level and his sense of color was original, daring even, better than many of her colleagues from graduate school (that wasn't saying much) and most of her teachers (that was saying even less). It was more pronounced than half of what you saw in New York galleries, another backhanded compliment. She only wished it weren't so . . . violent. Even the more abstract pieces were animated by an energy that unnerved her. All of his pictures were called *The Pretty Hides the Big Stupid.*

■   ■   ■

Jenny did not retire after all, despite her stroke. One side of her face had collapsed and she thought twice as much makeup helped to disguise this sorry fact. It didn't. She looked like melted candles, which kept Joan in a constant state of agitation. Joan paced the small aisle they worked in like a recently caged animal. More painful yet, Sammy, after the Melissa incident, had begun to treat her with a condescending friendliness that Joan recognized because she used it herself, with the infirm and the insane. She couldn't eat doughnuts. Any breakfast sweet made her nauseous. When she stopped being able to put sugar in her coffee, she quit.

The card shop wasn't bad, but it was slow. She didn't know how they stayed in business, but she and Flora kept it spotless. There was nothing else to do. They made sure "To a Fine Nephew on His Graduation" hadn't strayed into the BEREAVEDs. They polished the crystal circus figurines, careful not to snap the elephant's trunk or the aerialist's arm. They restacked erasers. They rearranged stationery. The desperate gratitude of their "Thank you"s after they rung up "On This Your Anniversary" unnerved patrons. But the smell of the paper heaped around them comforted Joan. It smelled like innocence.

Flora was pleasant but dotty. She flounced around the store in her pastels like a contessa hosting a tea party, revising sprays of scented paper flowers that went for a dime a pop. She was terminally excited, full of ideas. For Mother's Day she planned to dye aprons—bought with her own money—pink. She planned to tie them end from end and drape them from the ceiling. Like Jenny, Flora had three favorite subjects; her's were her illustrious Virginia genealogy, the arts, her daughters. They were actually all the same subject. The daughters were in the arts and of the lineage, descended from "a Spotswood, yes, oh my, even the royal governor himself." Joan vaguely remembered a great-great-aunt on her father's side, Bitsy, who'd worn veils, but that was as genealogical as she got. Flora's nattering made Joan unutterably tired. She spent the afternoons in a torpor, wacky greeting card poems chattering in her head: "You're not old, just filled with mold, and burnished gold, the farm's been sold, Achoo! a cold." While Flora went on about Spring—poor child, that was her real name—who choreographed people dressed as barnyard animals at a theme park in the Midwest, or Jeanne—pronounced to rhyme with "done"—who wrote radio jingles for a furniture store in town, or Anastasia, who . . .

■　　■　　■

Daryl's torso was winter white and hair was beginning to mist his legs. Joan hoped Kyle had talked to him about sex. The lawn mower was far enough away to be a pleasant hum.

A velvet blanket of cut grass lay across the ground and seemed to revive the surprisingly sticky spring air. Daryl's shoes were burned green. Joan sipped at her tea as she clipped the hedge. She had cut them last weekend, but they were thicker than ever. If the doughnut shop had made Joan long for Saturday nights, the card shop made her crave daylight. She had the unspoken hope that if she nurtured the ground it would stop eating her house. So far, so good. It was holding steady at an eleven-and-three-quarter-inch decline.

If Melissa had been there she would have been bitching and moaning and hung over. But she wasn't there. On her eighteenth birthday, Melissa had packed grocery bags and boxes marked RECORDS. She had called a cab. She didn't say good-bye. She lived in a studio downtown and managed the ear-piercing joint. She called every now and again to tell whomever picked up the phone that she was still alive. Her phone number was unlisted and she would not give it out. Her whole life seemed like one long reproach to Joan's.

Something heavy, a piece of bark, perhaps, fell into Joan's hair, but when she knocked at it, it tangled more. It was sharp like a stick and would not come loose. It bit her. Two perfect dots of blood rose on her hand. She ran towards Daryl, slapping her hair and frantically shaking her head. He couldn't hear her over the mower.

"Get it out, get it out," she was screaming as the engine died.

"What? What is it?"

"GET IT OUT OF MY HAIR!"

He pulled her arms down. She tried to hit him. It was one of the bugs. A big fucker. Daryl tried to pick it out. "HURRY," his mother yelled. It bit him. It drew blood. The pain was enormous and deep. They hadn't done that last summer. He snapped it in two. They were strong, but they were still bugs.

"I killed it," he said.

"Get it out of my hair."

They had to cut it out with the hedge clippers. Joan sat the rest of the day in a bandanna, on a lawn chair, wielding a shovel. She must have smashed twenty of the insects. At dusk, Daryl rinsed the shovel of goo with the garden hose. That evening she bought a gallon of extra-strength poison, a nozzle to spray it with, and a blue mask that made her look like a surgeon. She also made an appointment at the beauty parlor.

■   ■   ■

The team was having pizza after the game, a Friday night ritual. You could tell when they lost. They talked quietly amongst themselves about how Daryl had been robbed, I mean robbed, on that cross-court shot. That baby had been in there. They had all seen it. When they lost they ate two pizzas instead of four. They did not high-five until their palms stung. They did not spit Coke.

Mike whispered to Daryl, his breath warm and salty, "Listen, man, if we can get to my house, I can get this chick that lives two blocks over to come over and blow both of us."

"Shit," Daryl said.

"I'm not shitting you, man. I mean she's fat, but shit, a blow job's a blow job, you know what I mean?"

Daryl didn't but he wished he did. "I can't, man. My old lady's picking me up."

Mike shrugged. "It's your loss. Think about me when you're slamming the old ham tonight. This bitch is seventeen and she goes all the way down, man, all the way."

Daryl felt such a mixture of fear and lust that he couldn't tell one from the other. He bit through his pepperoni and extra cheese and chipped a tooth.

Real attractive.

■   ■   ■

Suzy inspired tenderness in Kyle. Her moans were long and tinged with disbelief and he loved them. One of her eyes was blue, and one was green, and he loved them. After sex she'd smell like wet grass and he loved it. He licked the balls of her feet, her scalp, the pink, wrinkled rose of her asshole. Nothing was dirty with her. He loved feeling the insideness of her. He loved to fuck her slowly and for a long time, browsing, meandering, discovering circuitous paths to orgasms that surprised him in the violence of their relief.

He was old enough to know that part of it was novelty. He and Joan had wrung the possibilities of their bodies dry. One night, when he'd had one too many, when he thought he'd given it to her good, like the old days, Joan said she felt like she'd been raped. She had tried to push him off, but she'd done that before and it hadn't meant anything. He might have been a little rough. He couldn't remember. Afterwards, after she'd said that word, he could barely stand to peck her good-bye in the morning. Afterwards, the thought of intimacy between them brimmed him with a directionless disgust. It wasn't for himself, and it wasn't for his wife, and it wandered him, escaping at odd moments. Looking down from his truck, Kyle could loathe the stranger below him who ate tuna fish in her Toyota while fiddling with the radio, neglecting some onion, or was it celery, above her lip.

Suzy was like finding a garden that was mysterious and familiar at once, where you wanted to touch each petal, every leaf, the singular blades of grass, the black earth, the cobblestones, the pollen-scented air. You wanted the burst of new experience while savoring, at the exact same moment, each sensation as its own realm. He could spend an afternoon exploring her mouth with his tongue, his finger, his cock; its slick velvet softly bitten or swollen with him: there was no end of kissing her. The moments were alcoves where she was hidden, and where he eternally and unexpectedly stumbled across her within himself.

Suzy turned up the radio on her bedstand and lit a cigarette. She was not pretty, certainly not as pretty as Joan. There was a stubborn carelessness to her appearance that seemed to imply that all worry about looks was officially declared over. Her hair was dreary, her breasts were mannish, and her hips puddled around her when she sat. She wore uncomfortably short dresses. Her one vanity was her pubic hair, which she kept manicured. She didn't wear panties and he loved casually inserting a finger inside her when they were out. She'd sigh but it was difficult to name the human noise as pleasure or exasperation. It didn't sound like either. She seemed to accept the finger as inevitable because it was there, like a sneeze or a sudden break in the weather.

She owned the things you needed to live: a bed, a couch, a toaster, a toothbrush. But nothing seemed chosen for charm or beauty. There were no mementos, no pictures, nothing old, nothing odd, nothing sprinkled with the residue of sentiment or nostalgia or longing. Only her enormous television seemed new, cared-for, expensive, but there was no comfortable place to watch it from, not one. She sat right up to it, flicking channels with no apparent reason or interest, on the edge of a cheap, pink child's rocker with pandas quilted on the headrest. One of the bowed, wooden slats had shattered. He had thought the small, lopsided chair a clue to her, but no; she'd found it already broken in the laundry room and didn't know why she'd lugged it three flights.

He said, "Tell me."

It was a game he played in his hunger to know her. After they made love, they had to recount a story from their past, the sort of chatter that sprang up naturally between lovers; but with her nothing seemed to happen of its own accord. Except sex.

"One time," she said, "I was baking brownies for my brother's birthday and I burned them really bad."

"What happened?"

"Nothing. We went out and bought some more."

All her stories were like that.

■   ■   ■

The night of the earthquake, Joan called Mr. Belmont at midnight, not realizing her rattling knickknacks and shuddering walls were an uncomfortable planet fussing with its layers, thinking instead that her house was making one abrupt and final descent. But her whimsical home hadn't budged. It sank in accordance with its own unfathomable laws, which were not natural ones. Her foundation would be buried in a year, maybe two. The precipice of the front porch would be level with the yard; the patio would be crumbs. Last week a neighbor's dog had lamed itself in the patio's cracked concrete and she'd wasted half a week's paycheck, tears, and a sleepless night having the mutt put to sleep. She didn't like being called a murderess. For legal protection she nailed NO TRESPASSING signs to pine trees, a Belmont suggestion.

"Girderizing" her house was still an unattractive option, and funds had been allocated to stash the Demerests in the Holiday Inn off Route 60. But relocation included signing all rights to her home over to the city, and there was no guarantee of reimbursement if "the structure was terminated." After all, who could determine what was an unacceptable level of sinkage, or if the house was sinking at all? Perhaps the ground was rising. Would that constitute sinkage? They'd be back at square one, defining terms, regrouping committees. The Sinking Committee wouldn't feel comfortable with questions concerning the earth's upward movement. It might be best to stay put for the present.

Kyle was fucking some whore. He always had the most pleasant, most plausible excuses for his late arrivals. Joan's various reactions—murderous, indifferent, murderously indifferent—seemed to have almost no bearing on the affair itself, were so mercurial that they might have been governed by the moon, subtle shifts of the wind, the rotating lunch specials at the cafeteria near the card shop. Joan had become mysterious to herself. It was true that with age came wisdom, but wisdom turned out to be as baffling as ignorance. Knowledge was formalized confusion.

■ ■ ■

Brenda could see Sherry's mother and father crying in gray folding chairs by the small, white coffin. The wind had fiddled with the square, black collar of her black dress and she righted it. She wished she'd sprinkled perfume on her handkerchief. The funeral home smelled like science class crossed with a florist shop. The pen in the crease of the sign-in book was a pathetic Bic and the cap was missing. Brenda tried out her new signature. It was still all wrong, undignified, girlish. She'd have to keep practicing. With the teaspoon, she dipped two mints from the bowl also on the table. She was being polite. She approved of masking body odors but it did seem like a funny time to be worrying about your breath.

She'd left Kyle in the car reading sports headlines from a newspaper and drinking a beer. She'd made him park a block away. It was too embarrassing. He wasn't even wearing a suit. Joan was at home. Sherry's family had moved two years ago and they'd never been friendly with the Demerests. Only the girls had been close. Or had they? Now that Sherry was dead, Brenda was certain they must have been.

Joan hadn't wanted Brenda to go. "When's the last time you talked to her?"

"But we played together," Brenda had said.

"I just don't want you upsetting yourself if you don't have to."

"But we really did play together."

"I know, sweetie, it's just that you're still so young and . . . O.K. But I can't go with you. I just can't. It's too much. A child. I don't want to feel that if I don't have to. Her poor parents."

No one else was there alone. They seemed to be whispering condolences—a phrase Brenda had picked up from television—to the parents, then looking into the white coffin, then crying. Several of the women had to be helped to their seats. Brenda wasn't sure she wanted people looking at her after she was dead, though she did want lots of tears and fainting. She ate two more mints to buy time.

She skipped the parents and went straight for Sherry. That's what she was here for, to see what death was.

She had to tippy-toe a little. It was Sherry all right, and she didn't look natural or asleep or peaceful: she looked dead. She was ten and she'd been run over by a garbage truck and the brand-new doll cradled in her arms didn't look like much comfort. The green velvet dress, the pink satin lining, the bow in Sherry's hair: Brenda didn't like it one bit. Sherry's flesh color was weirder in its way than a Band-Aid, and all the pink satin lining in the world couldn't change that. "Sherry," she said to herself, "I know it isn't you." It seemed important that someone admit that.

Tippy-toeing was making Brenda dizzy. The sweet unnatural aliveness of the flowers was making her dizzy. Her hands found the brass handles. They'd lift Sherry by those. Brenda let go and weaved into a man who'd walked up.

"Are you all right?" he asked.

"I'm twelve," she said, though she didn't know why.

"Who's your mother?"

Now she knew what she felt. Pissed. She stared hard at the coffin, focusing until it was no longer a marshmallow of white fuzz, but a box with a dead thing in it.

"Is your mother here?" the man asked.

She stepped away and looked up his long, blue suit until she found his concerned face. "None of your business," she said.

She didn't run until she got outside, but then she galloped, her new patent-leather shoes cracking over the pavement. Street lamps blotched the road with dull, gray light. The air was cool and not drenched with flowers.

The overhead light was still on. Kyle was asleep with the paper over his face. Typical. A clumsily smashed cigarette smoldered in the ashtray and the beer between his legs was close to spilling. The car reeked.

"What?" he said when she slammed the door. Then, "Oh." The beer spilled as he was crackling his paper shut. "Shit," he said.

"Daddy."

"Sorry, darling. I spilt my beer."

She made a disgusted sound.

"How was it?" he asked.

"Fine."

"Oh."

He turned the ignition and she snapped her seat belt shut.

"When I die," she said, "I want you to burn me up."

"What?" he said, turning up his high beams.

"You know. Creamerated."

"Cremated?"

"Whatever."

"I think your mother was right about you coming here tonight."

"Daddy. Promise me."

"Darling, I don't want to promise a thing like that."

"Promise me."

"I think we should talk to your mother about this."

She beat her fists on the glove compartment and said, "Do it, do it, do it . . ."

"All right, all right."

"Thank you."

He shifted into drive. "Do you want an ice cream or something? I could go for one."

"O.K. I guess I'm kind of hungry."

■   ■   ■

Kevin liked two people: Miss Rhodes, the art teacher, and his mother, whose attention he forced upon himself when she arrived home stunned by the card shop. When she watched the news, he crawled into her lap. When she read the paper, he made her do it aloud, though the world was scary, bad. He colored while he listened. The world in the paper was the Big Stupid and the colors he made walking around were the opposite of the Big Stupid. Miss Rhodes kept the drawings he did at school, but he threw away the ones he drew at home, though his mother liked them. They weren't fun when they were finished. Joan asked how he made them so pretty and he shrugged. He didn't say Mr. Tartar anymore because people thought Mr. Tartar was the Big Stupid when really they were. These days Kevin practically had to think his whole head off to conjure Mr. Tartar, who usually came when Kevin was between awake and asleep.

When his mother cooked, he helped. Her food was ugly and he tried to pretty it, but she'd say, "We're going to eat it, not hang it on a wall." He sprinkled Joan's perfume on his pillow, to smell her while he slept. He *was* to her, and since he was to her, he was, and it made him safe.

His father wasn't, even when he was. He was an uh-huh or a nod in Kevin's life. He came and he went, like phrases that dot time.

Melissa, the big one, had moved, and he was glad. She

called once, and he picked up the phone because he was there and it was ringing, and she said hi what are you doing and he said drawing and she said that's nice and it went on like that for a few minutes and then it was over and then he hated it. It was talking with no talking in it.

Brenda-ugly was stupider than ever with her cheers. If she wasn't on the phone, she forced him to watch when she babysat. He thought she must have jumped her brains out, splat. She'd say, "I know you're going to like this one. I made it up myself," and it would be the other ones, only different. Pukey.

Daryl played balls with him, and Kevin hated balls—they bounced away. Daryl wasn't mean-stupid but he got in the way. Kevin was sick of the in-the-wayness of the most of life. Like Daryl now, doing stretchies at the top of the stairs. More ball stuff. Kevin couldn't stand to hate it anymore. He was walking-around but he wondered if other people were as much as him.

Kevin's brother couldn't see him. Daryl blew his cheeks in and out. It was easy. Kevin walked. Kevin stood. Kevin pushed. Daryl fell. His ankle went twisty and big and blue. Kevin watched it swell like a time-lapsed photography flower blooming. Daryl not all the way cried, but almost. Yes. He was walking-around too. As much as Kevin. Maybe more right now with his Big Pain.

■　■　■

Not sprained, but torn. Daryl had to sit the rest of the season out, on the bench, in his Ace bandage, cheering. Each afternoon, Coach soaked the foot in Epsom salts while the team practiced. Daryl hated the bench but the intern at the emergency room—he'd played ball in college—gave Daryl two distinct choices: lay low for the three weeks left of the season or forget a college career.

Daryl sat on the sidelines, his injury elevated on an overturned bucket, while the team lost. They didn't have a prayer for the play-offs; but at least the varsity coach had reassured him that he was in next year whether he could make tryouts or not. Mike made the bench half-bearable. He knew the name of every girl who walked by and how far she'd go.

Daryl's bandaged foot was on the coffee table. He and his mother were watching "The Waltons." His dad was out. Daryl bit his brownie. Brenda had baked a special batch with hazelnuts and marshmallows especially for him.

Kevin was in his room, making *vroom* noises. Daryl hadn't told anyone that the accident hadn't been one. The push wouldn't settle down as real in Daryl's head. He rolled the incident over and over: Kevin hadn't seen him; Daryl had imagined the pint-sized hands on his back; it was a practical joke that got out of hand. But Kevin didn't joke; he laughed at his drawings. Sometimes. But that was all and even then the laugh wasn't one, not a laugh as others laughed them; it meant something else. Daryl could not forget the curious look on Kevin's face. He could not forget Kevin standing there with the arms he'd pushed Daryl with dangling innocently at his sides, as if Daryl were an experiment he'd conducted.

"Mom?" Daryl said.

"Hmmmm?" Joan asked distractedly. John-Boy couldn't decide whether or not he should go to college. Daryl figured he would. It was the last show of the season.

Daryl couldn't remember his rehearsed opening. It seemed increasingly strange that he'd waited a week to tell. Maybe it was too late. Maybe they wouldn't believe him.

"You know my accident?" he said.

"We're old friends," she said.

"Well, it kind-of wasn't an accident." Cute Mary Ellen's top lip was tremulous.

"What do you mean?"

"Kevin pushed me."

"On purpose?"

"I think so." Daryl's heart pounded as though he'd just run off the court.

Quietly, Joan said, "Goddamn him." Then she screamed, "Kevin Wayne Demerest, get your ass in here right this second."

■   ■   ■

Joan and Kyle ordered Surf 'n' Turfs, but she did not go to the salad bar. She didn't want to fill up. They always gave you too much food here. She'd save Daryl some lobster. Brenda was dieting. Joan still had not forgiven Kevin. She didn't know how to. Daryl and his mother had agreed to keep "it" from his father. Daryl's basketball career was like a newborn to Kyle and he had all of a recent father's fierce protectiveness concerning it. Joan thought it entirely possible that Kyle would kill Kevin if he knew.

She was wearing the dress she'd bought for last year's Christmas parties, and she'd had her hair done during lunch. She felt strange, as if she were dressed as a wife for Halloween. She was too nervous to walk past tables to the ladies room.

Joan wondered what Kyle had gotten her. He was erratic with gifts. One year he'd give her a diamond, the next a Mr. Coffee, at a time when she hadn't drunk coffee. She couldn't remember if the fifteenth anniversary was a pearl or an alabaster or an ivory, though it was posted somewhere in the shop. Whatever it was, slaves leading elephants bearing rubies and hand lotion wouldn't be enough.

He had agreed to give up Suzy. That he had chosen such an ordinary woman, a toll collector, had added unexpected depth to the multicolors of Joan's emotional bruises. His choice implied an ultimate need she had never satisfied, and she despised him for the waste of it all. When she had confronted the hapless girl, Joan in her car, Suzy's hand

expectantly suspended in midair for its quarter the duration
of the conversation, a line of honking traffic behind them,
Suzy had pushed her neck-length hair behind her ears with
her unfrozen hand and said with a vacancy that made Joan
feel marriage had never existed, "Whatever Kyle wants."
She'd let Joan through without paying.

"Here's to one heck of a gal," Kyle said, toasting his wife
with his whiskey sour.

"I'll drink to that," Joan said.

"Should we open presents now or later?"

"You know I can't wait."

He hit at his pockets. "I hope I brought it."

"I do too or you'll be having divorce for dessert."

"Ah." He pulled an envelope from inside his jacket.
"Here it is." If it was a card, she was going to cut off his
dick and mail it to Suzy, who'd gotten more use out of it
recently than Joan had. You hated what you worked with.
She'd lay money most butchers were vegetarians.

"What is it?" she asked.

"Open it and see."

It was a card, a cheap card. She hoped Suzy wasn't
squeamish.

"Have I mentioned my job?" she asked.

"Yeah, sure."

"I work in a card shop."

"I know, I know. Open the fucking thing before you
think about cutting my dick off."

Great minds might not think alike, but married ones did.
Two tickets fluttered to the bread plate. She held one up
to the candle. There were crumbs on it. Acapulco. They'd
talked about Mexico since before they were married, but
she had long since relegated it to the kingdom of subjects
you talked about but really didn't expect to happen—like
death. She began to cry, and hated herself for it. She didn't
want him to know their life together could still move her.
He didn't deserve it.

To cover she said, "I suppose I should thank Suzy for making you guilty enough to be this extravagant."

She'd gotten him a tire iron. It was in the trunk of the car with a bow on it. There was no card.

■   ■   ■

Melissa drove around the block for the sixth time. She wished the windows weren't blacked out. She'd seen women coming and going, solitary and in groups, but she wanted to see jukebox glow, some reassurance that she wasn't going to be auctioned off to a bull dyke with tattoos and a Harley. The last time she'd come this close, a woman fitting that description had roared up and staggered in. Melissa had floored it home, rehearsing her recant to Case: "No, really, I want to suck cock and give birth."

The car behind her beeped. The light was green again. She took it as a sign. She parked behind the bank across the street where she'd seen other cars pull in. She smoked a cigarette. Two women a couple of spaces down were sharing a joint. The one behind the wheel saw Melissa looking and motioned her over. Melissa shook her head no and made tracks for the bar. She stood on the curb for a full minute, pretended to be looking for something she'd dropped in the gutter. A long-haired guy on a bike whizzed by and called her a dyke. My God, she thought, I haven't even gone in yet and already I'm showing. She started back for the car but saw the two joint smokers headed towards her, felt suspicious, and turned back.

She went straight to the bar and ordered a Heineken. She normally drank Rheingold because it was cheap, but she wanted to seem sophisticated. She chugged it, lit a cigarette, and ordered another one. She hadn't looked at anyone yet. She concentrated on the wall, which was carpeted. She felt like she was in Jumper's van.

She began by looking at hands. No one was drinking

Heineken. Maybe it wasn't sophisticated. Maybe lesbians weren't sophisticated. She couldn't know. She'd never seen a book, a photograph, or a movie about lesbians. She wondered how Wendy had known about them, how anyone knew about them. They were like great bargains—you heard about them but where did you find them? She'd found this place mentioned on the bathroom wall at the Sears that anchored one end of the mall where she worked.

The second beer calmed her, and she ordered a third. She'd brought plenty of money, as if she were going on a long trip fraught with potential emergencies. The music pounded. Disco. Her old friends would have hated it. She wasn't sure she liked it herself, but had decided to like anything they wouldn't. She'd bought purple boots for this reason. This was the first time she'd dared to wear them.

It was a dark, crummy place. Red and blue lights flashed on a dance floor the size of a dining room table. Women jammed it, making a high-pitched *woo-woo* sound. No one seemed to be dancing with anyone in particular. She liked that. One group of four passed a small brown bottle from nose to nose and it caused them to dance more wildly. She made a note to try it.

She still wasn't sure that she was a lesbian. Screwing Case hadn't been bad. She supposed she could do it for the rest of her life if she had to. The couple beside her kissed. She couldn't look. The woman on the other side of her said, "Hi."

"Hi," Melissa said, her heart skipping rope in her chest.

"I'm Fancy." Fancy held out her hand.

"I'm Melissa." She pretended not to see the hand. Her palms were sweaty and she couldn't touch another woman's hand, not in this place. She still wanted to go to college.

Fancy was wearing a flannel shirt. Her hair had been dyed within an inch of its life and was orangey blond. It looked toxic. She had, dear God, a faint moustache. Melissa licked her upper lip, which was still mercifully bare. Maybe the small brown bottle was liquid male hormones. She didn't know if she had a type yet, but Fancy would never be it.

"I've never seen you here before," Fancy said.

"No," Melissa said, an answer which she felt summed up her whole life. She was disheartened that Fancy's come-on hadn't been any more original than your average dumb jock's. These lesbians were a disappointing lot.

"You want to dance?" Fancy asked.

"I can't," Melissa said.

"Ooohhh . . ." she said, "you got a girlfriend."

"Actually, I have scoliosis." She didn't know what scoliosis was, but she hoped it sounded contagious to Fancy.

"Oh, man, so many women are sick these days. Want another beer?"

"No thanks," Melissa said, setting her empty bottle on the bar. "I have to get going. I'm getting married."

"Oh," Fancy said, "a tourist."

■　　■　　■

When Kyle came into the office, Trish said, "Mr. McGee wants to see you," with practiced indifference. She did not look up from her rubber stamping. Herb had left his wife for a friend of his daughter's. Trish had a brief fling with Scientology. She'd cut her hair short recently and it had the odd effect of making her look more feminine. There were two cigarettes smoldering in her Florida ashtray, their filters iced pink from her lips.

Mr. McGee was on the phone. He motioned Kyle to the wide, soft, black chair that swallowed you whole. It made you feel small and young and faintly ridiculous, like an adolescent sent to the assistant principal for bed wetting. Mr. McGee's desk was in important disarray. This was a man with things on his mind. His coffee cup said Big Cheese and had a cartoon of a Swiss cheese with mouse legs kicking from its closed smile. There was a bologna sandwich, half in its plastic Baggie, with a bite missing. His gray moustache was crumb-speckled and his tie was unknotted. He set the phone down briskly.

"Well, Kyle," he said.

"Yes sir."

"How's things at home?"

"Good, good."

"Glad to hear it. That Joan's a fine woman."

"Thank you," Kyle said, as if he were somehow responsible for her goodness.

Mr. McGee tapped his nose, a nervous tic the guys mimicked behind his back. "I'll get straight to the point. I need a man who knows my business to keep an eye on the warehouse. You've been with McGee how long?"

"Eight years."

"That's a good long time."

"Thank you," Kyle said, uneasily congratulating himself on his perserverance.

"So what do you say?"

"Huh?"

"Are you my warehouse man?"

It was a question, but it didn't seem like one. "Uh . . . sure . . . I guess."

"Good. I've got a man coming in on Monday, Vietnam vet, just had a set of twins; inexperienced, but he seems decent. I want you to show him the ropes. Think you can handle it?"

"Sure."

"Now, I want you to understand that the warehouse isn't going to be as much money at first; but for a man with a little gumption, it's a golden opportunity."

"I can't really afford a cut in pay, sir. I mean with Joan working we get by but . . ."

"I'll understand, of course, if you feel you can't take it."

"Why not give it to the new guy?"

"I need him out on the front lines."

"Oh."

"Tell you what. You train Adam next week and think about it. No need to make a decision like this off the cuff. You're a good man, Kyle, and I'd hate to lose you, but whatever you decide, no hard feelings."

Mr. McGee extended his hand. The enormous gold wedding band welded to his finger was scratched and dim. The hand seemed a hundred years away to Kyle, sunk as he was, deeply, in the soft, black chair.

■　　■　　■

Brenda was not happy with the new cheers. Angela, head cheerleader and all-around numbskull, did variations of the jump and swing. She got her rhymes from a rhyming dictionary Brenda had discovered hidden in Angela's locker. Last week she'd had them chanting "Fight, fight, fight; something, something, blight." She'd still be worrying over the second line if Miss Truesdale, their faculty adviser, hadn't suggested that "blight" was over the heads of most teenaged sports fans. Miss Truesdale was a grave woman who wore a rape whistle at all times and treated cheering as if it were a formerly austere art that had fallen into decadence.

Brenda made Daryl and Kyle call her during halftimes so she could study the pros. Her bible was "Jumping Jehosephat!," a magisterial study published by *Teen* magazine chronicling the history of cheering with photographs of the great squads. Yale '44–48 would probably never be equaled due to the imaginative brilliance of their leader, Deb Apple, and their rigorous athleticism. There were diagrams with arrows and stick cheerleaders outlining the more venerable moves. The sixties had been an era of great innovation and the seventies seemed stymied by comparison. Where were the pom-pom visionaries of today? Brenda wondered.

Brenda knew where one was, at Anderson Junior High, and weekly rehearsed her acceptance speech, her Silver

Megaphone—a Lifetime Achievement Award given annually—clutched to her sweatered breast, misting over as she thanked her idol, Deb, for sustenance and courage during those times when she was under the yoke of clods like Angela. The Apple Hall of Fame was in Delaware. There was one anecdote in "Jumping" about a misguided group of orchard owners who'd shown up once. Brenda was trying to organize a field trip there.

She wanted to bring boys back into the cheering fold. There would be so much more you could accomplish. You could backflip from their manly shoulders. Deb thought the decline of male "bouncers," as she affectionately called the clan, accounted for most of the amateur clowning she saw today. Brenda had tried to interest Louis, who was never going to make it as a quarterback. He'd said no way. She wanted to change cheering's image. She wanted to build human pyramids, spell names with their bodies, use sparklers, involve the players who sat on the bench, incorporate animals into the formations. She could see herself astride a tranquilized and declawed tiger. These were frontiers where only pioneers could or should go. Angela didn't have the stuff, that indefinable quality that separated the bounders from the mere leapers.

"Miss Truesdale," Brenda said, after rehearsal. Miss Truesdale insisted they were rehearsing, not practicing. Brenda liked the rigor and artistry the word implied.

"Yes, Brenda?" she said, not looking up from the notebook she was scribbling into.

"I know this is terrible, but I think I accidentally put my stuff in Angela's locker and I just wouldn't feel right going through it myself."

"Is there something there you have to have tonight?"

"My science book." Miss Truesdale taught science.

"Very well, Brenda. I have a master key, but please don't let this happen again. The root of strong cheering is—"

"A nimble mind as well as a nimble body," Brenda said, finishing Miss Truesdale's favorite phrase.

Brenda stood behind while Miss Truesdale unlatched Angela's locker. There was a hairy mole on the back of Miss Truesdale's neck, and Brenda had to squelch the impulse to suggest a good dermatologist. There was a whole section in "Jumping" on blemishes and their remedies. The girls' locker room was stale and she tried not to breathe through her nose.

"I don't see anything," Miss Truesdale said.

You will, Brenda thought. She waited. Miss Truesdale's left shoulder twitched, then twitched again, then her whole back froze. Speechless, she pulled out the small, blue Trojan packet Brenda had stolen from Daryl's room. She held by it the edge with the outermost tips of her fingers, as if it were already bloated with the very stuff it was designed to contain.

"What's that?" Brenda asked.

As head cheerleader, her first order of business would be the school colors, which clashed.

■   ■   ■

Kyle sat entranced by the television. He hadn't felt like eating. Melissa speared another piece of lettuce glowing with orange dressing. In her new life, she did not eat lettuce. For breakfast, it was a Coke and a smoke, which her new girlfriend, Trixie, called the breakfast of champions. For lunch she caught a burger, a slice of pizza. Dinner was a Happy Hour steam table. She didn't grocery shop. She lived in gay bars.

Daryl said, "So what's it like out there in the real world?"

"O.K.," Melissa said.

He still limped from his "fall," if that's what you could call being pushed down a flight of stairs by your seven-year-old brother. That's what her family called it. While layering lasagna noodles, Joan had asked Melissa's advice about Kevin, evidence of her desperation. Shocked, Melissa suggested the first solution that came to mind—a psychiatrist. Trixie had stopped her halfhearted and increasingly tedious suicide attempts—aspirin overdoses, inconsequentially slashed wrists, loose nooses—since she'd jumped the therapy train. They took her antidepressants before they went dancing at For Women Only.

"You know, Melissa," Brenda said, "you could be a very attractive person if you tried. There's this great article in *Teen* this month called 'The Eyes Have It,' about how to change your whole life with a little mascara and an eyebrow pencil. You know, the eyes are the windows to the soul."

"Blow me," Melissa said.

"Please, Melissa," Joan said, "you're supposed to be one of the adults around here."

Melissa shut the windows to her soul.

"I was only trying to help," Brenda said, flashing the pert smile she'd recently developed. "If Melissa doesn't want a boyfriend, that's her problem."

"It's not a problem," Melissa said.

"Melissa doesn't have time for a boyfriend," Joan said. "She hardly has time for her family."

Melissa did not wonder why people butchered their families, but rather why it wasn't routine. She hoped Trixie had refilled her prescription.

■　　■　　■

The porch was not what it had been. Daryl could sit on it with his feet resting comfortably on the ground. It was cold, but Daryl would have braved thirty degrees less to get out of the house. His parents were arguing again.

The house across the street hadn't budged. Neither had the one beside it, nor the one beside that. He wondered how much of life was pure luck. In basketball, you could practice yourself into a better player; but without talent, you weren't going nowhere. The luck of the talent came first. It presupposed everything. Except a bum ankle. That was another kind of luck that outranked talent.

When he tuned back in, they'd stopped yelling.

"Just leave," his mother said. She sounded more tired than mad.

"Why do I have to leave?" Kyle asked. He seemed genuinely puzzled.

"It's good manners, Kyle. You're the one with the girlfriend."

So that was it. The older Daryl got, the harder it was to love his father. Kyle couldn't seem to get some essential thing right. He didn't have a talent for life.

Luck.

"I really tried to give her up," Kyle said.

"I really don't care." Daryl could tell that she did. "I just want this to be over. I want to get on with things."

"I don't."

"Stop this torture." Daryl didn't move during the pause that followed, and when she finally spoke, "Please," her voice ragged and torn and stained with grief, it socked Daryl in the sternum.

The storm door opened and Kyle said, "What are you doing here?"

"I still live here," Daryl said. Sarcastic as hell.

The cuff on the back of his head didn't hurt, but Kyle's class ring did. "Go to your room," Kyle said.

Daryl sat there. He refused to rub the spot where the ring had gotten him.

"It's cold out here," Kyle said.

Daryl got up. Kyle was blocking the door. Daryl tried to get past him without looking. It was like trying to drive around a state with your eyes closed.

Kyle stepped off the porch and as the storm door eased shut behind Daryl, Kyle said, "I really tried, Daryl. You gotta give me that."

The problem was, Daryl did believe him, and he wished he didn't. It would almost be better if Kyle didn't try. Less sad.

1980

In their way, the girders were magnificent—smooth, indestructible; three Ls of steel that fit snugly into the right angles formed by the house meeting the ground. Each leg was sixteen feet long and a foot wide, and they were screwed into Joan's home by gigantic bolts that necessarily nosed through holes the size of dinner plates into the various rooms. Kevin had painted his "interior overhang," as Mr. Belmont dubbed it, with exact likenesses, as sober as death masks, of each family member. Rust already sprinkled the girders and Joan had replaced her out-of-date signs with even more prominent and vibrant ones warning children away from this irresistible and potentially dangerous playground equipment. She had not forgotten the lame dog. She planted ivy, hoping it would weave itself thickly and greenly around the gleaming support system, and camouflage it into the ordinary. Like latticework. Or shutters.

Kevin held the unopened Pepsi bottle over one of the girders.

"I christen you the *Enterprise*," he said, smashing the bottle over one of the steel beams. Glass and Pepsi sprayed everywhere. His sweater got soaked.

He went around front where Joan was raking up leaves. "How far are we from the Arco galaxy, Lieutenant Uhura?"

"Not far enough," she said glumly. Arco was the insecticide she'd enlisted in her war against the bizarre, hearty bugs her neighbors thought she was exaggerating. A brisk fall had shooed most of them away, but occasionally one of the kids would show up with two small, pinkish bumps that itched out of all proportion to their size and resisted the balm of calamine lotion. Daryl had discovered, during a lemonade craze, that lemon juice calmed the crazy itching and perhaps hurried their healing, but the latter quality may have been the wishful imagination of the desperate. A gallon of Real-Lemon lay on its side in the vegetable bin of the refrigerator.

"Put up the force field," Kevin said. "Melissa of the evil Romulan galaxy is bearing down on us."

Joan looked up and, sure enough, there was Melissa's blue Mustang pulling into the driveway. A rare cameo. Melissa found the house, the girders, the bugs, all of it, sidesplitting, and Joan hated her for it.

"I'm afraid," Joan said to Kirk, "that she's already broken through."

■　　■　　■

Melissa had planned to spend the month between when her old lease ended and her new apartment became available at Trixie's. But Trixie bashed herself and half of North America into consciousness with the eardrum-goring wails of Donna Summer. After a week she became alarmingly vocal on the subject of Melissa's hips. Melissa thought Trixie should use deodorant, even if it was a patriarchal plot, even if it did mask her woman-scent. Trixie's dissatisfaction with Melissa's hips found its final expression between Pam's—one in a series of roommates—legs. Melissa had come home from work at the usual time to find Trixie's gymnastically inclined tongue doing an Olga Korbut in Pam's cunt, her traitorous hands massaging Pam's rugby-firmed hips. Rather than stuff her ex-girlfriend up Pam's womb, Melissa's first impulse, she packed quietly, carefully snapped the Donna Summer oeuvre into cornflakes, and sprinkled the vinyl confetti across the bed where she and Trixie had committed their crimes. Eating pussy was a felony in Virginia. "Felonious cunnilingus" was Melissa's favorite phrase.

The phone rang. Melissa was staying at her mother's. It was only a few days before her new lease started. She considered not answering. It was never for her.

"Hello?"

"I want every single one of those records replaced, you bitch."

"I'm sorry, sir, you must have the wrong number."

"Does your mother know you're a lesbian?"

"Does your father know you steal his prescription pads and forge his signature?"

End of story.

Joan and her daughter did not discuss the absences that seemed to constitute Melissa's life in her family's eyes. Melissa had brought up the introductory English class she'd started at Randolph E. Mooney Community College, but Joan, who thought education was noble, was also suspicious of anyone who had too much of it, and the conversation loped off into nothingness.

They talked about work. Melissa would mention an ancient, crackpot method of ear-piercing she'd seen at the last beauty convention, and Joan would respond with an anecdote from her new job at the hardware store, which she'd taken, in part, because she could get her poison at cost. Joan's stories usually featured her coworker Clarissa, who was forever mouthing off about company policy. In the latest, Clarissa had eaten her yogurt while ringing up handsaws and three-way plugs to protest half-hour lunches. She'd won fifteen more minutes when Accounts Receivable got tired of tens and twenties encrusted with yogurt.

Friendly Daryl tried to describe shots he'd seen in the NBA play-offs and bored Melissa would say, a starchy quality in her voice, "That's interesting, Daryl," and embarrass them both.

Kevin was as mysterious to her as electricity or death.

This unexpected truce Melissa seemed to have reached with her family was in some ways worse than the enraged, circuitous route she'd braved to attain it. Hatred was at least passionate. Her new standing was like the third or fourth cup of tea made from the same flow-through bag. She sometimes felt she was adrift above them, connected by the fragile, bloody, inevitable umbilical cord she had mistakenly thought had been severed; she was like an astronaut, hovering over the mother ship, and slowly realizing the door is shut forever and the oxygen won't last.

These fits of panicked despair would send her hurtling towards any tenuous possibility of contact, even with Brenda.

She knocked on Brenda's locked door.

"Yes?" Brenda said.

"What are you doing?" Melissa asked.

"Curling my eyelashes."

"Oh. How do you do that?"

"With an eyelash curler," Brenda said, her voice curdled with disbelief.

"Oh. Does it hurt?"

"Of course not."

"Does it really work?"

"No, I do it because it doesn't work."

"Oh. Sorry. I guess that's a stupid question."

Long, long pause.

"Melissa?" Brenda asked, invisible to her sister behind the locked door.

"Yes?"

"Why are you still there?"

■   ■   ■

Mr. Carstairs sat behind his thick glasses; the second fingers of his hands formed a temple whose peak rested in the middle of his upper lip. He looked like a giant bug, its hunger sated, considering its prey out of boredom. His office was so clean and exact that it felt alphabetized, as if neurosis was something you could organize away. There was a fishbowl of brightly colored suckers and the light of the fluorescent lamps buzzing from the ceiling shattered in their crinkled cellophane.

"Well, Kevin," Mr. Carstairs said, "how do you feel about Daddy moving away?"

"Nothing."

"You must feel something—happy, sad?"

"Not happy and not sad."

"Did you like Daddy?"

"Daddy was there."

"What do you mean?"

"Daddy was there."

"Do you see Daddy often?"

"No."

"How does that make you feel?"

"Nothing."

Mr. Carstairs rubbed one of his magnified eyes. "Do you think you could draw me a picture of Daddy?"

"Yes."

Mr. Carstairs pushed a pad and a short crystal vase of sharpened crayons across the desk. "Take your time," he said.

Kevin picked black, an ominous choice.

"Why did you choose that color, Kevin?"

"It's like the charcoal things Miss Rhodes gives me to draw."

"Who is Miss Rhodes?"

"The art teacher."

"Do you like art?"

"I can't draw if you're going to talk."

"Excuse me."

Mr. Carstairs had scarcely clicked his pen to make notes when Kevin pushed the pad back, knocking over the crystal vase, scattering crayons. A pink one rolled onto Mr. Carstair's lap. Kevin was either hostile or clumsy. In either case, he was not apologetic.

"That was quick," Mr. Carstairs said.

"I'm a good drawer." Mr. Carstairs was so startled by the complexity of line and subtlety of shading that at first he didn't notice that the father was missing an ear, was unsmiling, was all head and no body—revelatory detail. In his sudden anxiety, he smudged the chin and never detected the phrase "The Pretty Hides the Big Stupid" threaded into the hair.

■　　■　　■

They thudded in a herd around the gym. Coach started every practice with laps. The team smiled like a pack of mental defectives as they made the hated rounds. If the ex-drill sergeant detected so much as a flicker of a frown, you'd end up doing a few extra ones by yourself. The only thing worse than laps was laps by yourself.

"How do you like them laps, boys?" Coach roared as they flowed past.

"Great, sir," they chorused back, more vigorously than the time before, but not as heartily as the next time. They couldn't stop until he was satisfied with their enthusiasm. They'd learned to modulate their voices. If you started at the peak of your lungs, you spent the rest of the run trying to live up to it and usually didn't succeed. On those days he called them a bunch of pussies when he finally let them stop. Daryl thought that was going too far but he wasn't going to whine about it. Coach hated whiners. Whiners were pussies with opinions. Teachers could be whiners. So could assistant principals. Anyone who disagreed with Coach qualified.

Daryl actually liked the rigor, the ritual, the badass routine. He liked the sweat and the after-practice exhaustion. He could be something, and this was it, and the laps and the unspoken conspiracy against Coach, and the unspoken conspiracy with Coach were part of his becoming.

"How's that ankle?" Coach asked when they were done.

"Good," Daryl said.

It almost never bothered him. Sometimes, when laps were elongated, but there were Epsom salts and heating pads and massages. Mike said all Daryl needed was a good blow job. Daryl would have been willing to risk that particular therapy if only he could have found a willing nurse.

"You're O.K.," Coach said. It was his idea of a compliment.

"Thanks, Coach," Daryl said.

"If that ankle ever bothers you, we can talk. There's laps"—he winked—"and then there's the guys who don't need to run them."

"Thanks, Coach."

"We can always talk," he said, clapping Daryl on the shoulders. "Always."

■   ■   ■

Suzy didn't have a stereo because she didn't listen to music. When she drove she hopped from station to station, like a stone skipping across water, until she found news. Since the gigantic bolts had burrowed into Joan's life, rendering her walls decoratively useless, Joan had given Kyle the large pictures of dreamy Spaniards, the interlocking shelves of knickknacks. Except for the starburst clock that ran fast, Suzy's apartment had been barren of frou-frou, and her formerly austere walls seemed to totter under Kyle's gaudy, ragtag possessions, like an old mother superior done up to turn tricks.

Folded pizza boxes, dilapidated take-out cartons, and wrinkled burger bags littered wobbly tables and frayed rugs, like the paper rubble of a costly junk-food war. Kyle had rediscovered Fig Newtons, and their boxes, in various stages of emptiness, were scattered about; in the bathroom, for example, to be picked at while he shit or shaved or showered, until the cookies dampened and deteriorated and were dismissed as inedible into the small, dented tin trash can already overflowing with tampons or tissues stained with lipstick or torn by tears.

At first, they had drenched themselves in sex, fucking three, four times a day, sometimes twice in a row. They did it sitting, standing, in the shower, in the car, on their sides, under assumed names, with Suzy on top, with Suzy in her toll booth hat, with Kyle tied to the bed by dish towels. They fucked when they were exhausted from fucking, in the morning, during lunch breaks, while Suzy watched kids playing tag in the parking lot three stories down, while Kyle watched basketball. They used syrups and French ticklers and ribbed condoms and leather jock straps and peek-a-boo bras and edible panties and cherry-flavored lubricants. They talked dirty. They fucked in complete silence. By daylight, by nightlight, by no light. Quick fucks. Loving fucks. Languorous fucks. Furious fucks. Kyle felt his body had been jolted awake. He had the stamina of a fourteen-year-old, the strength of two Kyles, the limberness of a Chinese acrobat, the endurance of a marathon runner, the expertise of a brain surgeon, the imagination of Picasso, the daring of a Russian spy, the resources of Merlin. His hard-ons were harder, his cunnilingus more cunning. Their kisses were full of their souls. For months they'd wandered the dailiness of their lives bruised, bitten, scratched, sore. Muscles their complex couplings discovered ached.

Now they made love once a day. It was good but it had changed, and nests of nipple clamps and cartons of cock rings would not change it back. They had tired.

Thursdays at eight, they watched "The Waltons." Suzy had so few favorites in life that Kyle insisted they watch it together, even when an important game was on. They were usually naked, a habit from the ferocious fucking days they hadn't bothered to break. Suzy liked to curl up, her cheek on her hands cupped as if for prayer and resting on his thigh. He'd moved the couch to a comfortable watching position. He'd asked her to remove the child's rocker and she'd set it just outside the door, where it had lingered until Kyle, inexplicably enraged by its broken presence, had kicked it down the staircase. He didn't know who had finally removed it.

He did not miss his family, though a sound as silly as deodorant hissing or the sight of a balled-up sock would unexpectedly balloon a startlingly precise picture inside him of, say, Joan brushing her teeth on tiptoe, her robe casually open, the soft, sweet slope of her belly resting gently against the sink and undulating with the miracle of her breath; images that sucked the blood from his chest and froze his heart.

"I love it when they have the old lady moonshiners on," Suzy said.

"Yeah," Kyle said, "me too."

He wondered if one day the memory of her hair spilled across her white, freckled shoulder would also freeze his heart, and knew the answer as he wondered the question: the seeds of regret were planted everywhere, in the slightest gesture, in the most insignificant glance, and were only waiting for the rich mulch of heartbreak or death to bloom.

■　　■　　■

The conditions in which customers browsed through Bowers Hardware amazed Joan. A woman in bedroom slippers and a sheer scarf loosely tied over curlers yawned or scratched her pregnant belly as she tested hedge clippers, snipping at the air, or peered into a length of garden hose to ascertain God knows what. It was beyond casual. Joan would have hated to see the cow's kitchen. Clarissa noticed

her too, but Clarissa noticed everything: grown men innocently picking their nose; minuscule aberrations on clothing
in places most people wouldn't think to look; two-year-olds
eating screws; how handsome a teenaged boy would be if
he'd shave that moustache; a crack in the ceiling twenty feet
away and eighteen feet high; shoplifters; the brand of perfume Marcy was trying this week to trap men; lipstick on
your teeth; a crumb she brushed off your collar. She could
place people to the town by their accents.

"She's a real winner," Clarissa said, referring to the cow.
It was her favorite descriptive phrase. But instead of sound-
ing harsh, as it would have in most mouths, in Clarissa's
voice it was edged with sorrow, as if ugliness and stupidity
were the stubborn failures of a willful world she'd long since
resigned herself to, content now to ruefully mark the passage
of the parade of error.

She had three children, one of them foreign-looking, but
she had been married only once, when she was a fourteen-
year-old dropout, to a born-again preacher exactly twice her
age. Her father had the marriage annulled. His one noble
act, she said, other than having the courtesy to slam his car
into a tree a year later, finally giving her mother some peace.
She said she'd married the born-again because she was fat
and he'd been the sole suitor of her adolescence, if you
could call blow jobs in the church parking lot courtship.
He'd moved to a desperate parish in North Carolina after
the annulment. Clarissa was thin now and ate yogurt for
lunch seven days a week, fifty-two weeks a year, even on
Thanksgiving, though she still baked a turkey for her boys.
She had discipline. She was a problem solver.

She also had a beautician's license, but dipping her fingers
into strange hair had given her the willies and she'd packed
up her scissors in the middle of a permanent and split. She'd
do friends and had given Joan a cut that took five years off
her face.

She was funny and attributed her success with men (if

you could call a different one every week success) to her blond hair and black eyebrows, both of which she dyed. She said it sparked their curiosity as to what color they'd find down below. She talked about dicks shamelessly, while near-blind old ladies bought light bulbs, while she changed the dollars of stock boys into quarters for the Coke machine: "He was all right if what you wanted was a side of meat with your potatoes." She owned a house forty-five minutes from town, where she could afford one, and saved bonds to send her kids to college.

Their fingers hectored at the cash register. An endless procession of products that kept the world nailed, bolted, hinged, locked, and in general put together, flowed by in numbing numbers. There were frantic days when a quip tossed off by Clarissa had saved Joan's life just as surely as if she'd pulled her from the drink half-dead and resuscitated her with her own breath.

■   ■   ■

Kevin had been peering at the chalky lumps of mummies for a good half an hour. Their faces were still remarkably expressive, haughty even, given their current predicament. Kevin was going to convert his room into a museum when he got home. He'd move the furniture to the basement and sleep on the cool floor like a monk. He'd crowd the walls with drawings, different ones every day. He'd hang black curtains and light his paintings by flashlights dangling from the ceiling. It would be faintly sinister. He'd charge ten cents for children and a quarter for adults. There would be no optional donations.

"Do they sell popcorn here?" he asked.

"No," Miss Rhodes laughed.

He'd sell popcorn. His mother would pop it and he would dye it, stuff it into twist-tied sandwich Baggies, and sell them for a nickel apiece. About one Saturday a month Miss

Rhodes took him places, usually to look at pictures, though once they'd attended a pretty movie playing at a rundown theater owned by a man and a woman who looked like versions of each other: ponytails, earrings, no shoes. Kevin could not decide if the man looked like the woman or if the woman looked like the man. They hadn't wanted him to see the movie because of the naked bodies in it, but Sandy had explained—they were her friends—that he was an artist, and they'd wordlessly let him through the turnstile. He wondered what else drawing could get him that he wasn't supposed to have.

Today they bypassed the Greeks, where they always got snagged, and headed straight for the Moderns, which they'd never made it to. Their shoes echoed on the marble floors and Kevin craned his neck to look up into the ceilings taller than his whole house. Sandy steered him towards a large brown and blue painting of a violin and fruit, broken up and put back together, but not right, like jigsaw puzzles inadvertently mixed together.

"What do you think?" Miss Rhodes asked. She always asked that.

"Why did they break it?"

"They wanted to show objects from multiple perspectives."

"They want to see it all ways, but they still want to see it one way."

"You don't like it?"

"No."

"But this is the tradition your art springs from."

"Un-uh. It comes from Mr. Tartar, even if Mr. Carstairs says he isn't real."

"Don't listen to that wicked man."

"Can we go see the Jesus paintings with all the tiny clear stuff and the bright, bright color?"

"But the color isn't walking around." She still liked the phrase, though Kevin was outgrowing it.

"That's why I like them," he said.

"O.K.," she sighed. "Next time, we'll try Matisse. His colors skip rope."

■   ■   ■

Joan and the children she lived with rarely had time for one another. Even Kevin had receded from her. She saw Melissa, who stopped by once a week after work, more than she saw Brenda, whose bedroom was across the hall from Joan's. Brenda had stormed junior high. She was a cheerleader, the first beauty editor of the school newspaper, and an honorary member of the glee club, honorary because she couldn't sing. She'd been kicked off the debate team for frivolity but didn't hold the good opinion of math geeks in high regard. She organized bake sales and car washes and chaired Mr. Legs Night in which the most glorious example of eighth-grade male limbs was awarded a trophy. She had nearly bankrupted Joan voting for Louis. The cheering squad had made a fortune at a quarter a ballot and now had a fat wad of cash Brenda was lobbying to have allocated for a field trip to some crackpot museum of pep in Delaware.

"All in the Family" was on. Joan was too tired to read by the time the dinner dishes were stacked away. She could still smell the spaghetti sauce she'd simmered in a Crock-Pot since before breakfast. She needed a man or a maid or a man who was a maid.

Daryl, home from practice early, had pushed his tennis shoes off and his dirty basketball sat between his legs. She almost told him to get his filthy ball off her nice, clean cushions, but they weren't nice or clean anymore and besides, she didn't go to his games. Kyle would be there.

"How's it been going?" she asked.

"O.K.," he said.

"O.K.? I thought you were the next Kareem Abdul Watchamacallit."

He spun the basketball on his finger. "Yep. That's right. Think you can handle having a superstar for a son?"

"I guess there are worse things."

The ball fell from his finger and bounced over to the television.

"I didn't know superstars dropped balls," she said.

"What would an old lady like you know?"

Joan stuck her tongue out.

"Very mature, Mother," he said, imitating Brenda.

They laughed.

■ ■ ■

For Joan's birthday, Melissa appeared to pierce her mother's ears.

"I don't like pain," Joan said.

"It doesn't hurt," Melissa said.

"Clip-ons are fine."

"Clip-ons are cheesy."

"I don't like pain."

"It'll be an expression of your newfound independence."

Joan didn't understand how holes in her ears expressed independence, but it was the reason that swamped her aversion. Maybe it was because she'd never thought of herself as independent. Maybe it was because she hoped she was.

It hurt, not terribly, and the small diamond chips were snazzy. Joan kissed Melissa after she looked in the mirror, surprising them both. She hadn't kissed her oldest daughter in ten years. Melissa kept reminding her mother all afternoon to stop fiddling with her freshly wounded ears.

Daryl gave Joan oven mitts, butterflies scampering across them, as if to mock the independence Melissa had so freely granted her. It was an unfortunate reminder of his father's similar propensity for bad gifts, and Joan thought a gift-buying school for men should be founded by someone like herself, who had suffered birthdays and Christmases at their clumsy hands. It would emphasize originality, extravagance, impracticality.

Still, she kissed him.

Brenda threatened Kevin into painting the bolt faces happy. There was a chink in Kevin's talent—he could not paint smiles—and the new, improved Demerests were worse than the old dour models. Their upturned mouths looked as if they'd learned smiling from a textbook with no illustrations. It was horrible. Ugly. Only Kevin's unchanged, grim-lipped self-portrait looked natural. Joan wondered if she should inform Dr. Carstairs. Brenda broke the paintbrush. Kevin lunged for her with the shattered edge of the tool but Brenda's cheer-trained body bounded from harm's way.

Brenda, dressed like a midget Donna Reed and eager to apply her newly acquired home-ec skills, made lunch, which she corrected into luncheon. Her apron looked starched enough to crack. Melissa, unused to her sister's greed for normality, which tripped casually and frequently into the bizarre, was disconcerted, but the others paid no mind. It was Brenda.

The luncheon was like her. A Cheese Whiz fondue. A melee of Campbell's soups followed. Then a strangely gorgeous congealed beet salad with unshelled peanuts that Kevin wanted for his museum. The peanuts were like little satellites frozen in the act of orbiting one another in a martian night sky. It was only Jell-O, but it hinted at the eternal, the sublime. Melissa stared at her sister in fear and awe. Brenda crinkled her nose and smiled back, nibbling vinegar-scented Bibb lettuce. She said she was dieting but Melissa thought it entirely possible that her sister was slowly poisoning them.

There was a duck-shaped meatloaf surrounded by ducklings carved from potatoes nesting in a glade of carrots. Bits of black olive formed eyes, hinted at feathers, defined little beaks. It was insane. Brenda chattered vacantly and nonsensically to her stunned family about Louis, cheekbones, bake sales, and Daryl's basketball career, which she knew better than he did.

The store-bought chocolate cake was shocking in its simplicity.

"Sorry," she said, slicing with authority, "I didn't have time to bake."

■　　■　　■

Mike smelled like gas. He'd just filled the tank of his mean machine. He usually smelled like Brut. Daryl pulled on his beer. He'd gotten to like the taste, actually craved one after practice. He put his foot up on the glove compartment.

"Whoa," Mike said, "I just hit that with the Shinyl Vinyl."

"Sorry, man," Daryl said.

Mike kept beat to a Cars song on the steering wheel. He drove like that.

"Hey, man," he said, "what are we going to do?"

"The Moon?" The Moon was a crater where people hung out.

"Naw, man. It's Wednesday. Won't be anything there but some skeevy chicks you wouldn't let your dog fuck."

"We could check out Broad, see if there's anybody worth racing."

"No competition, man. The Car is too bad for them."

"Then you got me, bro."

"Hey, man, I heard about this X-rated movie place where they don't I.D. It's run by Japs or something."

"I don't know, man. It's kind of late."

"Aw, man, don't be such a fucking pussy."

"All right, hop to it, bro."

"All right," Mike said, drumrolling the steering wheel.

There was a spot in front of the Beaux Arts Theater. Downtown was desolate, crummy.

"I hope nobody fucks with your car," Daryl said.

Mike gave it a hard think. "Naw, man. Nobody fucks with the Car."

A tiny, waxy, pockmarked Asian man took their money. Under the Gro-Lite on his desk sat an English-Vietnamese dictionary, open to the Ss. He had *success* underlined. Suck. Sex. Daryl saw sex coded into everything. He wondered if fucking was different in Vietnamese, not that he had an English standard to measure from. He was the last sixteen-year-old male virgin on the planet. He couldn't even get his last girlfriend to touch it, whereas a large segment of Moody High's female population had sucked Mike's cock. And swallowed.

Daryl felt he should inform the foreigner that he was reading under a plant lamp; but a small, dry pocket of air between his heart and his tongue silenced him. The same man took their tickets. During those, what, ten steps, from the booth to the door, Daryl had managed to foolishly crush his ticket into his jeans pocket where his large clumsy hand no longer fit. He ended pulling the pocket out into a rabbit's ear, scattering change onto a theater floor sticky with . . . he didn't want to think about it. The popcorn was a lifeless yellow anyway. The versatile theater operator expertly blew lint from the ticket before depositing it in his shirt pocket, which had a pen guard. He ushered them in with an unexpectedly dramatic arc of his arm.

"You like soda, pwease?" he said, smiling a smile startling in its size.

Daryl shook his head no, his heart chugging bluntly in his neck.

The lighted screen made the dark an absolute black. Mike pulled him into an aisle of seats and Daryl half-fell on a stranger sitting in the next row. The chairs creaked. When his eyes adjusted, he saw that the only other person in the theater was the gray crewcut he'd knocked into.

"Let's move down," Mike whispered. "He might be a pervert or something."

An older flabby man with sideburns and a huge dick fucked a woman in a red corset bent over a desk. The speakers were old and a blizzard of static blew through her frantic moans, which were as loud as the gale of a hurricane. Daryl wanted to plug his fingers in his ears, but it wouldn't be cool. When the guy came he pulled his monster dick out and shot on her back. As big as he was, you would have thought there would have been more than a few large blobs, but there wasn't. Daryl came more than that and he was half that size. He felt superior.

The woman in the corset was the star. She was not a good actress. She moaned crazily, almost before the guy got in her, and wouldn't shut up: "Oh yes," "Harder," "It feels so good." Daryl thought if it felt that good she wouldn't be able to talk about it. If talking was part of sex, Daryl was in trouble. He couldn't talk to girls regular.

The men were like the first one, his father's age, not in great shape. The women were young, elaborately coiffed and made up, as if in apology for their nakedness. He'd seen women flat and immobile in magazines, but seeing them in motion was another universe. The flat-paper women conformed to the mind's wishes, but women moving had their own wants. It excited him. It was repellant. It added a fearful dose of the unknown, another's desire, that competed with your own: two ungovernables.

The repetition made him queasy, and by her fourth encounter, with an alleged set of twins who bore so little resemblance to one another you almost believed it, the frail nausea had subsided into boredom and his dick went limp. The actress's faked rapture bore about as much resemblance to the real thing as the pine-tree-scented deodorizer Mike had dangling from the rearview mirror did to the robust, minty odor it was the sad, pale mimic of. A woman masturbated. He didn't know girls did too. He was surprised she didn't cut herself on her fierce red nails.

His attention wandered to the enormous domed ceiling. He squinted. Angels, clouds, gold: heavenly stuff. A gigantic figure, God probably, in billowy robes seemed to be pointing at the screen. Daryl couldn't make out the face, squinted harder, until he realized there wasn't one. It had fallen away, as if from grief, leaving behind a large, blank mask of craggy white plaster.

"Gross," Mike said.

Daryl looked quickly back. Two chicks ate each other out while the dude watching jerked off. Mike and Daryl didn't stay for the second feature. The Asian man was studying by the dim, gray glow of the Gro-Lite. They couldn't hear him in the booth, but they could see the English words contorting his face, as if they were too large and awkward for his mouth, like the gruesomely large dick the porno queen had tackled with her seemingly elastic jaws, with more spirit than success. The air was blessedly cool.

"I got a fucking boner that won't quit," Mike said. "Imagine getting paid to screw, man. Un-fucking-believable."

Someone had fucked with the Car. They'd snapped off the antenna and scratched FAGGOT into the hood's immaculate, expensive paint. Enraged, crying, Mike went back to the booth and screamed at the uncomprehending English student, who smiled in panic, pushed three dollars back through the small half-moon hole in the window, which sent Mike's fist crashing through the glass, slicing his wrist.

Daryl called his mother from the emergency room, bumming a dime from a chain smoker who'd forgotten her glasses and was waiting for word on her husband, whose heart had jammed, then stopped. Bare chested, his soaked T-shirt still tied around Mike's wrist, Daryl had listened while she meandered through her purse and her story: he'd been fine one minute, then, poof, during a margarine commercial . . . Daryl was anxious for his dime. The man was dead before Daryl could get back to thank the dim-eyed woman again.

All that remained of the wife were two freshly lit cigarettes, one of which Daryl picked up, though he'd never smoked before.

In the car on the way over, Mike, insisting he could drive, had said, "Those fucking gooks killed my brother."

Mike had a dead brother. Girls masturbated. Death nabbed you at homely moments, during commercials. Daryl felt sluggish with knowledge. He picked up the other cigarette and went in search of a light.

■　■　■

The light was buttery and the grass was sweet. You could taste spring. The day's warmth hinted at perfection's attainment. Brenda needed no such hints. She believed perfection not only possible, but necessary. Too bad its vehicle, the human race, was such a sorry lot. They fell, sweated, missed steps, forgot lines, kept gum hidden in their mouths. Brenda felt as if she'd been asked to draw with crayons that broke in midstroke. Even food, though it had no will and could be measured in cups, was subject to impenetrable laws beyond perfection's slender-fingered grasp: cakes collapsed, cookies crumbled, recipes followed to the milli-ounce bumbled.

"O.K., you guys," she said. "Bea, more pep, please. We are encouraging our warriors. Dee, could I have a smile, please? Thank you. You know, you have the best teeth of any of us. Flash them with pride. Philomena, I hate to embarrass you in front of the other girls again, but that perfume has got to go. I can smell it all the way over here."

She had chosen Philomena for her exotic name, a disastrous decision. Philomena didn't understand that a boy was an accessory to a cheerleader's life, like a great purse, only it took you to dances. The boys called her Philomena Fillerup.

"And Hilary," Brenda said, "your jumps don't have the height they used to. What gives? Your technique used to be flawless."

Hilary. Even bent over backward, she had grace, poise, style. She was only a seventh-grader, but Brenda imagined them sailing as one to their mutual destiny in the Pep Hall of Fame on clouds of pom-poms, swept along by the gales of their own greatness.

"I don't know, Bren." Only Hilary dared to shorten their leader's name. "Maybe it's because you're such a fucking cunt that all the rest of us are ready to quit."

Brenda suddenly felt like a paper doll: flat and small and perfectly made, but powerless to affect the world. People outside of her family were capable of disliking her. She hadn't known. She couldn't lose Hilary. They'd never make the Regionals, much less the Nationals.

"Fifty demerits," she said, an absurd amount that would take lifetimes to work off. "With time off for good behavior," she added, knowing only that it sounded good, gave her an out. "Now, you guys," she said, breathing as if they'd just completed the Tarantula, a complicated formation she'd spent weeks honing to its current muscular shape, "I'm not trying to be mean. I just want us to be the best."

"We understand," Philomena Fillerup said.

Why couldn't she be Hilary?

■   ■   ■

The warehouse was silent and dark and smelled of cured tobacco. The only person Kyle saw was Lebanese Sammy, the other janitor. Sammy laughed to himself in his thick accent and didn't watch basketball and shuffled around, not doing much. There wasn't much to do. Kyle daydreamed of Lebanon, envisioning himself in a turban, a saber sashed at his side, though Sammy wore the same khakis and flannel every day, even during the warehouse's punishing summer humidity. Kyle's fantasies were fuzzy, indistinct: grapes, hordes, harems, billowing striped tents, camels and gold, silken rope were the sole means of transportation. All in the dizzy colors of the "I Dream of Jeannie" bottled apartment.

Sammy chewed his peculiar lunches loudly. The meats smelled of murder, as if they needed a good chewing.

"So, Samboy," Kyle said, "what did you do over there in the old country?"

"Teacher," Sammy said.

"Oh yeah? What'd you teach, oil embargoes?"

"Philosophy."

"Philosophy, huh? Well, how's this for philosophy: screw them before they screw you."

"Perfect for your country."

"America's a hell of a country."

"I can't complain."

"You're damn right you can't. None of us can."

Though, recently, Kyle felt very much like complaining. Americans were free, but he sometimes wondered: free to be what?

■　　■　　■

Mr. Mesmer spoke slowly, methodically. He was handsome, but without desire blurring her vision, Melissa appreciated his beauty the way she had come to appreciate a perfectly designed and flawlessly executed pair of diamond studs. She liked the classroom—the hard, functional chairs, the antiseptic smell of chalk. She was alive when she was here.

After the way she had careened through high school, it sometimes seemed an accident that she was alive. There had been casualties: overdoses, drunken drownings, car crashes, the girl strangled by her boyfriend, another who fainted during gym, cracked her skull, and didn't wake up, but died two years later in a nursing home, a fifty-pound fetus. Jumper had pumped Wendy full of kids and left her. Wendy lived with her mother, who'd gotten her into the assistant manager program at the drugstore chain Mrs. Wright had been with for thirty years. It could have been Melissa, any of it, and it wasn't simply the sly trick of her sexuality that had spared her, though that was part of it. Mysteriously, she had been infiltrated by the desire to be more than the life her mother and the cramped opportunities of her class had imagined for her.

During Mesmer's break, she smoked, leaned against the wall. A fellow student in a ponytail, glasses, and an earring bummed a cigarette and hung around. She moved to the other wall.

"Don't worry," he said, "I'm not into dykes."

"Excuse me," she said. She didn't consider herself dykey, but none of the women who were did.

"I've seen you at the bar."

He meant, and she knew he meant, Liaisons, the men's bar, which had once been a warehouse. Lesbians went on Saturdays, fed up with the claustrophobic dance floor of For Women Only.

"Oh," she said.

"You always look so grief-stricken there."

"You would too if you couldn't turn around without running into an ex-girlfriend."

"I'm Neil."

"Melissa."

"Listen, Melissa, the trick, pardon the pun, is to get so drunk that you forget you ever slept with them, except sometimes you end up sleeping with them again, and it is depressing to wake up to the same bad lay twice."

"Twice? I went out with a woman for three months who thought cunnilingus was something that grew on a rock and had calloused fingers that still make me ouch to remember them."

"What do you say we blow this popsicle stand and drink martinis and become best friends?"

"Sorry, I have to ace this class if I'm going to transfer to a real college this fall."

"There are real colleges?"

"I mean not a community one."

"I know, you're right. Me too."

131

"You're transferring too?"

"Yep, as an English major."

"I'm an English major too."

"Favorite author?"

"Flaubert."

"Favorite singer?"

"Janis Joplin."

"Hello, soul mate." Neil extended his hand.

"Rain check on the martinis?" Melissa said, shaking on their Siamese souls.

"Deal. I think we're late for the second half of Dreamboat's sermon on *Antigone*."

"I think I have a crush on Antigone."

■　　■　　■

Sometimes Kevin played "The Staring Game" to keep the self buried that Mr. Carstairs's sneaky questions tried to dig out. Today he sneezed.

"Bless you," the shrink said.

"Thank you," Kevin said back, as if it were a switchblade he'd pulled from his back pocket.

"We're very polite today, aren't we?"

"My mom likes me to be polite."

"But we don't always do what Mommy likes, do we?"

"Sometimes."

"But sometimes it's to trick us, isn't it?"

Kevin studied the bowl of suckers. The colors slammed against one another and light twinkled in the cellophane wrinkles. Very soon, it would be all he wanted to draw; to draw it and draw it and draw it until it was out of him. He could put all the other lines and all the other colors from all the other pictures into the suckers. Then maybe the drawing would be gone from inside him. Lately, he was more interested in commerce. His museum was a mild success. The kids liked the colored popcorn and he liked the nickels. Money was pleasant.

"How do you paint like that?" Mr. Carstairs asked.

"For the hundredth, billionth time, I don't know."

"What do you think when you paint?"

"Nothing."

"You must think something."

"There is no thinking."

Kevin thought Mr. Carstairs hated life because he wanted to draw, but it didn't need to get out of him, so he couldn't. The suckers were pretty and stupid. They weren't hiding anything.

■   ■   ■

Joan couldn't decide about Pink Passion. Brenda had recommended it in her last beauty column, but maybe it only worked on eighth-grade fingers. Brenda had drawerfuls of sample-sized cosmetics. Joan was slightly awed by Brenda's breeze through life, accomplishing, accomplishing, accomplishing. Where had she learned it?

Giving in again, Joan dipped the small brush into the thick, pink paint. Kevin was in his room hanging tomorrow's show. Mr. Carstairs said Kevin was coming along nicely, but Kevin said all they ever talked about was "how drawing happens." Psychology gave Joan the creeps.

Gravel crackled in the driveway. Daryl, probably. He would rib her no end for this color. She layered a last beam of pink over her thumbnail. Brenda was right. It was "perfectly perky pink," too perky for a grown woman. It was done now. The front door opened and closed. It wasn't Daryl. No "Hi, Mom"; no screen door slapping shut behind him: the walk was heavy.

Kyle had lost weight and grown a beard, which suited him. He was almost handsome. Joan resented the implication that his old self was an allergic reaction to their marriage.

"Have you got the money?" she asked.

"Money, money, money. That's all you seem to think about these days. As my friend Sammy would say . . ." He couldn't remember what Sammy would say. Kyle was drunk.

"Scram."

"Money can't buy happiness, Joan."

"But it can buy food, shoes, and pay mortgages. Get out."

"Is that any way to talk to your husband?"

"Ex-husband."

"We're not divorced."

"In my mind, we are divorced."

Kyle scratched his head while he considered this. He walked over to an armchair and sat down. He said, "I don't know if I love her."

Men amazed Joan. She said, "If you don't leave, I'm going to kill you."

"I don't feel about her the way I felt about you."

"You're older."

"I think I want to come home."

Joan screwed the brush back into the fingernail paint bottle. She went into the kitchen and opened the silverware drawer. The butcher knife wasn't there. "I'm looking for the butcher knife," she warned him.

"This is my home too," he said, sobbing, daring to sob.

The butcher knife was in the dishwasher. He'd given it to her two Christmases ago; now, coconut shrapnel was scattered festively across its blade, the debris of a cake Brenda had made that called for, God help the little maniac, the milk and pulp of two whole coconuts. It smelled divine baking, but Joan could not bring herself to eat any food constructed from such a bossy recipe. She wiped the knife on her slacks, something she would usually not do, but it seemed fussy to use a dish towel when you were going to shove a knife into someone you once loved. She got Pink

Passion on her blouse and cursed Kyle silently. The stain would never come out.

"I have found the butcher knife," she announced.

She walked to the armchair. Beer and grief had doubled him over. His face was in his hands. His shoulders shook. He'd always cried like that. Silently. He still wore Aqua Velva, blue mint. She'd bet he still liked corn on the cob, hitting all the vegetable stands in summer, appraising each batch for color, texture, sweetness, scent. He would have made an excellent county fair judge.

She gashed his arm. A thick mouth of blood formed and slid in competing lines down to his elbow, where it dripped in great casual drops into black flowery stains on the carpet. She wondered if she had any Comet left under the sink. He looked up at Joan, then over to his bloody arm with the bewildered face of a child who cannot connect clocks with time.

She had wanted to kill him, but she couldn't, and she was glad that she couldn't.

"Now," she said, "get out."

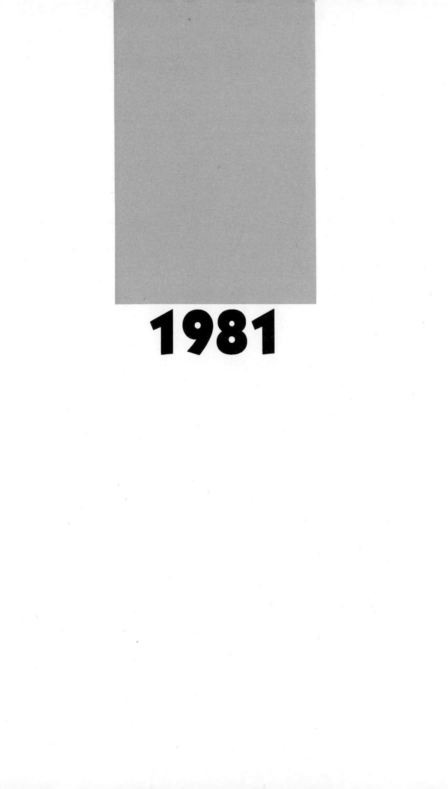

1981

Footsteps echoed in the shining, pink marble lobby of the courthouse. Brenda sat at one end of a burnished mahogany bench. At the other end, a man in a loosened tie went through a briefcase, ashes from his cigarette flickering over the papers he shuffled.

Joan hadn't wanted Brenda to come but Brenda had insisted that she'd be scarred for life if she was excluded from this legal ritual of dissolution. Scarring her children for life was one of Joan's pet fears and she had nervously relented, but at the last minute she wouldn't let Brenda into the courtroom. Brenda was gearing up to pitch a fit when she noticed her mother's pocketbook vibrating in Joan's clenched, trembling hand.

Brenda wondered if the man with the briefcase was a lawyer. She liked lawyers. She sometimes imagined herself in navy blue, her hair pulled into a stern chignon, making closing arguments. Surprise witnesses. Order in the court. The chair. She'd prosecute and approach the bench and raise objections. Naturally, the law wasn't perfect. There were technicalities and parole and, worst of all, a jury of your peers. She knew who peers were. Other people.

"Going over a brief?" she said knowingly.

"Yeah," he said, eyes funny. "Wanna see?"

"I'd love to," she said in a crisp, legal voice.

She scooted over. He definitely wasn't wearing cologne and it was a mistake. His open briefcase covered his lap and his left hand moved peculiarly under it. He was a strange, disappointing lawyer. Still, it would be fun to see live legal documents, except there weren't any. There was a transistor radio and cigarette butts and orange peels and a greasy bottle of Vaseline Intensive Care and pictures of naked women, wrinkled and smudged where he'd ripped them from magazines. Women bent over and smiled between their legs. They smiled as they mashed their giant breasts together. They smiled up from white, furry rugs as they kicked their high-heeled feet in the air. She couldn't imagine what they were smiling about.

The man moved the briefcase forward. His hand moved up and down the dick poking through his zipper. The head was a red, wrinkled plum and it was oozing. She had felt Louis pressed up against her through his pants, but she'd never thought they'd look like . . . that. She was angry. She could feel something ruining inside her and he was ruining it.

"You're not a lawyer," she said.

"Huh?" He moved his briefcase back. His prick nosed over the edge of it.

"Why are you doing this?" she asked, looking up, straight into his pervert eyes. She really wanted to know.

"Do you like it, baby?" he whispered, stroking again.

"I hate you."

"Keep talking, baby."

She slammed the briefcase shut. He gagged on his pain. It echoed. He jumped up, clutching himself, spilling the briefcase. Cigarette butts and orange peels and dirty pictures skittered over the smooth marble floor. He ran, hunched over, his hands cupped over his hurt dick, like someone in one of those humiliating relay races on "Battle of the Network Stars."

140

"I hope it's broken," Brenda yelled after him.

She dumped the briefcase and its disgusting contents into a wire-mesh trash can and went to the ladies room. She couldn't stop washing. She must have been in there fifteen minutes. Her face was red with rubbing. Joan was waiting for her when she came out.

"You're flushed," her mother said.

"It's just that awful bathroom soap," Brenda said.

"Well," Joan sighed, "it's over."

"Men are scum."

"Don't talk about your father that way."

"Please, Mother. I'm practically grown up."

"He's still your father."

"Mom," Brenda started. She knew she should tell her mother what had happened, but Joan already had enough to worry about. Besides, it was over. Some weirdo with a brief-case. Who cared? Brenda hoped his stupid dick would fall off.

"What?" Joan said.

"Nothing."

"I guess you're sad too."

"Kind of."

"Let's go shopping. I think the Sears credit card is in my name."

■   ■   ■

Joan was glad the vacation was over. Kevin had blackened Brenda's eye with her own hairbrush. Daryl had told Joan many times that he hated her—that phase. Brenda had thrown Daryl's shoes into the Atlantic, saying they stunk, which they did. They had moved to another motel when Kevin was caught spitting off the balcony of the first one. Sand was a malevolent force intent on destroying Joan's life. And she'd nearly fucked a boy Melissa's age who she'd skinny-dipped with after midnight, after daiquiris. They'd been

141

on a raft, about two seconds from lift-off, when Brenda appeared, spectral in her nightgown, to inform her that Kevin was crying from a nightmare. Joan had awarded herself second place in the Fort Lauderdale Unfit Mothers Sweepstakes, the grand prize going to a woman from Cleveland who had drowned her infant daughter and made the national news.

She turned off the radio as she pulled into the driveway. The yard was alarming. Hedges threatening and thick. Flowers, violently colored, hung their enormous petaled heads over the beds as if gasping for breath. The pine tree seemed to have grown a foot. The bugs, sluggish from the buffet of poisons she'd left out, heaved themselves through the jungle. One perk of her insanely fertile soil was the ivy blanketing the bizarre steel beams that had held her house steady for a year; except the bottom legs of the metal Ls were gone. And where was her porch? The lower molding of the front door was lightly kissing the ground, the way you might peck a third cousin at a family reunion. The house hadn't sunk in a year, and now, in a week, the rest of the foundation had said its sayonara to sunlight.

Her temples beat satanically. Home was where you lived your important life. It was where you sang to yourself while shaving your legs. It was where you stored Kotex and coupons and cans of soup. It was where love unleashed its horrible earnestness, and died its thousand lingering deaths. It wasn't that home was where the heart was; home was where the heat was. Home was where the people connected to you by the intimate telepathy of blood could be counted on to help you destroy your life. Joan would not forgive this betrayal, this abdication. She had as much right to her foundry of neurosis as anyone.

"You kids get this stuff in," she said, shutting off the ignition.

The porch was seamlessly level with the yard. She went straight for the phone.

"Hello," the secretary said.

"This is Joan Demerest. I have an urgent message for Mr. Belmont."

"Mr. Belmont's in a meeting."

"I would call this dire."

"I'm sorry."

"Fine. Would you kindly tell that good-for-nothing that if he doesn't get his goddamned ass over here, pronto, to remove these fucking beams from my fucking house, I'll have the lousy son of a bitches taken down myself to be deposited in his personal yard where he can shove them up his ass for all I care. Got that?"

"All but the last part."

■   ■   ■

Clarissa clicked her ice in her empty glass. In the mirror, Joan tried her left profile, then her right profile, gauging which side of her date she should sit on. She was forty, she had wrinkled slightly, her chin sagged. Makeup and the magic of Clarissa's hairstyling hands helped; but passing for thirty wasn't the same as being twenty.

Clarissa said, "Goddamn it, quit your primping. He's Larry's brother, not Robert Redford."

"I'm too dressed up?"

"For God's sake, let's go upstairs and find that hooch before you comb the hair right out your head."

"I wish women still wore wigs."

Clarissa pulled her from the shifting, magnetic image in the mirror. "Well, they don't, except the ones peddling their butts on Broad Street."

They settled onto the living room furniture Joan had bought with her tax return. It was white and brocaded with green flowers, and no one was allowed to sit on it when Joan wasn't around to monitor dirty clothes and slap feet from the armrests. She'd won the house outright in the settlement. Clarissa smelled nice.

"What are you wearing?" Joan asked.

"Aviance," Clarissa said, va-va-vooming her shoulders. "I'm gonna have an Aviance night, oh yeah." She high-kicked a foot.

"Can I borrow some?"

"You already got three kinds on. You're going to smell like a goddamned whorehouse."

They were drinking bourbon and Diet Coke. It tasted flat to Joan, but when she complained, all Clarissa said was "Figure," and Joan suffered Nutrasweet.

"Tell me about him again," Joan said.

"All right," Clarissa sighed. "He's thirty-eight, divorced four years. Two daughters, eight and fourteen, who he hasn't seen in two years since his ex ran off with them to Texas."

"Awful."

"Yeah. He's kind of funny and likes to play the guitar when he's had a couple. He's medium cute, bearded, six two, six three"—she made that uncertain, wavy motion with her hand—"and if he's anything like his brother, he's got a dick down to his knee."

"Oh, I don't care about that."

"Let's put it this way—it's a nice bonus."

They met the boys at Blue Heaven, the one dance joint Clarissa hadn't seen Suzy and Kyle at. It was small, smoky, dark. Joan nervously lost count of how many drinks she'd had. She kept forgetting the table wobbled. Her finger itched.

Wade was an O.K. dancer, not much on rhythm, but he had spirit. A married man forced his number on Joan while she waited in line for the bathroom. The drummer of the band winked at her, but later she noticed him blowing kisses to a braless woman with earrings that scraped her shoulders like wild pendulums when she danced.

Clarissa kept Joan in stitches: dancing barefoot; grinding unashamedly against Larry on the dance floor, then slyly pointing to the work she'd accomplished under his zipper; ordering round after round; mimicking everything their poor waitress did behind her back; whooping out of nowhere. Joan had never had such a time.

As soon as she woke the next morning she pulled Wade's big, hairy body back on top of hers. One-night stands were underrated. Fucking without the accumulations of marriage was liberating. They figured out the mazes of one another's bodies, turning corner after unexpected corner. Even his beard scratching her thighs was erotic because it was new, though she could already feel how she would tire of it. She was glad he'd been married, and wondered which of the moves he'd tried with her had been honed on his ex-wife's body. Which had he made up on the spot? She was surprised when a trick that curled Kyle's toes didn't elicit the same ecstasy in Wade; surprised and pleased by his exact, unique sexuality, like encouraging her finger up his ass while they screwed.

Clarissa had been right; he was like his brother and it was more than a nice bonus. It was a marvel. She was surprised when he didn't go pale and light-headed when the blood rushed from his torso to fill it up. She wanted to borrow his cock for an afternoon and carry it in a jar to Suzy's to show Kyle. She wouldn't say a word, just stand there, smirking.

She didn't love Wade, and though she'd only known him for an evening, she knew it like a fact that she wouldn't love him. He was a nice man with a big peter who bought her drinks and led her proprietorially by the elbow to the dance floor. That was enough.

■　　■　　■

Pansy sighed again. The date was not going well. Daryl had rented the tux and bought the corsage. He'd taken her for a fancy dinner at La Belle Boite on Kyle's generously donated credit card. He'd sneaked in a pint of vodka to spike their plastic cups of punch. Joan had given him a few dancing pointers. He'd actually read an article in one of Brenda's dumb teen mags called "Don't Be a Dud Date." And he still was. First class. King Blockhead.

The band did another Doobie Brothers song.

"Do you want to dance?" he yelled over the music.

Pansy smiled and shook her head no, her Farah-Fawcetted hair bobbing, but falling right back into place when she was done. Hair that stopped on a dime—Pansy was gorgeous. She wore lots of perfume. Around corners, you smelled her before you saw her. At dinner, she hadn't gotten so much as a crumb caught in the corner of her mouth, and the French words on the menu had flowed from her mouth like honey. It had given him a hard-on.

She beckoned him to lean down.

"Huh?" he said. He couldn't believe he'd said that. The teen article should have been called "Don't Be a Daryl Date."

"Have you been to the Bahamas or something?" Her sweet girl's breath opened a passage straight from his ear to his groin. Her father owned a lumberyard and she didn't realize that most people didn't get to go to the Bahamas. Daryl knew why she'd asked. He'd been wondering too.

"Nah," he said, real casual.

"You look sort of sunburned or something."

"I'm outside a lot. Practice and stuff."

Her eyes roved over his face.

"Can I touch it?" she asked.

For one panicked second he thought she meant *it.* "Uh, sure," he said.

She touched a fingertip to his cheek and held it there for several delirious seconds, as if he were a cake she was testing for doneness. Her perfectly shaped and perfectly red nail rested just below his eye. His heart beat so hard he was sure she could feel it through his face. He tried to look natural.

"Gross," she said. Then seeing his face: "I mean have you considered a good moisturizer?" And when that didn't help: "I mean it's not bad or anything. It's just so dry."

"Do you know a good one?" he asked.

"Well," she said, wiping her finger on the paper table-cloth, "no. I mean boys don't use moisturizer, do they?"

"I don't."

She smiled again. It was like a wall you bumped into. She looked back out at the prom. It hadn't been just a song, but a whole Doobie Brothers medley. Pansy's perfume tortured Daryl with promises she would never keep. He decided to spike his punch some more. Mike said when you couldn't get laid, you could always get drunk. He and his date had left half an hour ago. Daryl started for the bathroom, then remembered bathrooms had mirrors, and stopped.

■   ■   ■

They de-homosexualized the apartment. The Holly Near records, *Our Bodies, Ourselves*, the snapshot of Neil in drag, the rally flyer, the bottle of poppers Neil kept in the freezer; it was all crammed behind Neil's bedroom door, which was then locked. Melissa drove him nuts. Was the mannequin too campy, her combat boots too dykey, the orchid he'd bought too vaginal? She made Neil swear: no tricks.

Brenda had invited herself over to spend a Saturday night and as much as Melissa did not want heterosexuality's arrogance and infuriatingly serene assurance marauding through the only place where she was fearlessly herself, her brutal genes won the weekend. Kinship was like slow-acting poison you gulped in with your first bloody squalling breath.

Brenda remarked on Sappho the cat's indifference to its weekend alias, Muffin; was appalled by a beggar who'd waved while peeing just outside the living room window; and expressed mild surprise when a caller (she'd beaten them to the phone) asked for Miss Neil. Still, she was charmed by her host, embarrassed by her taste for Andy Gibb, vocal in her admiration of Melissa's independence, and incurious as to the contents of the closed room.

All in all, a success.

Neil left to visit a "cousin" and Melissa tested the quiche with a fork. It needed a few more minutes. As she sliced avocado for salad, the B-52's stopped, and Brenda, who'd been dying to change it, didn't. Melissa suddenly knew what was meant by ominous silence. She went into the living room, wiping her hands on her jeans. Brenda was poised rigidly on the absolute edge of the couch, as if practicing a posture from a Victorian etiquette book.

"Bren?" Melissa said. "Are you all right? There's plenty of other records. I think an old Bruce album may be hidden under there somewhere."

Brenda didn't answer. Melissa moved cautiously towards her. Her stomach switched to the churn-and-burn cycle. "Bren? Is anything wrong?"

"Melissa, I think you should pack a bag and come home with me tonight."

"Why, sweetie?" Dread nosing out any familiarity the pet name implied.

Brenda nodded stiffly at the coffee table. It was the slightest gesture, imperceptible to any but a panicked sister's eye. *Hot Butt Half-Back*, one of Neil's favorite pictorials, was the object of Brenda's rigor mortis. Its cover was a badly cropped photograph of three naked men, one of whom would have been the bologna had they been a sandwich. There were the scantest references to the sport alluded to in the periodical's title: a crumpled jock strap on the floor, a pair of shoulder pads, and an unfortunately lit background of gym lockers.

"I found that under a couch cushion," Brenda said.

"I wonder how it got there," Melissa tried.

Brenda looked at her sister with all the withering sarcasm a ninth-grader could muster. "Don't be naive."

"Neil?" Melissa suggested.

"Obviously. You're living with a . . . a . . . "

"Homosexual?" Melissa guessed.

"I knew it from the minute I walked in here."

"Do you really think so?"

Brenda gagged her disbelief.

Melissa said, "I suppose I should take you home and discuss this with Neil when he returns from his aunt's."

"His cousin's," Brenda said, dryly.

"I can't keep up with him. He's always off with one of them."

"People are going to think you're one too."

"Of his family?"

"Don't be retarded. And just be glad I found out before some blabby stranger did."

"Thanks," Melissa said inanely.

"Don't mention it," Brenda said, as if the unpleasant gratitude of others was a fact of her life to which she'd become accustomed.

When Melissa didn't throw Neil and his magazines out, Brenda stopped speaking to her. Joan proclaimed her grief over Melissa's life-style. Daryl, when she stopped by to retrieve a forgotten book, said in the strange haiku of adolescent boys, "Gosh, Mel, fags, bad news." His skin was the color of half-faded sunburn and papery looking.

Oddly, they never considered that she might be guilty of a similar crime. When they thought about it at all, most people seemed to imagine homosexuality as an alien spore highly contagious to school-age children, but to which immediate family had an unquestionable immunity. At least you knew when people were black.

Melissa was relieved to be on the outs with her family again. It fit her like an old favorite coat.

■　　■　　■

Daryl had itched, then reddened, then flaked. Then he turned green. His skin acquired a toughness and a faint iridescence. It was more of a soft, shiny armor than gently layered epidermis. From twenty feet away he looked like any other lanky boy of seventeen, a driver's license warm in his wallet, strategies for getting laid crisscrossing his hormone-flooded circuits. At ten feet he took on a slight luminesence, and at five, a definite amphibian glow. His cock was green and his erections were green too. His hair remained blond on his head and walnut on his arms, his chest, his legs. His pubic hair was familiarly dark and thick. His toenails retained their white, beaten-up looks and his fingernails their pinkish charm, like a gentle, mocking reminder of his former hue. His mother wasn't lying when she reassured him he wasn't ugly. He wasn't. He was the same attractive young man, only green.

As was Joan's right index finger. Like Daryl's, the nail was untainted. The green faded just below the knuckle except for three thin ravines across her palm, like new life lines. But it was, however subtle, unmistakably green, as real and jarring as a sudden pothole on an otherwise evenly paved road.

Daryl sat greenly. Other patients, mostly adolescent girls with sweetheart rings and harried-looking mothers, tried not to look at him. Their eyes seemed sprained with not-looking. Their not-looks stuffed the room. Daryl tried not to think green but his not-thinking was like their not-looking. Green informed it. He'd stare at his face for hours in the mirror. His eyes were still wet and soft and blue and oddly dim, and the eyebrows looked bleached. He'd pulled, tugged, folded, pinched his skin. Tiny, translucent scraps of it fluttered to the sink like a new form of precipitation, each one as intricate and unique as a snowflake. He shed like a creature in metamorphosis but there was green beneath green. He had pricked his finger to find out how deep it went, only slightly relieved when the blood was red, rich, and human.

Joan sometimes swore her finger had gone numb and constantly bit at it. She refused anesthetics when they did painful seven-layer extractions, fearing the numbness would stay like an unwanted guest. Daryl knew instinctively that this was as far as it would go and Dr. Hartley had confirmed that whatever it was, the malady seemed to have run its course. Daryl experienced no numbness, though it might have been welcome, and he jerked off ferociously, frequently, the globs of come warm and wet on his breath-pumped belly. He started tasting it as if there might be a clue in the normal color, the ordinary consistency. His fantasies were wild: two, three, ten girls, all races, shapes, and sizes. He was always himself and powerful and not green.

"The doctor will see you now," the receptionist said, smiling as if all this had been predicted.

Dr. Hartley's office was typical: bright and white and silver and furnished with menacing, futuristic objects. It had the dead, clean smell meant to be reassuring. Dr. Hartley wore turtlenecks under her white smocks and moved with the delicacy of a retired dancer. She poked, pricked, prodded, scraped, made slides, took temperatures.

"Any changes?" she asked.

"No," they said.

"You've been using the soap and the distilled water twice a day?"

"Yes," they said.

"And you apply the cream at night?"

"Yes," they said.

"I'd like to try an antibiotic that's been remarkably successful in extreme cases of psoriasis and hives. This may be some sort of virus. Any other family members exhibiting symptoms?"

"No."

"Well, that's something. You should know that we have discovered some irregular compounds at the molecular level and I'm thinking of transferring your case over to the university, where I could have access to a range of equipment and opinions. Any objections?"

"If it will help," Joan said.

The doctor played with her stethoscope as she spoke. "I know this is difficult, but you seem to be in perfect physical shape otherwise. Though I do wish you, Mrs. Demerest, would quit smoking. You're not sick, you're not dying, and there's every cause for optimism. We've only begun to research this. Please be patient, try not to despair, and feel free to call me at any time if something develops."

"We will," they said.

■　　■　　■

Kyle folded the package of Cheez Doodles in half. He found Sammy sweeping behind a stack of Marlboro 100 Lites, and handed him the bent cellophane bag, his fingers still orange. "Eat them in good health, my friend," he said, clapping Sammy on the back. He didn't tell anyone, just opened the door and walked into the amazing sunlight. They sent him a check three weeks later, minus the cost of the five McGee shirts hanging uselessly in his closet.

That had been three months ago. The first week he kicked back, cracking a beer at ten, catching "The Price Is Right" at eleven, not shaving, shooting baskets, napping, cooking a little dinner. At a yard sale he bought a guitar with a hairline crack, a manual called "Picking and Grinning: Twelve Easy Lessons," and a yellowed "You're Looking at Country Songbook" with a forgotten, signed photo of Chet Atkins pressed between its pages. All for ten dollars. He suspended Chet in the frame of the dresser mirror and every morning said, "Howdy, Atkins," before he got out of bed.

The lessons were easy. Applying them to the songbook was hard. He had learned to pick a fair version of "Wings of a Dove" that Suzy could recognize from any room in the apartment.

"Recognize this?" he'd say.

She always did.

He wanted to master a couple of others because A) playing the same damn song was getting tiresome and B) "Wings" was about God and made him uncomfortable. He couldn't sing it on the footstool in his underwear. His voice, which he also worked on, wasn't anywhere near as good as his playing.

He kept meaning to look for a job. He'd buy the paper, scan the Help Wanteds with a cup of coffee and a McGee pen. He'd circle the jobs he felt qualified for. There weren't many. Either you needed a college degree of any moron with half a brain and two hands could do them. He might not have gone to college, but he wasn't stupid, though it seemed his one qualification was that he could drive—the ads he usually marked said "Driver's License Required." He never made it to the interviews. One thing or another— his guitar, his car needing an oil change, just plain fatigue— got in the way. Suzy left him a five on top of her jewelry box each morning and that kept him in six-packs and cigarettes.

He tried another chord of "Green, Green Grass of Home" and fucked it up again. You needed the hands of a chimp to hit that sucker. His fingers ached. Suzy was on the couch in her bra. They'd stopped going around naked. He wore his underwear—the elastic shot in most pairs—and she stripped down to her bra when she got home from work.

She sipped her Diet Coke and said, "Are you ever going to get a job again?"

"Well, sure," he said.

"I'm not criticizing. I just need to know."

"The day a Demerest man lets a woman support him is the day I eat this guitar." He strummed for emphasis. He was being funny, but Suzy never laughed, not at him, not at TV, not at anything. Only if you tickled her, which she detested, and once during sex. That time he'd stopped screwing and asked her why she laughed. She'd said, "I was just imagining if an earthquake or something happened and they found us hundreds of years from now like this." Kyle hadn't thought it was funny. "You think of stuff when we're making love?" "Only sometimes," she'd said.

Right now she said, "I was thinking about quitting my job."

"What for?" he asked.

"I don't know. I'm just tired of it. Sometimes taking quarters all day long from people makes me want to kill myself."

"Aw, you don't mean that."

"Sometimes the interstate seems too long. I can't see where it ends from my booth. It just fades out. And I'll think, I bet if you took this road from here to where it ends it wouldn't be no different. You'd just keep running up on people like us."

"We're not so bad."

She flicked something from her bra. She needed a new one. "I guess not," she said. She sat her Coke down and it fell over, empty.

■　　■　　■

Disco was like a migraine: it pounded in your temples and had to be experienced in almost total darkness. Melissa's eyes followed the same woman all evening, a wiry, hypnotic dancer, the flashing light sparking off her blazing silver belt. Melissa watched her laugh and order beers and play pinball, any moment when the beautiful stranger could be caught unaware by Melissa's longing.

By the bar, Neil made out with a leather number who looked to have been carved from the last of a race of giant oaks. Tonight's paramour tilted Neil's head roughly, latched the poppers to his nose, then kissed him. Long, deep kisses. As they kissed, Neil's hands clenched and unclenched the back of the brute's jacket, rippling the light that had melted there. Melissa couldn't see Giant Oak's hands, but whatever they were doing, she was certain it wasn't tentative with desire.

Neil whispered, the man nodded, and Neil crossed the dance floor. He took Melissa by the shoulders. She blew smoke in his eyes.

"Is your heart on fire?" she asked.

"No, but my honeypot is."

"How'd you know I was standing here?"

"You always stand here."

"Your nose is raw."

"All my orifices will be raw when he's finished with me."

"You're going home with that Nazi?"

"He's my 'Intro to Psych' professor."

"Please tell me that's a joke."

He shook his head no and pecked her nose.

She said, "Don't forget about brunch tomorrow, if you think you'll be able to sit."

"Can I bring Psych 101?"

"Not dressed like that you can't."

He kissed her again, this time on the forehead, and drifted back through the throng of thrashing dancers, as if he had discovered a secret path that required an insistent calm in the traveler before revealing itself. Giant Oak, one of his limbs fallen over Neil's shoulder, waved good-bye to her. He had the earnest smile of a social worker or a Girl Scout hawking cookies. It didn't go with his chaps.

When Melissa thought to look again, the silver belt wasn't sparking anywhere in Liaison's darkness. Melissa began the tedious search for her jacket, which she misplaced every Saturday.

■   ■   ■

They kicked Joan upstairs. Clarissa, who'd been there two, three years longer, they left at the cash register. She said she didn't mind as long as they gave her a raise every six months and an extra three days' vacation each year. Company policy.

The new position's official title was Assistant to the Store Manager, but Joan thought you could just as easily have called it secretary. They'd paid for her to take typing at the community college where Melissa had started. She answered phones, filed, made coffee, ran out for sandwiches, and kept Mr. Kratz to his schedule. It was easy and reassured her that she was efficient, competent, capable of accomplishing goals—sensations often absent from her real life. At the office, spelling could be corrected, dust polished away, hours on time cards tallied to the minute and multiplied by their wage to the cent. In life, getting your house ungirderized was a study in failure; you couldn't organize a pervert out of Melissa's apartment. She sometimes thought that the error, disgrace, and longing of life were a conspiracy by businessmen that made you crave the clarity of employment.

■   ■   ■

Mr. Carstairs was still scribbling in his notebook from the session before Kevin's. The suckers were the same ones. Mr. Carstairs didn't give them out. It was like they were fake, but they weren't.

He closed his notebook and looked up. "What are we going to draw today?"

"Nothing," Kevin said.

"We have to draw something."

"I'm tired of drawing."

"Are you tired of drawing at home too?"

"Maybe."

The office was totally odorless. It was like being in a closed Tupperware bowl. Mr. Carstairs cracked his knuckles.

"Kevin, we're trying to figure out why you can draw and all the other little boys and girls who come here can't."

"I don't care about the other boys and girls."

"And that, my friend," he said, hitting his finger on the table, "might just be your problem. You should care about those other boys and girls because it hardly seems fair that you can draw and they can't, now does it?"

"I don't care."

"I'm going to teach you to care, but I can't do that unless you draw for me."

"No."

"Kevin, I can't have you going around pushing people down staircases."

"I said I was sorry two years ago."

"Sorry isn't enough." He pushed the pad over the desk.

"I can draw fifty million billion pictures and you still won't be able to do it." He had never said this out loud.

Mr. Carstairs wet his lips, which he did five or six times a session. "Kevin, you are going to do this. We can sit here fifty minutes a week for the next five years, but you will draw for me. You may have genius, notice I said *may*—those types of tests are under fire—but I have power. Besides, what is one little drawing when you'll do hundreds, thousands, in your lifetime?" He paused. "Please."

Kevin wished he could sneak up behind Mr. Carstairs and push him down something. "Say pretty please," he said.

"Pretty please."

"Can I have a sucker?"

"One per drawing."

■　　　■　　　■

At nine, Kevin had his first show. Sandy gave it for him in the elementary school art room. A friend of hers printed the invitations for free. They were glossy and postcard-sized and didn't have a picture of Kevin's suckers because he wouldn't allow them to be reproduced. "It makes it something else," he said. One side gave the date and location of the opening. The other was black with the phrase "More Suckers" burning through in white. Sandy invited the teachers of Anderson Elementary, Kevin's family, her friends, the mayor, the curator of the local Civil War Museum (the one from the real museum wouldn't come), a regionally famous watercolorist, and the newspaper's arts reporter, who mostly covered movies. She transformed the art room into as gallerylike a space as was possible, which wasn't very, as there was masking tape that read "newsprint" and "rubber cement" curling from the cabinets. There were sinks and a chalkboard. There were long tables that came up to your knee and miniature chairs stacked against the walls.

Sandy wore a black leather dress and spiked her hair. She had crudités and wine for the adults. Kevin, in slicked-back hair and an Easter Sunday suit a size too small, sat at a table selling cups of Kool-Aid, bags of colored popcorn, and two trays of Joan's brownies. Sandy was distressed by this mercenary injection into the blood of art, but Kevin had insisted, just as he had insisted that she invite his fourth-grade class so there would be someone to buy his goodies. But she had been firm in denying his request that Joan dress as a gypsy and tell fortunes from the supply closet for a quarter.

Joan stood around in a pants suit, a plastic cup of pee-colored wine held like a ballast to her chest. The room stunk of glue. The guests seemed puzzled. There was no place to sit. By seven o'clock Kevin had made five dollars, a low figure by his estimate.

Except for her friends, no one liked the work. Sandy wasn't surprised. These people wouldn't qualify as philistines. They were connoisseurs of the crass, valuers of the vulgar, revilers of the real. They couldn't understand art because there was no Top Forty describing it and it couldn't be eaten. Though they could have eaten part of these pictures. Kevin had taped actual suckers—and stale, faded ones in cracked cellophane at that—to the center of each painting. The suckers made Sandy uncomfortable and she had been the first among her friends to champion Beauys, but Kevin had been vehement: the forlorn candy was essential. She decided that Kevin was entering a self-referential phase.

The newspaper critic gave the show a paragraph in the Sunday edition, dismissing it as a curiosity.

■   ■   ■

Real college. A four-year one. Melissa had imagined that it would be like France, people in berets sitting around smoky cafes sipping cognac and discussing the Meaning of Life. She would roam halls dazzled with knowledge. She would be dusted by the wisdom of a race of Olympians, gigantic with enlightenment. She would glide on a gossamer carpet spun from ideas, over an earth teeming with numbskulls and swollen with ignorance.

Instead, she had Dr. Wilmuth for French, who had never recovered from the *je ne sais quoi* of a youth misspent in Paris, and told pointless anecdotes that ended with a high-pitched laugh meant to stun her barbarously American students into sophistication. There was Dr. Brock, biology, who spoke about the mysteries of the human body as if they were of no more interest than a platter of flapjacks. She needed a large coffee, black, for his lectures. Dr. Trinceri had enough enthusiasm for ten logic professors and his Italian accent would have been knee-weakening had it not swathed his English into musical gibberish.

She was so grateful for Dr. Jones that had marriage been a prerequisite for his Art History 102 class, she would have impaled herself on the wedding altar to express her devotion. He must have weighed three hundred pounds and he wheezed, but between wheezes there was a rigorous elegance to his constructions that made her swoon. He described the Notre Dame cathedral as if he'd built it himself, the lights and darks of Carravagio as the stuff of tragedy, Cezanne's mountain with such immediacy that the brushes seemed to be drying in a room nearby. He was witty, angry, and his girth seemed the result of his having gulped down anything—sculpture, breezes, entire civilizations—that crossed his path: the whole of life seemed to be inside him.

Then there were the others, proof that knowledge wasn't wisdom. That was the final disappointment. They could stuff you with facts until your toes split and your cerebellum smoked, but facts would never be passion and grace, a way of being. It made Dr. Joneses and it made Dr. Brocks. It didn't automatically dance, subtly shimmering around the edges of perception, but seemed, if anything, to make you more yourself; exactly what Melissa had not wanted.

■   ■   ■

Joan read about visualization in *The Skin We're In*. The article "I Can See Myself" was a series of testimonies attributing remarkable recoveries from shingles, skin cancer, and, of course, acne, to this mutant of meditation. You imagined yourself as healthy. You marshalled the body's strike forces and sicced them on intruders. The American Association of Dermatologists approved visualization in conjunction with customary pharmacological procedure. Dr. Hartley told them flat out she thought it was blarney, and Joan countered testily that it couldn't possibly be any less effective than any of the treatments the lily white–skinned doctor and her colleagues had experimented with.

Joan listened to Daryl breathing, stretched out beside her on the carpet. She focused on her finger, gently prodding green-killers towards it from her brain, her heart, her chakras, whatever the hell they were. A crick tried to assert itself in her neck and her feet went nonexistent, like reverse phantom limb syndrome. She peeked. They were there but her stockings had run at the big toe. They were forever running there, and it made her feel clumsy, awkward, prehuman. She would never forget the time . . .

Her finger! It was green. She slowly flooded it a peach, fleshy color which it stayed about two seconds before going vermillion. She willed the human shade back. Focused. She held it slightly longer this time, but strained so desperately for her natural pigment that she lost control of her ordinary nail, which grew two feet. She nipped it with an ancient pair of clippers she hadn't thought about in years. Lanie had borrowed them after Hilly's first stroke, or was it the second . . .

A small snore rippled through Daryl's nose.

■ ■ ■

Melissa and eleven other females—English, journalism, and art majors—were kicking around the idea of a women's newsletter, not necessarily lesbian. It was not going well. A rapier-thin radical, dressed, oddly, as if she were off to teach kindergarten, had them living on an edenic commune wiped clean of men inside of an hour. The project had to be of portfolio quality or the Layout and Design major was out. The journalism faction wanted all hard news. Melissa was relieved when the phone rang, until she heard her father's voice.

"How's about a cookout this weekend?" he asked.

His guilt, Melissa knew, had provoked the call and the cookout; and she could feel herself being drawn towards it trancelike, as if her father's remorse over strained, tenuous familial relations were a telepathic field with the unopposable forces of science and nature at its center. Nothing provoked her helplessness like the competitive griefs of her family.

"Sure," she said.

They pretended Daryl wasn't green, a feat destined for

the Futility Hall of Fame. Melissa asked him how school was and he looked away from the television long enough for her to register the depth of his contempt. He'd quit playing basketball. The banality of anything you said bounced back from his predicament with deadening impact.

He wasn't bright green. From across the room he looked almost normal, that is, you knew that something was off, but you couldn't decide what it was. It wasn't until you were next to him that the flaky dryness and disorienting color became evident. He had the soft patina of aged bronze. A medicinal scent hovered around him. Brenda gave him a plate heaped with cookout food and he ate only the hot dog, which he wiped clean of condiments with the bun. The savagery of the gesture was touching in its calculation. Melissa had made a point to kiss him when she came in, and he'd jerked away as if scalded.

Kevin sat beside his brother all afternoon, pretending absorption with midday movies and car races. He sat with an animal stillness, and Melissa wondered if he was trying by osmosis to decipher Daryl or if he realized, as they all suspected, that this was all that could be done. He sat at his post on the couch like a sentry and it was impossible to tell if it was a generous act of a predatory one.

Kyle and Suzy seemed like foreign actors who'd learned their lines phonetically. You sensed they didn't get out much. They were both on unemployment. Even their clothes looked like they'd been whipped up by a European who had learned American culture from manuals explicating sitcoms. She wore sandals, loose shorts down to her knees, and a peach halter top that seemed designed to expose her breasts. He wore flip-flops, garish plaid cut-offs, and a T-shirt split at the shoulder by a row of variously shaped and sized holes. Their apartment had the same detached, almost hallucinatory anonymity. Only the smoke drifting in from the grill seemed to have any substance. Melissa wanted to scream at several juxtapositions of the day, but she was afraid that no one would notice.

"Anybody want to hear the next Chet Atkins?" Kyle asked.

"Dad," Kevin said, "we're trying to watch TV."

Suzy, the only one who seemed genuinely unaffected by Daryl's skin, sat down beside him on the arm of the couch and said, "I bet Daryl would like to hear his father play."

Brenda, Their Lady of Perpetual Good Cheer, said, "Of course we would."

"Where did you learn to play the guitar?" Melissa asked.

"Right here in this apartment," Kyle said.

"Do whatever you want," Daryl said.

"I think Daryl hates me," Kevin said, as if this were the conclusion he'd been circling all day.

"Oh, bullshit," Kyle said.

"Daddy, don't cuss," Brenda said, pinching him.

"Daryl doesn't hate anyone," Suzy said. She lifted his hand and put her lips to it. The kiss was unaffected. Some inevitable law seemed to be on its side. Daryl did not pull away as he had with the others, but studiously watched the television.

He said, "I wish I'd died that day you pushed me down the stairs."

Kevin said, quietly, "I didn't realize how real everything was then."

"It is?" Melissa said, as if she'd been hypnotized into it.

■   ■   ■

Other mothers did not have boyfriends who creaked down the stairs just before dawn to avoid detection. Other fathers did not have girlfriends who dressed and acted like they were from a parallel universe. Other houses stayed on top of the ground where they belonged.

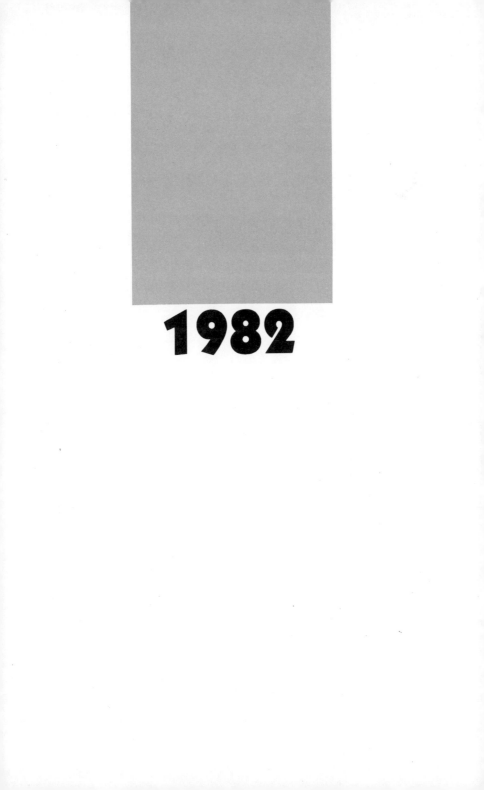

1982

Joan and Daryl waited in Dr. Hartley's office instead of the waiting room. Joan had insisted. When strangers stared, Daryl was liable as not to shout "Boo" or touch them and whisper "Now you've got it." A month ago an older woman had asked how it happened and he'd said, "I screwed some ivy. Chlorophyll will fuck you up."

They tested Joan once a month, Daryl once a week. They had decided the two must have been exposed to some chemical, but they couldn't figure out what since the rest of the family remained unaffected. Joan and Daryl had answered endless rounds of questions, together, separately, orally. Today's little exam was written. They had been drilled by Dr. Hartley, quizzed by committee. Specialists had come into their house. They had spit until they were dry and shit until they were empty. The fiber of their clothes had been scrutinized, their water and their detergent analyzed.

Mr. Belmont's men had dismantled the ivy-thickened superstructure and carried it off. Brenda had been relieved that the embarrassing atrocity was gone, though it was now her job to sweep the soil that collected just inside the front door. To keep the dirt out, Joan had considered installing a six-inch-high board across the threshold, but she worried that then her life would be littered with sprained ankles and broken wrists. A foot of earth was mashed against the sliding Plexiglas doors that had formerly led to the patio, which was now just a memory. Kevin liked to draw the revealed slab of earth, threaded with grass roots and earthworms. He also liked to draw Daryl while Daryl watched TV, which was what he did when he wasn't being tested or working in the yard. Daryl wasn't going back to school in the fall. He was going to get his G.E.D.

Sometimes Joan blamed herself. Sometimes she blamed God. Lately, she blamed the bugs, which had returned with a vengeance this summer. She sprayed every day and raked up their stunned bodies. There was a four-foot, fire-scarred, ashy blot at the very edge of the backyard where she incinerated the sons of bitches. She watched with bloodless joy as they blackened and crisped and curled into their deaths. She liked the sizzle. She cursed them. There were always more the next day. Daryl cut the grass daily, clipped the hedges, weeded the fantastic flowers—roses the size and color of bludgeoned infant heads. The tomatoes were more like cantaloupes: thick skinned, pregnant with seeds, bloated. The vines would have snapped under them had they not been the width and strength of jump ropes. She sent photographs of her whacked-out garden prizes to gardening magazines, using toasters and basketballs for scale, but no one cared. A man in Butte had grown a watermelon the size of a pig. A woman in La Jolla had raised tulips you could stick your whole face in, dusting it a resinous yellow. When Joan explained that she hadn't purposely cultivated them, the editors were even less impressed. She should see some of the stuff coming out of Hawaii.

But this wasn't Hawaii.

More's the pity, they said.

Joan listened to Daryl's pen scratching over the paper. She thought his skin was beautiful. She chewed on her pen cap. She could still smell the rubbing alcohol where they'd pricked her finger. If it hadn't been for Daryl, she would have stopped all this testing, but there might be a filament of optimism still burning, however feebly, inside him. The coals of her hope weren't even warm. It was all dry, gray, ashy.

■　　■　　■

Blue Heaven was empty for a Wednesday. Clarissa was in the ladies room powdering and Joan was humming a song she couldn't remember the name of. Benny was cleaning the mirror over the bar, spraying it with Windex and wiping it with a paper towel, though Joan and Clarissa, together and separately, had told him that vinegar and newspaper worked better. It was an old mirror, spotted and warped and slightly gray. In it, scenes looked more like memories of themselves than reflections of their presence in the world: men playing pool for a quarter a ball, a woman punching her favorite song into the jukebox for the fifteenth time, a couple smooching in the back booth. Joan pushed the pretzels she ate unconsciously away from her. She needed a new glove. This one was dingy. A man in the mirror watched Joan. He didn't look the Blue Heaven type. He wore a baby blue sweater and he wasn't drinking a long-necked Bud but some frothy thing with fruit in it. His face was pudgy, innocent, and he was young, not even thirty. Joan looked away as he approached and saw that Clarissa and Ed were the ones smooching in the booth. Clarissa liked to sleep with him every now and again. It was a casual thing.

"Hi," the guy said, perching on the edge of the barstool, his knee already touching hers. She repositioned her leg and he moved it back with his hand. "That feels nice," he said.

"I try to avoid touching legs with strangers."

"I'm Ray," he said, holding out his hand. He had nice nails with large half-moons. She shook it with her ungloved hand. "Now we're not strangers anymore."

"I know plenty of first names, but I wouldn't exactly call them friends."

"I like disco and pretty women in nice-smelling perfume. I like pizza and cuddling and my mother's name is Mary. Can I buy you a beer?"

"Sure," she said, "why not?"

He bought her four and convinced her to do a shot of tequila with him. Clarissa and Ed left. Ray offered Joan a lift home since Clarissa had driven. He was eager like a boy. He smoked awkwardly, like a boy. He didn't seem quite adult in anything. When they danced to a slow song he playfully bit her neck and ear. When he told her he was in town on business she laughed and asked him if it was a lemonade stand. He laughed too, though she was sure he didn't understand. She wasn't surprised to hear he hadn't been married—he wasn't coarse enough to have been through a divorce. He lived with his mother.

In the car she sensed something was wrong. He smiled mechanically at her.

"Can we turn on the radio?" she asked. She wanted to hear his voice to reassure herself.

"No," he said, "I don't like music."

"What about disco?"

"I lied."

The car smelled brand new. It was a Pinto.

"Is this a rental?" she asked.

"Yep."

"You know what? I left my wallet back at the Blue Heaven."

"No you didn't. I saw it in your purse before we left."

"Did you?"

He slapped her. "Don't ever lie to me."

He parked behind an abandoned gas station about a mile from Blue Heaven. He rested his forehead on the steering wheel.

"Don't hurt me," she said.

"Shut up. You're confusing me."

The new smell all around her seemed to make it worse, more tragic. She put her hand on the doorknob, cold even through her glove. She looked for something to kill him with. There was a nail file in her purse but she would never get to it in time. He leaned back, arching his neck over the headrest. The dashboard glowed green and the headlights lit rocks and trash and fallen branches on the pavement. The men's room door had been thrown against the hurricane fence blocking the woods; she could see the sink and the paper towel dispenser through the hole where the door had been. There was a frightening clarity to the edges of things, as if it had all been lovingly razored into existence. His Adam's apple rolled in his throat. She was stone sober. A tear rolled down his temple and vanished into his hair. She bashed his Adam's apple with her fist. He made an inhuman choking noise.

She ran, thinking the word, *Run*. It was all she could think. She could not have feelings. She would not have feelings. Horror would collapse her. Her legs moved numbly, dumbly forward. Cars passed. Her heart was a balloon. When she saw Benny's car still parked at Blue Heaven she cried, great gulps of sobs erupting with the force of something born.

They never found him.

■ ■ ■

Daryl heard the Mustang growling before he saw it. The bugs slowly and methodically ate the grass he'd mown. Joan would be by later to murder them.

Mike got out of the car and walked up to the porch playing his imaginary drum set. He perched on the arm of Daryl's lawn chair and tapped Daryl's knee to finish out the solo.

"Hey, dude," he said.

"Hey," Daryl said.

"Haven't seen you much lately."

"Yeah, well, I don't know about you, but being green keeps me pretty busy."

"Hey, well, listen, man, like I got this job at my father's shop and, you know, I got this old lady, and I got to keep her satisfied. Not much time for the boys."

"You got a girlfriend?"

"Yeah, man, Nina, twenty, cosmetology school, a woman, not some fucking high school chick. And she fucking looks, man, a babe, kind of classy too, likes to go to restaurants, sensitive movies, makes me toe the line."

Mike stood up and stretched and scratched his underarm. He was at ease in the world, always had been. Daryl had hoped that one day he could be, but now that would never happen.

"I want to get laid," Daryl said.

"Hmmm . . ." Mike said.

"I mean it, man."

"Well, speaking as a former man of the world, it seems to me you got a few options here. You got your hookers."

"If I got to pay for it, I don't want it."

"Cool. How's about this? There's this school for the blind . . ."

"Forget it, man. She's got to fucking know I'm green."

"If you don't mind my saying so, you're getting a little picky. What's a fucking blind chick going to know from green? It would be like trying to describe pussy to somebody who's never had it. It can't be done."

"I want to get laid."

"No, man, you want to be loved. Two entirely different things. If you really want to get fucked, I'll call Glenda. She's fat, she's twenty-five, but she fucks. She ran a train with four dudes from the basketball team last week."

Mr. Moran was watering his yard next door. He'd asked Daryl the day before what kind of fertilizer they used and

Daryl had said, "Monkey shit. We get it from the zoo." Old Man Moran had nodded seriously. Mike still wore the same cologne. At least Glenda would have to look. This is what his life would be like: settling for less and less until there was nothing left to settle for.

"Call the bitch," Daryl said.

"That's the spirit," Mike said. "I knew my man wouldn't roll over and play dead."

"Fucking-A. Call her."

■   ■   ■

The key always caught in this particular lock. Room twenty-nine. The brass 2 was missing and had left the ghost of itself in brown, dried glue on the door. Kyle's cleaning cart was behind him. He was low on Fantastik. As he jiggled the knob he cussed to himself, and when his half-empty pack of cheese–peanut butter crackers fell from his shirt pocket, he cussed out loud. He hoped a hooker or a drag queen had used the room last. They were relatively neat. You might find a fingernail in the sheets, the TV on. Simple stuff. The passion of adulterers was always messy, ostentatious: mattresses askew, damp spots on the carpet, you were liable to find anything in the bathroom. They were also more likely to hide the Bible in the nightstand drawer. They never left the TV on, though. As an ex-married man, Kyle understood. Television wasn't ferocious enough. It was leftovers, mortgages, and heart gone stale.

Finally. It always gave just when you thought you'd have to call a locksmith. He pushed the door open. You had to push hard. It resisted the shag carpet. He pulled the cart over the threshold. Bottles and spray cans and plastic handles clinked like a drunken toast at a small wedding. The damn bed was still buzzing. Was this the one that stuck? Or was it Seventeen? Maybe he'd lie down for a sec after he changed the sheets. The vibrations didn't exactly relax him, but he liked feeling the tremor in the base of his spine. His back bothered him sometimes.

He felt for the light switch. All the rooms of the Cantina were trapped in a perpetual dusk. Even at noon, little patches of gloom clung to the corners like vampire bats. At least he'd gotten used to the sex musk. People never smelled more like animals than right after they'd fucked. He went through a can of deodorizer a day: Country Pine, Lemon Zest, Lilies of the Field. Nothing masked it.

A guy was still asleep on the bed, like something out of "The Three Bears." He was on his back and the covers were rumpled around him. He looked about Kyle's age, maybe a little older. Gray misted his sideburns. He was vibrating and his mouth was open. Sleep humiliated you. Only people who loved you should see you do it.

"Hey, buddy," Kyle said, "your hour's up."

He hoped the guy wasn't drunk. That would really hold Kyle up.

"Hey, buddy," he yelled, "get up. It's closing time."

Nothing.

"Come on, pal. I got a job to do."

He didn't like this. It didn't look good. Something was definitely wrong. He went over and touched the guy's naked, hairy, freckled shoulder. Kyle wanted to be sure before he thought anything drastic. The guy's skin was cool as a wall in a cellar. His lips were the color of grape Kool-Aid, and now that Kyle looked closer, the poor sucker's right eye was still open. The guy was gone. The bed vibrated through the stranger's body and into Kyle's hand. Kyle jerked his hand away and shook it, as if he'd been burned.

Kyle had seen dead bodies before, but only in coffins. This was different. There was nothing between him and it. He felt like a mirror had been shoved in his face. The guy was naked. His pants hung over the ratty armchair and change had spilled from the pockets, dimes, nickels, quarters, pennies: for toll, for coffee, for tips.

Kyle needed this to mean, but it resisted meaning. It just was. It was like strolling through a place you knew intimately—your own backyard—and suddenly falling down the hole you'd always known was there. Something shifted, something slipped, something subtle. He knew what belief was, now that it was gone.

■ ■ ■

Melissa didn't know half the people crowding the small living room. Neil, though he couldn't be there, had cleaned the apartment. It looked nice. She rarely saw him, though they had a check-in dinner once a week. He was forever in New York or Washington. There was always someone: the French Canadian journalist, the married, retired surgeon, the auto mechanic who'd tried to slug the infidelity out of him. When there was no steady there were blocks and baths and bathrooms and back rooms and bookstores and bushes. There were beautiful Puerto Ricans wanting blow jobs in their cars. There were interior decorators disguised as drill sergeants. There were orgies in swimming pools. There were weekends of a dozen men and more. Melissa devoured the details. She couldn't decide if he was life-hungry, liberated, or if he was acting out a terrible drama of self-hatred on various darkened stages; if the endless lines of stiff, slick pricks and gallons of semen were meant to satisfy or to mortify. He called her a prude and spouted Foucault, Lacan. She couldn't argue with the hard wisdom of Frenchmen.

Neil was brilliant, sailed into the honors program while she was left paddling around on the raft of her limitations. His paper on the homoerotic imagery of horses in Gide was to be published, unheard of for a sophomore.

She resented him, but it was a minor envy, occasionally irritating, salved by his assurance of her brilliance, which she knew wasn't there: she lacked the suppleness of an original thinker.

He had cleaned the apartment. He had snuck by Joan's for an armful of the wondrous roses heaped in a new vase on the TV (he watched, she didn't). He'd bought a gallon of white, a gallon of red, a flotilla of clear plastic wine cups, a mountain of tortilla chips. He'd prepared a vat of guacamole. It wouldn't have been done otherwise. The Piercing Pagoda, where she'd returned again this summer, sucked her dry of time.

She hated the job. To ward off mall-ness she spiked her hair and wore a pink triangle, which she claimed to like for its color and shape when a customer asked what it meant. The hairdressers from Thalheimers didn't have to ask and winked when they strolled by on break. The one with the perfect moustache gave her his card and said, "I'll give you spikes, Mary. To Jesus." The triangle's code protected her from stretch pants, large pretzels, her family, high school hard-ons, three kids and a divorce racked up before age twenty-five: the shudder producers. She could have spent her life cataloging them.

"All right," she said to the gathering, "if everyone could please be seated."

Neil had arranged the chairs. He thought of everything. An exceptionally cute woman couldn't get a dipped chip into her laughing mouth and guacamole splatted on the floor.

"Sorry, sorry," she said to no one in particular and wiped it up with a cocktail napkin. She didn't sit, but leaned against the card table.

"Thank you," Melissa said when they were settled. "You all know why we're here. Next month there's a Gay Pride Day in most cities across the country, and I think it's high time we had our own. I think if we all really worked together we could rally five, maybe ten, thousand people. It's time we shook this city up, let them know we're here."

"I think there should be a separate day for lesbians," said the older woman, a transplanted New Yorker who ran the feminist bookstore/natural food co-op.

They were off, interrupting, raising blood pressure. Cigarettes piled up in the ashtrays like fallen soldiers. The New York feminist opened a window and stood by it because of the smoke, an excuse for her to shout louder, though the breeze was a relief. A psychologist and a Special Advisor on Human Rights to the Mayor ran out for more wine. Neil's guacamole, which had probably decimated several avocado groves in California, disappeared. The New York feminist and the man who owned the other progressive bookstore in town (Melissa recognized her handiwork in his ear and it turned out she'd done him while she was still in high school) embraced at one point after two and a half years of cold-shouldered silence.

Five hours and uncountable scars later, Melissa said, hoarsely, a fist of fear clenching her heart, "Anything else?"

"Yeah," said the cute woman, Veronica, who had not moved from the card table. She ran the Rape Crisis Center. Discussion had warmed the room, if not their hearts, and she had stripped down to a tank top. She had muscular arms and sumptuous breasts. Even her sweat was pretty and she had sleepy eyes that gave Melissa stomach twitters.

Activists groaned.

"O.K." Melissa sighed. She felt like they'd been playing baseball with her brain using real bats; everyone stepping up to the plate a slugger.

"Will you be my date?" Veronica asked.

The heat rose up in Melissa's face. Let Neil tell her two sailors had fistfucked him under a pier, and she'd calmly bite from her cookie as she pressed for clarification: Did they wear gloves? Who'd thought to bring the Crisco? (Neil, of course.) Didn't he worry about sand? But let an attractive woman ask her out and she blushed. She couldn't ever remember blushing, which embarrassed her further. She felt she was blazing like the hot center of the sun.

"Go for it, girl," the New York feminist said, uncharacteristically, Melissa thought.

Joan was sure painting had something to do with Kevin needing psychology. She didn't like psychology or evasive Mr. Carstairs, and if it hadn't been for the painfully vivid memory of Daryl balled up at the foot of the stairs cradling his swollen, colored ankle and moaning, she would have halted the sessions. But there was the memory, and though Kevin seemed fine, she knew from interviews on the six o'clock news with the former neighbors of psychopaths, that it was always the nice ones who worked in pet stores and had beautiful rose bushes who hacked children up and stored them in doggie bags in the freezer. Joan knew surfaces were tricks, but she was perfectly willing to be tricked so long as it didn't involve her family. Kevin was her baby. She could have picked him from a coliseum of children by the sweet, straw smell of his hair. Her love for her children was the one thing she hadn't had to learn and she did not want them turning out wrong or bad. Whatever that was. Increasingly, she didn't know.

She tapped on Kevin's door, a formality she tried to stick to even in a rage. Hilly had been forever barging into Joan's childhood rooms.

"What, Mom?" Kevin asked.

"Can I come in?" she said.

"Sure."

The odor of turpentine and paint swarmed around her. His furniture was crammed up against one wall and plastic drop cloths had transformed the floor into an arctic wasteland. The green splats might have been oases, the red and yellow and orange streaks a sunset reflecting on the ice, the serious brown smudges faint-hearted attempts by the earth's soil to reassert itself against the glittering snow. It crackled when you walked across it. Kevin was lying on his belly munching an Oreo and painting. He never seemed up to much, almost seemed bored. Then you saw the paintings.

"How's it going?" she asked.

"Fine," he said.

"That's Daryl, huh?"

"Sort of."

"You mean sort of because it's a painting?"

"Mmmm . . . I mean it's sort of Daryl and sort of me and sort of our house sinking and sort of the sky."

"Do you think if we lived in a regular house you wouldn't need to do it so much?"

"This is a regular house."

"We're sinking."

"I like the sinking."

"Wouldn't you like an apartment better? With a swimming pool?"

"No."

"We could get one with a patio to cook out on."

He swirled the brush into a wad of gold on the old Seen-Say he used as a palette. "Don't worry, Mommy," he said. "Think about the sky or something." He flecked Daryl's eye gold, tilted his head quizzically, squinted, then flecked again.

Joan thought about the sky. It was vast and blue and pitiless.

Now she was really depressed.

■   ■   ■

Joan wanted to fix dinner for Melissa's birthday.

"Only if I can bring a friend," Melissa said.

"Of course you can bring a friend," Joan said.

"Her name is Veronica." They'd been seeing one another for a month.

"Like in the Archies," Joan said.

179

"Yeah. She's a woman."

"I figured," Joan said, puzzled.

Nothing short of Melissa clearing the table with her arm, hoisting Veronica upon it, and shredding Veronica's panties with her pussy-crazed mouth would alert her family to her lesbianism. When they asked about boyfriends, she replied in no's ringing with the death of boyfriends. She could have snuffed their willed stupidity in one blunt pronouncement, but the fact that was a declaration, "I am a lesbian," wandered inside her like a ghost of itself. One late afternoon— she always envisioned it during the faded light before dusk—as Joan rattled on about life as she lived it and Brenda hot-combed her hair, the words would flutter from her mouth as unexpectedly as butterflies or bats and make her real to her family.

Daryl was watching "Lost in Space" when they arrived. It had gone into syndication.

"He's not that green," Veronica whispered.

"Try telling him that," Melissa suggested.

Brenda picked at her food as if it were a conspiracy she were mulling over. A portrait of Daryl, Melissa's birthday present, was leaned against the wall. Kevin was amazing. The painting looked more like Daryl than Daryl did. It almost replaced him. Its background was a frighteningly realistic block of earth riddled with roots and worms that rose imperceptibly into a jarringly beautiful haze of pastels. A crumbled sucker, still in its dried wrapper, was tacked to his cheek. Its sadness ached in Melissa's chest.

Joan was decked. Her hair was immaculate, her makeup applied with the care of a plastic surgeon. Her dress was too much. A hideous silver sunburst medallion, the width of a good-sized coffee cup, swung gently when she bent towards her fork. She was undamageably beautiful. Exactness couldn't scar it, polyester couldn't disfigure it, age had enhanced it. It was as if she'd been spun from a mysterious silk whose hues were enhanced by time.

Melissa slid another spatula of lasagna onto her plate. She was starving. Veronica kept toe-pinching her thighs.

"How's the G.E.D. coming?" Melissa asked Daryl.

"O.K.," he said.

"Are you planning to go to college?" Veronica asked, stroking Melissa's knee with her foot.

"No," he said.

"Daryl was a basketball star," Brenda said.

"Oh really?" Veronica said.

"And still could be," Joan added.

"This conversation is queero," Kevin said.

"Adults are boring, aren't they?" Veronica said.

"Kevin thinks he's better than everybody," Brenda said.

"He is," Daryl said.

"All my children are special," Joan said.

"How am I special?" Melissa asked.

"You like girls," Kevin said.

Melissa dropped thirty psychic floors.

"Kevin," Brenda corrected, "it's her roommate who's the fag, not her. You're awfully stupid for somebody who's supposed to be so smart." She turned to Veronica. "Do you know about Melissa's roommate?"

"Yes, I do," she said.

"Leave room for birthday cake," Joan sang out.

Melissa tried to say, "Kevin's right," but instead said, "Gertrude Stein," confusing even Veronica.

Joan began collecting plates though no one was through.

■　　■　　■

Brenda clipped Louis's tie on. She dabbed a faint bit of Polo on his collar. He could be so cute when he wanted to be. She held her hand under his mouth.

"Gum, please," she said.

He stuck out his tongue and crossed his eyes. Not much was left of the Juicy Fruit but the tracks of his teeth. Still, it was wet. Like his tongue. In her mouth. Ugh. Brenda ignored sex the way she'd learned to ignore the rudeness of people who could further her and Louis's bid for class president: you took what you needed from them and pretended the rest of them didn't exist. Other people knew Wayne and Cindy and Alice. Brenda knew Great Poster Maker, Writes Editorials for the School Newspaper, Good for Errands, like an Indian. She had trouble with names. She was working on it.

She patted his coat pocket for the index cards she'd neatly stenciled with broad generalizations that didn't mean much of anything. She'd learned this tactic from watching Ronald Reagan on TV and had modified it for her own use: Something About the Family, Something About School Spirit, Something About Lowering the Price of School Lunches. The simplicity and ease with which people were manipulated was marvelous.

"Smile," she said. Louis's smile brimmed with the optimistic idiocy that worked so well for Reagan. There were no consequences in it. It was America and it was beautiful.

"It's easy to smile when I'm with you," he said. As a fellow flatterer, Brenda took it for what it was worth: he wanted a blow job after the debate.

"Now," she said, tweaking his pert little nose, "remember. Keep calling her by her full name so people won't forget she's Jewish. They won't know why, but it'll make them suspicious."

"Weinstock."

"Right. And right at the end say something about her pro-abortion stand like she's had one. Like, 'Well, of course you're for abortion.' Like that."

"How am I going to bring that up?"

"Just do it. People love hearing about abortion. It gets them all excited. And if she denies it, say something about how you hate rumors too."

"What rumors?"

"My rumors."

"Nobody's going to buy that. She can't even get a date."

"That makes it even worse. People will meet us halfway. They'll believe the worst if we give them a chance."

"I don't know, Bren."

"Trust me."

■　　■　　■

They held the Gay Pride rally in a small local park. About a thousand people showed up, though the local news put the figure more at four hundred. A handful of badly dressed fundamentalists carrying the same tired "God Didn't Create Adam and Steve" signs walked up and down the same strip of sidewalk, like felons taking exercise. One young Christian girl, who Veronica wanted to corrupt behind the drooping branches of a maple, could not stop weeping. The girl's sincerity disturbed Melissa. Heaven and Hell were real places to these people; you got to them through the vehicle of your own death. Though they lived in the same land of microwaves and mobile homes and machine guns that she did, they also existed in a landscape of prophecy and miracle where the devil was as real and substantial as the sap-flooded leaves whispering over Melissa's head.

Every size, shape, and color of gay person was there: a thin black lesbian in a beret with a three-year-old on her back; three fat, pink, sunburned men all dressed as Divine; the women's soccer team, last year's regional champions, in identical pink T-shirts; men who could have been any-thing—deli clerks, diving instructors, dog catchers; and about a dozen or so men and women sweating it out in their leathers. Melissa wore sunglasses and half-hoped, half-feared that she'd make the news. Neil was in shorts and sneakers and no shirt. He kissed his new boyfriend, a theater major named Al, each time a news camera glided by.

The speeches were dull, exhortatory, and the speakers

were awkward, stiff, but to be standing out in the open, not cornered in some bar, and to say yes to the self, to be uninvisible, to hoot and holler and harangue against the devouring "No" crowded all around them, moved Melissa and she allowed the smallest spot of hope to sneak past the terror and guilt, past doubt and suspicion, past all the sentries guarding her despair. There were moments when it seemed their common joy and rage, which were strangely indistinguishable from one another, would propel them twenty, forty, sixty feet into the air. She looked around her with a tender amazement that would not be stunted when her gaze bumped across the blue and black and silver of helmeted policemen whose mouths were configurations of amusement disfigured by contempt, the kind of mangled smiles one kept in reserve for the pathetic and absurd.

She fell in love with Veronica.

■　　■　　■

Mr. Carstairs looked to Sandy like something that had been cultured in a petri dish by a Freudian cult. He seemed more vegetable than animal. Kevin had been right: the office was malignantly odorless. The suckers were on the desk, not arbitrary, formal devices, but intensely personal expressions of his private torture sessions with the good doctor. Sandy dressed threateningly: black leather, sunglasses, hair sprayed and spiked into a severe block, thickly painted, bloody red lips hinting at recent carnage and subsequent feasting. She looked like a witch gone corporate.

"Can I help you?" a surprised Mr. Carstairs asked.

"As a matter of fact you can," she said, opening her briefcase with a snap that echoed of the guillotine.

"My dear . . ." he began, but Sandy lowered her sunglasses with two fingernails filed into claws and flattened him with the full force of her boredom and power.

"Mr. Demerest won't be in today," she said, crisply.

"And who are you?"

"The friend of genius and the enemy of psychology," she said, pushing a button on the tape player sitting serenely inside the red velvet lining of the briefcase.

Mr. Carstairs's disembodied voice said, "Kevin, have you ever heard the pitiful cries of the mad?"

Kevin's taped voice said, "No."

"At any rate, I don't think you'd enjoy them as your daily companion, or their distorted faces, or the smell of their fear—and your own, or the institutional food, or the strait-jacket I'd have them cart you away in. I want that seascape, young man. Now."

"You can make me draw it, but you can't make it not stupid."

"Your childish aesthetic is of no interest to me."

"And I still want—"

Sandy clicked it off. "Kevin won't be returning," she said.

"Naturally, I understand how you, not being a profes-sional, might misinterpret Kevin's and my exchange . . ."

Sandy slammed the briefcase shut. "Can it, clown."

"But, of course, if Kevin wishes to terminate, I'm cer-tainly open to that."

"Good."

"Though I wouldn't stand anywhere that I could conceiv-ably be pushed from if I were you."

"Kevin has never forgiven himself for that."

"An equally destructive impulse to my mind."

"You're a nut."

"We're all nuts, my dear; but I am a nut with an impres-sive collection of drawings by a miniature Jasper Johns."

■   ■   ■

At first, Daryl had considered them pity calls, probably encouraged by his father. He had been cool towards Suzy and had expressed his impatience by sighing and answering

Brenda liked the sameness of the guests of the Sadie Hawkins dance: bare feet, flannel shirts, rolled-up jeans. She'd freckled her face with magic marker and tightly pig-tailed her hair. She'd volunteered to work refreshments again. Louis, adorable in his straw hat, danced with every other unattached girl in the gym, even the fat ones. She hadn't planned to jerk him off until next year, but she might have to revise her strategy. Louis was popular. He genuinely liked people, even the fat ones.

Brenda liked the idea of people—you couldn't stage football games without them—but the idea in practice didn't work. Take the fat girl dancing with Louis. Penny. Those same hips bounced just as bigly when she waddled to the blackboard to show off her Algebra I savvy. She thought she was so smart, but not smart enough, apparently, to hop the next diet to thinness, normality, a boyfriend.

Louis lacked ambition. He could have been class president but he was more interested in tug-of-warring over the breast issue. All right, he could feel them through her blouse but that was it. All right, he could feel under the bra that would remain snapped shut. All right, he could see them, but no mouth-to-nipple contact and that was final.

Louis made out and she schemed. Her best ideas came with his tongue wiggling around hers, like the kissing booth at Winter Carnival. She understood how girls fell. Boys, with nothing to occupy their horny minds, had persistence on their side. Girls, distracted by organization and upkeep, couldn't muster a comparable resistance. Left to males, there would be no dances, no clubs, no officers of clubs. There would be one gigantic, darkened parking lot stacked with jacked-up cars and coolers of beer where they fucked out what brains they had. There would be an equally enormous locker room nearby to brag in. Look at her father, shacked up with a girl who couldn't have been popular in high school. Men had to be stopped.

in monosyllables, conversational blocks that she leapt over with such deftness that he found himself talking when he didn't mean to. She called at no particular time on no particular day. Whenever the phone rang he experienced an involuntary pang of anticipation that was followed by delight when it proved to be her, or a small, grinding disappointment when it wasn't. This week he had waited until he couldn't wait. He called her. His father answered. Daryl hung up. She phoned back ten minutes later.

"It was you, wasn't it?" she said.

"Yeah," he said. "I guess."

"See how well I know you?"

"So?"

"You're still too young to know you hardly ever know anybody. Not really."

"I'm almost eighteen."

"I'm almost thirty."

"My dad's over forty."

"So?"

"So nothing. I just said it."

"Tonight's Kyle's gig at Roustabouts."

"I told you before, I don't want to go. It's embarrassing."

"I know that, and you know that, and I think even Roustabouts knows that, but he doesn't, and it would mean a lot to him if you came."

"Why should I care?"

"What's wrong with being kind?"

"Is that why you call me?"

"No."

"Why then?"

"I like you."

"Oh."

"If you come by I'll give you dinner on the house and sneak you a couple of beers. How about that?"

He didn't answer. Suzy was a waitress at Roustabouts and

she'd gotten Kyle his Wednesday night gig. They didn't pay him, but let him drink his weight in beer.

Suzy said, "See you tonight."

"Don't hold your breath."

He borrowed Joan's car. He hummed nervously along with the radio, not knowing any of the songs. He got there at ten-thirty. Roustabouts was gloomy, as dark as any one of ten thousand bars. He could have been anywhere. Kyle was well into his first set. He sat on a stool, lit by the glow of the jukebox. There was no spotlight. The ceiling didn't seem sturdy enough to accommodate its one flimsy chandelier; only two of twelve orange bulbs worked.

The crowd was small, mixed: a quartet of youngish double-daters in a booth; an old, unshaven fat man at the bar; three middle-aged women adorned in all the plumage they could muster; some road workers, leftovers from happy hour, arguing about tar and paint; an ancient black man asleep in a chair by the cigarette machine who seemed either wise or dead—Daryl couldn't decide. Patrons walked around Kyle to attain the restrooms, and he smiled broadly at each one as they passed. They nodded stiffly back.

Suzy waved frantically and snuffed out her cigarette when she saw Daryl. She walked towards him as if he might escape. He had shaved. His clothes were fresh. He'd slapped on Aqua Velva. He didn't feel as green. She rubbed his arm.

She sat him in the back booth, winking and saying it was the minors' corner. She brought him beer in a coffee cup.

"See," she said, "the world's not such a bad place. It's bad, but not that bad."

Daryl shrugged.

She brought him a meat loaf platter with cabbage and corn, a plastic basket of seed-sprinkled bread, and a red glass of water. He wasn't hungry. He and Joan had ordered pizza for dinner.

Suzy was fast. She swooped silently around the room: replaced pitchers of beer, shook her finger at the road workers whose comments Daryl couldn't overhear, put her ear to the black man's slightly open mouth to feel for his breath. She wasn't beautiful. She wasn't even pretty. Her uniform was too big and bunched around her. She kept pushing her hair behind her ears, not out of annoyance it seemed, but simply for something to do. She was bony and awkward for all of her speed. It was as if she'd never quite taken to walking. She seemed wounded in some secret way and Daryl couldn't take his eyes off her. She sat across from him between her rounds, gulping down a cigarette, picking crumbs from the table as she talked and flicking them into the ashtray. She'd unexpectedly touch his hand, the one that held the fork, as if what she said next might change his life, though it never did, or already had.

Between sets Kyle stopped by with his guitar. He wore Aqua Velva too. He had a job several afternoons a week cleaning rooms in a sex motel. The rest of the time he practiced music. He and Suzy lived in one room of a Victorian house downtown, but the old lady landlord, who kept guinea pigs and always smelled of straw and turds, was threatening to throw them out because of the hours they kept. Kyle didn't care. There were other widows, other rooms. He would miss the porch he drank beer in Slurpee cups from, telling Old Lady Boone it was tea. It was a porch to think from—she wouldn't let him practice there—a place to look at passersby and wonder what their problems were. He had recently come to the conclusion that everyone had problems, a revelation that embarrassed him in its simplicity.

"So," he said to Daryl, "is the old man the next Hank Williams or what?"

"You never can tell," Daryl said, sipping beer from his coffee cup.

"Oh, I know I'm not that all-fire good, but I got the urge, you know. I got to do it."

Suzy made a pit stop. "Beer, honey?"

"Bud."

"More coffee, Daryl?" she asked.

"Sure," he said, handing her his cup.

"She's a good woman" Kyle said.

"Uh-hm," Daryl said.

"Not that your mother isn't."

"Mmmm."

"Except she did cut me that one time."

"Oh well."

"You know, I could have prosecuted but I didn't. I was thinking of you kids."

"Thanks," Daryl said.

He could remember loving this man, back before everything happened. He tried to will the feeling's return by looking hard into Kyle's face and saying to himself, You are my father, but all he felt was a spasm of sadness that he could have mistaken for love. It faded almost before he felt it.

"One Bud, one coffee," Suzy said, seeming to materialize from the haze of smoke drifting through the bar.

"That's mighty funny-looking coffee," Kyle said.

"Did I say coffee?" she said. "I meant tea."

Kyle laughed.

She said, "It's time for the second set."

Kyle slapped Daryl's back and said, "Don't drink too much of that tea." He slung his guitar over his shoulder and ambled back to his perch. The old black man woke and clapped.

"Thank you," Kyle said, waving from his stool.

Suzy headed for the ladies room. Daryl waited thirty seconds, then followed. He hadn't planned to, but when he realized where she was going, he instantly decided to follow. It seemed more like a fact than a choice.

"My son," Kyle said, not missing a chord as Daryl strolled by.

Daryl opened the door to the men's room, looked over his shoulder, then sidled over to the ladies. The door was locked.

"Just a second," Suzy said when the doorknob rattled.

"It's me," he said, hoarsely.

"Huh?"

"Me. Daryl. It's me," he whispered as loud as he could.

"Ain't the men's working?"

"No."

He listened to the flush. He listened to the water gush from the faucet. He was damp and woozy and wondered if he was drunk. She opened the door and said, "I know the men's ain't broke."

She seemed even smaller in the light. Her neck was freckled. He couldn't look further up. She pulled him in by the wrist. She reached up and grabbed his neck, turning his head towards the mirror.

"Look at yourself," she said.

"I'm green," he said.

"No, not that. Look at yourself in that mirror and think about what we're about to do."

"I don't care."

"You will. These things have a way of sneaking up on you. This is wrong and I don't want any bullshit about that."

"So why are you doing it?"

"You need me more than he does and I need to be needed. It's the only thing that fills me up. I can't walk around the other way. It feels dead."

He watched his lips as he formed the words. "I want you and I don't care."

Her hand left his neck and traced the trail of ridges down his back with her knuckles.

"No," she said, "I'm afraid I don't either."

■　　■　　■

Brenda Demerest: beauty editor of the Fargo High newspaper; head junior varsity cheerleader; campaign manager for Louis Taylor's bid for class president, which had been won. He took office in the fall.

Her spoon rattled in the coffee cup. She was concocting a beauty potion from a mixture of bronzer and foundation that she hoped would hide her mother's green finger. This was her third attempt. The first had been too light and the skin had glowed strangely beneath the application. The second had been too dark, making Joan's finger look baked.

Joan studied her face in the mirror. She didn't care if she was pretty. The maniac from Blue Heaven had banished lust. She hadn't noticed she was empty of desire until Clarissa had pointed out the cute new guy in Garden Tools. Joan had looked at him with no more interest than she accorded the hose he was explaining to a customer. Afterwards, she wondered what she was alive for and immediately thought, Work, as if she had been fed the answer from a cue card. She became startingly efficient. She asked for a raise and got it. She scouted for another position in the company. Secretaries bored her. She wanted to run a show, improve it, make it work the way it should. A management spot opened in Power Tools. She asked for it. Mr. Kratz chuckled and told her men only bought power tools from other men. She read a book on power tools and came back the next day, telling Mr. Kratz everything he had ever wanted to know about drills, with facts to spare. They promoted a stock boy, citing his new baby as evidence of his need. Joan wondered why her three children living at home didn't count. She didn't ask. She set her sights higher, on Mr. Kratz himself. He was all bustle and no brains. She wanted his job. She was going to get it.

Brenda said, "O.K., Mother, this is it."

She dipped a fingernail brush into the peach solution. Joan stuck out her finger as if she were pointing to a patch Brenda had forgotten to dust. Brenda carefully applied what she hoped was finger-colored paint to Joan's skin. She leaned close and Joan could hear her breathe. Joan was sometimes struck by the wonder of the lives she had, with a strange mixture of serenity and terror, brought into the world. She watched her daughter's serious face and was glad for the distracting ordinariness of most of life. Who could live with this awe?

The cosmetic smelled practical and Joan found that soothing. Brenda's intently focused action seemed to embody the odd selfishness of love—her daughter was driven by embarrassment over the quirky failure of her mother's skin. Joan acutely felt the thingness of her body as the wet paint frothed slightly and slowly settled into dryness. She was an object that could be painted like furniture or aluminum siding and it was disquieting to be disabused of the superiority she naturally felt towards the mute, dead objects that outnumbered her. She felt no more important than anything else. She kept still. One small rivulet of fresh-colored liquid ran down her arm.

"There," Brenda said.

Joan inspected the new finger. "It looks pretty good."

"Rub it against something."

Joan sanded her finger against the vanity and left no trace of peach dust.

"It works." Brenda clapped.

"Estée Lauder," Joan said, "look out."

■　　■　　■

Joan waited a month before she made her move. She gradually applied the makeup Brenda had created so it would appear that her condition was disappearing on its own. She gently slacked off from pulling Mr. Kratz's part of the load. When they got to their monthly report meeting with the president, Mr. Bowers, her immediate boss would be behind, unprepared. Her victory had to be decisive but fortunately wouldn't require his destruction—an ineffectual helplessness would be sufficient to render him harmless. She watched the "Nightly Business Report" on PBS to arm herself with facts. She read the *Wall Street Journal* to strengthen her arsenal of rhetoric. She armored herself with clothes from *Dress for Success*. She dieted, not only to get into fighting shape, but also for the singular discipline of it. She could not influence her house's impulse towards the center of the planet or the soil's manic bid to reclaim her yard as its own or the bizarre twist her and her son's genes had taken: you lived with nature; you influenced men.

Mr. Bowers was a fat man who moved with a calm, elephantine grace, a diamond ring embedded into his pinky. He clasped his hands on the conference table and tapped his jewelled pinky when he was angry or impatient or bored. Sales were down. Mr. Kratz tried to cover with the same combination of good-old-boy charm and woozy economic generalizations that had worked for the past six months, but half a year was half a year and the pinky revved up almost immediately. That was Joan's cue. She pretended to take a few more notes and waited for an opening.

"I don't give a fuck about the economy," Mr. Bowers said.

"Excuse me, gentlemen," she said, "I know this really isn't my place but, you know, I have so little to do at home that I've been considering this issue a good deal and I think I may have a little suggestion."

Mr. Kratz smiled indulgently.

Mr. Bowers said, "Fine, fine, out with it. No one else around here seems able to come up with anything."

"Well," she said, going in for the kill, "you've always targeted the individual."

"And it's served me quite well," he said.

"Of course it has," she continued. "Our index growth is one of the highest in the city." She emphasized the "our." He nodded. "But, there's a whole market out there we've been neglecting, the contractor. Normally, it might be risky to offer the sort of volume prices we'd need to attract them, but the economy's booming and that means real estate, and that means buildings, and that means lots of nuts and bolts.

If we play our cards right, and I have some figures with projections back home, we could enter the contracting field ourselves and make megabucks." She leaned back and clasped her hands.

"What do you think, Kratz?" Mr. Bowers asked, his pinky stunned into repose.

"Well, sir, of course I'd have to look into it. It sounds a bit risky to me though."

"Mrs. . . ?"

"Demerest."

"Bring your charts and graphs and whatever by my office tomorrow and we'll discuss this matter further."

"Yes sir," she said, looking sturdily into Mr. Kratz's dim, startled eyes.

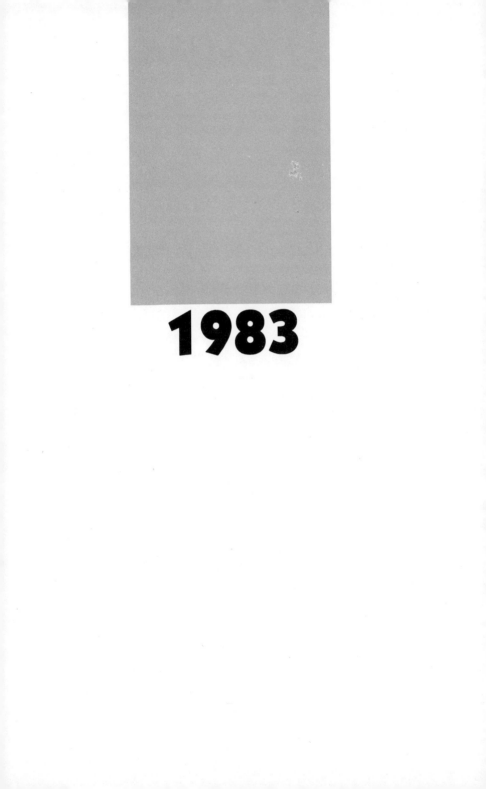

1983

The typewriter chattered alarmingly. Joan wondered if she could steal this woman. Her own secretary was a sweet, incompetent girl addicted to Valium and bikers. But exasperated Joan could not bring herself to fire a female, which she knew was foolish and misguidedly loyal.

Belmont's gal Friday had one flaw, a tarty perfume that smelled overpoweringly of cloves and cheap sex. Joan looked at her wristwatch for the tenth time in as many minutes. Her lunch hour was almost over. She was tired of waiting. She'd been waiting for years. Forever. For everything. She wasn't waiting one second longer. She stood up and walked towards his office.

"Mrs. Demerest," the secretary said to Joan.

"Ms.," Joan said as she opened Belmont's door.

He was working a crossword puzzle, a pen in one hand, an apple that was mostly core in the other. A cigarette burned in the ashtray. The room was glacial with air-conditioning and a symphony elaborately stitched the air, sewn by a small black radio that could not have looked blanker or stiller or muter.

"Well," he said, setting down the pen.

"Has my request for relocation and reimbursement been processed yet?" she asked.

"It's still in committee."

"My house has been sinking for five years and you have done absolutely nothing."

"Don't forget the girders."

"Nothing of substance."

"These things take time."

"Nothing on the first floor opens. It's all jammed with dirt."

"I'm very sorry. I really am."

"Sorry. Sorry. I'm sick of sorry. Sorry won't bring back my patio or my front porch."

"Don't forget, we were the ones who hauled the pieces of it away."

"And I'm very grateful, but that's not enough."

"I don't know what you expect me to do," he said, finishing off the apple and switching it for the lit cigarette.

"You could cut through all this red tape if you wanted to."

"You act like I enjoy all of this."

"I've contacted a lawyer."

"And what did he say?"

"She said I had a case."

"But you don't."

"She thinks I do."

"Oh, Mrs. Demerest," Belmont sighed. "Do what you feel you have to do."

"It's Ms. And I will."

■   ■   ■

The English faculty held its annual picnic in the park. Honors students were invited. All afternoon Melissa stuck by Neil, who was his usual effortlessly dazzling self. She had not slept well the night before, her mind buzzing with what she was going to talk about and to whom. She had been accepted into the honors program this past semester after two and a half years of stuffing herself with literature and spewing out her responses in paper after paper. She had labored. She didn't dare start an essay until she'd read at least three other critical appraisals, and she was never satisfied with her final product. After several drafts her insights still seemed leaden, her prose brittle.

Neil, by contrast, breezed in from weekends in D.C., stayed up all night under the steam of coffee, cigarettes, and some frightening reserve of energy, and tossed off whatever essays were due that week. Melissa wrung her themes from herself, certain, each time, that she had drained the last drop of intellectual energy she possessed. Nauseous with dread, she turned in her criticism, convinced that at last she would be exposed as the intellectual sham she had been desperately concealing. But the comments of her professors glowed, though not as brightly as they did for Neil.

Who had disappeared. Melissa knew he had enjoyed the public restroom nearby in the old days, before men had begun wasting away in New York, San Francisco, and, increasingly, D.C. She hoped he hadn't given in to temptation. He had loved getting fucked.

Melissa found herself trapped with three medievalists. She downed another hot dog out of boredom and sipped her warm beer. She wished she hadn't worn sandals. Her feet were ugly. She wished some alarmingly brilliant insight into "The Miller's Tale" would flash from her lips. She wished her thighs were smaller. She wished she was in Paris or some port bar in New Orleans. She wished perfume didn't make her sneeze. She wished she had been an army brat, or a topless dancer, or a roller derby queen, someone colorful with a chestful of anecdotes. She wished Blythe Danner would make more movies, better ones. She wished her Aunt Lanie hadn't died, not in the garden, not while picking tomatoes. She wished that she could find a hairdresser who

man." The music started. "Evergreen." A severe young
woman in thick glasses was at the organ. They had fertilized
the hedges recently. It stank. Daryl wished he'd brought a
beer with him. It was a hot, windless June night that dried
your throat to the consistency of old paper. The organist
played slowly, depressingly, as if the notes were long strings
of taffy and had to be stretched to the breaking point.
Mike's mother, Evelyn, was wearing a hat and sitting by a
bald man Daryl didn't recognize. Her husband's brain had
flooded with blood one Sunday afternoon last fall while he
was scraping paint from a windowsill. Daryl had thought
then that at least green wasn't dead. Mike had cried, his
head on Daryl's thigh, the new Camaro smelling of leather.
Daryl had rubbed Mike's neck. People forgot things like
that.

The organist eased into the here-comes-the-bride song.
Mike and his brother walked down the aisle. They looked
fucked up. The bride was a looker, a face courtesy of some
angel, and a body that swam your head with lust. Her wedding gown hovered around her. Mike had told Daryl before
the engagement that her come was nectar and that she
should be awarded a congressional medal for cocksucking.
She didn't seem the type that would scratch and wear
crotchless panties, but Mike said she was a banshee in bed.

Daryl had Suzy, who held his neck, bit his shoulder, and
squeezed her eyes tightly shut when she came. She had
bathed him. She had licked his eyelids, his belly button,
behind his knees. She had stopped sleeping with his father.
She kept meaning to leave him but Kyle had either lost
another job or she'd been too exhausted or she and Daryl
had argued. It was always something. He was giving her
until the end of the summer and then he was leaving with
or without her. He hoped.

He picked up his can of shaving cream. He walked over
to Mike's car. It was spotless. Traffic whooshed down the
interstate behind a grove of pines at the parking lot's edge.

The thick summer air was laced with their scent. He was damp under his T-shirt. He loved kissing away the dew of sweat that collected in the hair over Suzy's temples when they made love. He had planned to write FUCK YOU across the hood of Mike's car, but, remembering Suzy, and stabbed with a sudden remorse over what they were doing to his father, he instead sprayed GOOD LUCK DUDE across the windshield and left the can under the front wheel. The explosion would give them a good scare when they backed out.

■　■　■

"Kevin," Sandy said, "it's Henry Caplan. Some people spend their whole lives trying to get into a gallery of that stature." She'd sent him Kevin's slides on an off chance.

Kevin said, "The only important thing is for me to draw Daryl until the fall goes away from inside me."

"You were too young to realize what you were doing. How many times do we have to go through this?"

"It was bad and I did it."

"Fine. If that's what keeps you drawing, fine. But don't you want other people to look at them, to like them?"

"I don't care."

"You have to care."

"You sound like Mr. Carstairs."

She'd been in a group show at Caplan's just out of graduate school: Five New Painters. She'd "made" white six-by-six-foot canvases with one six-inch band of primary color unevenly dividing the picture plane. The three sixes were important to her because her mother had died her senior year of high school and her father had converted to an obscure brand of Christianity that considered any art that wasn't a forthright affirmation of the resurrection blasphemy. Mr. Rhodes regained his faith in matrimony, marrying a lapsed Catholic nun, and lost his faith in God, robbing her paintings of meaning. Some painters could have hung their faith on that one stripe of color, but Sandy wasn't one of them. She went into a decline from which she never expected to recover. At the opening, her life had seemed as spacious with possibility as a desert sky; and two years later she was matriculating for a certificate in elementary education.

"All right," she said, "I care. I want people to see this work even if you don't, and I'm going to call him."

■   ■   ■

Brenda's birthday. She didn't look sweet or sixteen. If anything, she looked preposterously middle-aged, like some loony mutation of the phrase "wife and mother." If Nancy Reagan, Brenda's latest icon, had sprung fully formed from the echoing head of her dunce husband, she might have looked like this. Brenda's hair was unnecessarily permed. Her face was a glaze of makeup. The red-and-white checked Adolpho knock-off that she had made from a pattern was a scarily precise fit. The various cheerleaders and class officers sat around chatting in a labored yet unconscious parody of boredom. Louis was the only one present who seemed to have the blood of adolescence coursing through him. He flirted and joked and Brenda treated him like a chimp who hadn't quite taken to captivity, but would if she had anything to do with it. Melissa and Veronica sat in appalled silence. Brenda was having the party at Melissa's, as a house sunk a good third into the earth did not seem quite Republican enough to her. She had tactfully asked if Neil would absent himself for the evening, and Melissa had replied that she could promise he wouldn't suck any minors off in the bathroom, but that was about it. Incredibly, during the bruised silence that followed, Melissa found herself apologiz-

ing and offering to make a nonalcoholic punch she'd had at
the last Lambda Ladies brouhaha. Brenda had declined the
offer.

As guests arrived she introduced Melissa as "my sister,
the radical," smiling and patting Melissa's shoulder as if Melissa were the last, touching example of a clumsy species
due for extinction. "Phyllis Schafly poisoning," Veronica
whispered.

Melissa snuck into her room, picked up *The Second Sex*,
and read passages at random to reassure herself that the
world was not utterly lost. She could hear the dull murmur
of the near dead gurgling from the terminal ward her living
room had become. A pair of arms enfolded her from behind,
the hands rubbing her belly, and moving up to massage her
breasts. At first, Melissa thought it was Veronica—who else
would dare? Then she smelled Brut after-shave. Then Louis
said, "I like you a lot."

Melissa elbowed him in the side, then swung around and
swatted him across the cheek with Simone de Beauvoir.
"What in the fuck do you think you're doing?" she asked.

"I like you," he said, one hand on his cheek, the other
on his side.

"I like David Bowie but that doesn't mean I'd go up and
grab his cock if I met him."

"I think you like me too."

"I think you're an arrogant little shit who thinks that's a
divining rod between his legs."

"I saw the way you were looking at me."

"You're confusing disbelief with lust."

"I love the way you talk."

"I hope you're drunk."

"A couple of us guys snuck some vodka in."

"Fine. You're a little loaded. So get back to your girlfriend's side, my sister, you boob, before you make a complete ass of yourself."

"You know, I've got a pretty big one."

"Louis, I don't care if you've got a python curled up under your zipper. Cocks—fat ones, small ones, flaccid ones, turgid ones, any ones—don't hold the slightest interest for me. *Comprende, muchacho?*"

"Huh?"

"I'm a dyke, Louis." She wished someone would rush in and pull out her tongue before she went any further. Why was she wasting this moment on some hormone-bloated, vodka-fogged clod?

"Get out of here," he said, grinning like the runner-up in a village idiot contest.

"A lesbian, a muff diver. I drink from The Well of Loneliness."

"You're yanking my chain."

"I like pussy, Louis. How much plainer can I be?"

"Wow," he said.

"You are a fount of eloquence."

■   ■   ■

Kyle wondered when it had happened. He couldn't remember. He knew there had to have been a time when he was a man with a wife, when he had been one of the men he now passed on his way home from work by bus who could be seen watering yards, when he had accepted work the way you accepted the inevitable green of spring grass or the fact that those two people were your parents and no one else or that your toes were shaped just so or any of the other seemingly immutable facts that existed whether you believed in them or not. He thought if he could pinpoint the moment when his belief had begun to falter, if he could isolate the infinitesimal instant, when he was tying his shoe or when his lips were still brushed against Joan's cheek but wouldn't be a split second later or—who knew—maybe during a particularly disastrous Redskins fumble he'd seen on TV, he could reverse this helpless decline. But scrutinize as he did, he could not locate that pivotal, thread-sized crack that separated what he had been from what he was now, a man who only half-listened, who had forgotten what it was like to glide through life with the unflappable security that all was correct and, by implication, that he was correctly placed. When had work come to seem pointless? His part-time job as an ice cream man was an activity he raced through, sometimes skipping lucrative, child-infested blocks or speeding up so they couldn't catch him. Suzy wouldn't sleep with him, wouldn't even kiss him while he jerked off; she wore nightgowns to bed and patted his shoulder good night. One morning, several months ago, she had unexpectedly mounted him, but there was a sad violence to her orgasm and he was almost certain she was thinking of someone else. He wondered if he would have to kill her if she tried to leave him. He hoped not. He still liked Suzy. He hoped that when she left she would do it as quietly and secretly as possible and spare him that decision. He couldn't blame her, but he was afraid of the pain that might rip through him on her departure, fearing he might need to inflict it upon her to rid himself of it. He sometimes now thought fear caused everything.

The tapes he made at home and sent to record companies came back and even their yellow, bulky envelopes had a brutal, unlistened-to quality. He couldn't stop playing, though. He sang as if his life depended on it because it did, and the sheer desperation of it sometimes startled people into acknowledging him on the street corner where he played for an hour at dusk. One evening he'd collected about ten dollars, but that was because one of the bills had been a five, which might have been dropped into his old peach can by accident.

■   ■   ■

Soaps hadn't helped. Not Ivory, not Liquid Joy, not dishwashing or laundry detergent, not the oatmeallike one created especially for allergies, not bars of it, not handfuls of green granules, not the spermy stuff you squirted from a tube. Neither had water: icy, soft, hard, holy, warm, cool, unholy, salted, sparkling, distilled, ammoniated; from taps, from rivers, from hot springs, from the mountains of Switzerland; in the form of rain, snow, whirlpools, rushing streams. All useless. Creams, facials, mudpacks, moisturizers, hot wax: kaput. Antibiotics, antifungals, antihistamines, tranquilizers: a big bust. Hypnosis, stress management: he was still green.

Daryl was not going back to the doctor.

■ ■ ■

Joan had read an article called "Strangers in a Strange Land" about the new estrangement of single working mothers from their daughters. These daughters dropped out, got pregnant, overdosed. Joan's conscience was maxed out. She couldn't take one more molecule of guilt. She couldn't tolerate another failure. The article had recommended lunch out as a contraceptive, shopping as crisis intervention, a trip to the beauty parlor as a key to higher SAT scores. Quality time. A tuna fish sandwich eaten together on a blanket in the backyard could stem the tide of ambulances and abortions waiting to cascade into a mother's life. Brenda seemed fine. In fact, she'd had to pencil Joan tentatively into her appointment book until she could confirm on Friday. Even this made Joan nervous. Overachievement was often mere compensation for neglect. Sometimes, girls who seemed to be doing the best ended up the worst. You couldn't tell.

From the looks of things, a lot of mothers had read the article. The restaurant was crammed with little tables of middle-aged women and adolescent girls in freshly cut hair. Waiters whisked through an obstacle course of shopping bags. Joan wondered if the study had been funded by restaurateurs and hairdressers. Maybe other women did this every weekend. Maybe Joan was the only one who'd been scared into lunch with her daughter.

Conspicuously, there were no little father-and-son duos. Joan hated how easily men got off. Where were the articles publicly denouncing them? They were apparently free to neglect their children as much as they liked.

Brenda seemed pleased with her new perm, though it looked strangely middle-aged and not at all like the other adolescent hair dangling over quiche and salad and Diet Coke. The hairdresser, a bony woman with rings on every finger, had tried to interest Brenda in something a little more contemporary, but Brenda had been adamant. The dress she'd picked out—no-nonsense but deceptively flattering— was something Joan might have bought for lunch with an important client. The day had made Brenda happy. She was even going to order dessert. Unheard of. Joan supposed she was glad she'd read the article, even if Brenda didn't seem in danger of becoming an unwed mother.

"How's school?" Joan asked.

"Busy," Brenda said.

"And Louis?"

"Louis is Louis."

"You don't sound very excited."

"I'm excited by what Louis can be."

"What does he want to be?"

"President."

"That's ambitious."

"Actually, he's not that ambitious."

"President's pretty ambitious."

"I guess I'm ambitious."

"What do you want to be?"

"The president's wife."

"Why not be president yourself?"

"Women can't be president."

"Says who?" Joan asked, sipping her coffee.

"People."

"Which people?"

"Everybody."

"I don't."

"Mother, I hope you're not turning into a big radical like Melissa. It's so retro."

"I have a job women usually don't do."

"I know; and another problem is our house. It's sinking."

"I've noticed."

"Why can't we move?"

"I'm in the middle of a lawsuit."

"I haven't been able to have anyone over, ever. It's totally embarrassing."

"I know, sweetheart. Believe me, I do. But . . ." But what, she thought. Was there an article about this? Could she take someone out to lunch to remedy it? "I promise," she said, "if this isn't settled by the end of the year, we'll move. Scout's honor. I should be able to afford something by then."

"What difference does it make? High school is practically over."

At least if Brenda, neglected and sinking, flung herself from her bedroom window, she wouldn't have far to go. She might sprain an ankle. That was about it. Joan knew from Melissa that she could only wait for her daughter to forgive her. It was almost a relief to pass the project along. Joan couldn't fix the past. Brenda would have to patch it. If she could.

■　　■　　■

It was an unseasonably warm March day and Melissa had the window open. She was sitting on a kitchen chair in nothing but a T-shirt. Her feet were propped up on the windowsill. She was reading Derrida and she had no idea what he was talking about. None. He seemed to be talking about possible energy sources on Mars or the mating rituals of an extinct species from a forgotten age or . . . The rhetoric was technical gobbledygoop.

She was stupid. She could accept that. Stupid people led perfectly plausible lives. They had favorite songs and cried when they were sad and developed head colds and ate out occasionally and fell in love with disastrous consequences just like everyone else. She'd have to break the news to Veronica gently. She'd understand if Veronica left her for a woman who understood Derrida. Naturally, she'd be bitter washing dishes for money and living in a rooming house and never being invited to Sayajit Ray film festivals but she supposed she'd manage. A half-life was better than no life at all.

She listened to Veronica's key catching in the lock; to Veronica, who almost never cursed, growl "Goddamn it"; to the door slamming into the wall; to—was that Veronica's purse being thrown against the wall? Maybe Veronica had already been informed that Melissa was a numbskull. She wasn't taking it well.

"Honey," Melissa said tentatively.

Veronica walked over, knelt, parted Melissa's legs, and crawled between them. She wrapped her arms around Melissa's waist, pressed her face into Melissa's pliant belly, then turned her head to the right. Melissa combed her fingers through Veronica's hair. It was beautiful: black, thick, soft.

"I love you," Veronica said.

"I love you too," Melissa said.

"And I hate men."

"But we love Neil."

"I hate all men except Neil."

"And that cute, old man who sells the carnations."

"And maybe him."

"You love your father."

"He's O.K."

"See? We mustn't be prejudiced."

"I can't take it anymore."

Melissa was always astonished by some part of Veronia. At this instant it was the unearthly white of her scalp. "Can't take what anymore, honey?" she asked.

"My job. I can't listen to women cry anymore. I cannot look at one more bruise, not one more. I do not want to hear 'And then he . . .' ever, ever again as long as I live. I don't want to sit there asking questions in my counsellor voice while they sit there in ripped blouses and broken zippers. I tell myself that I'm helping but I don't believe it anymore. There's too much wrong for it ever to be helped. I'm starting to feel hopeless."

"Quit."

"I can't quit. There aren't enough of us already."

"Some other do-gooder will take your place. You've been a very good girl. You've worked hard. Maybe it's time for a rest."

"But that'll mean they've won, that they've gotten to me. Another victory for the bad guys. No way. I can't quit."

Melissa leaned over, slid her hands down Veronica's back, kissed the nape of Veronica's neck.

"That feels good," Veronica whispered. "Do it again. You always revive me. You always remind me there's something good."

■　　　■　　　■

Brenda's squad placed third in the state finals, which was their ex-head cheerleader's unimaginative fault. There was no way, even with superhuman effort, that Brenda could repair the damage and get them to the nationals. She had been robbed of greatness, she would never be a Deb Apple. Also, more and more, she was sullen over her beauty column. Not about the column itself, which was expert, daring even, but over its effect. When she looked around her high school she still saw girls in earrings that elongated already bovine faces and eyelids drooping from too much mascara.

Her nose was still assaulted by clouds of cheap perfume, though she'd devoted a whole article to several delicate and inexpensive brands, experimenting with over a hundred varieties on her own sensitive skin to weed out the vulgar ones. They still used strawberry lip gloss and wore jeans and one poor dear had taken to trudging around in her boyfriend's leather jacket, shaving her head but for one green forelock, and, God help them all, piercing her nose like some Zulu priestess. It was this sort of willed ugliness that irked Brenda most. The pagan had been a modestly pretty girl who was too quick at Algebra for her own good and had never, evidently, seen Brenda's far-reaching advice in "Manners Are Beauty Too." Poise, diets in which you lost ten pounds in as many days, the sun and beauty, drugs and beauty, inner beauty: an unbeautiful world cast a deaf ear.

Being the wife—for she thought of herself as Louis's wife (she was going to have to let him do it this year so he'd stop sneaking fucks with tramps)—of a figurehead was also not everything the other girls probably thought it was. Brenda, at first, could not figure out how Nancy did it. Then she realized that of course Nancy was the wife of the president of the most powerful nation on earth while she was merely the wife of the former junior class, future senior class president. At her miserable level there were no foreign dignitaries to greet, no California retreats, no photo-ops, no helicopters, no intricate White House intrigues, no White House period. Decorating for Homecoming didn't cut it and Brenda wasn't even sure she'd make queen this year—standards had fallen that low. They had rejected her proposal that all the girls wear red on Nancy's birthday in tribute.

She floated on the sea of her disappointment, mulling over strategies, rejecting alternatives that seemed more of the same, setting her sights ever higher, while she listened to Louis's sexed-up breathing, while she mooned at him with eyes she hoped were glazed with passion, while his tongue wriggled in her ear, while his fingers dug around inside her as if he were searching for a button he'd lost, while his cock was in her mouth—she'd perfected her technique on a banana—while she remembered to moan. This was still her planning time, though occasionally he would distract her with some shock of pleasure. Once an orgasm had shaken her so badly that she determined never to have one again, no matter what he did with his limber tongue, his searching fingers.

She decided it was time to form a Young Republicans Club.

■   ■   ■

Talking Joan into the trip had been easy. She was busy luring contractors to Bowers Hardware and distracted by her lawsuit. After Sandy finished her monologue, swearing for Kevin's safety with her life and painting elaborate verbal pictures of his future success, Joan glanced up from the usual stack of serious-looking documents—all fine print and figures—and said, "Whatever you think is best."

The train ride was uneventful. Kevin asked for Coke after pack of peanuts after slice of pizza. He made her buy a pack of cards and teach him how to play gin rummy. She was a bad player and he started to trounce her almost at once and was bored again. She'd brought an *Artforum* for them to peruse and decide which galleries they'd hop, but Kevin pulled comic books from Daryl's old gym bag and said, after he'd finished the first one, that he might like to draw them one day.

"Why?" she asked.

"Because they are what they are and I bet they make you rich."

"Not as rich as Jasper Johns." She hated to make these low-grade plugs for high-brow art to focus him on his genius.

"Who's that?" he asked.

"Targets, flags."

"Oh yeah. Those are better than the comics in a different sort of way."

They stayed at the loft of a friend, Harriet. This was the part she had dreaded: the gossip about no-talents who had jockeyed their way to the middle, auctioning off pieces of their mediocre souls in low-rent Faustian deals; seeing Harriet's genuinely good paintings of bottles and full cups of water caught in the act of spinning and emptying themselves of their contents; the serious smell of turpentine and oil paint, which contrasted all too vividly with the scent of crayons and clay for Father's Day ashtrays that seemed to define Sandy's life; the inevitable question—why had she stopped?—posed after the bottle of good merlot Harriet always kept around; the fumbling answer, "I don't know . . . I didn't feel I was good enough. . . . Maybe I'll start again someday. . . ." The self-pity Sandy was usually so adroit at sidestepping was creeping up on her like some assailant in a dream you're running from in slow motion.

Their appointment with Henry Caplan was for late Saturday afternoon. They spent the day roaming. Kevin adored the roar of the subway trains. They went to three distinguished galleries in SoHo and Sandy would tell Kevin what she thought, hoping to prod him from his silence, but all he would say was, "Let's go." When she suggested a fourth show he used a phrase she hadn't heard since she'd first met him: "The pretty keeps trying to hide the big stupid but the big stupid keeps peeping through and that makes the pretty part of the big stupid. Why do they do that?"

"I don't know," Sandy said, not quite following what he meant.

"They should have places for people to pee so it doesn't smell like this," he said at the next subway stop.

"I'm tired," he said, leaning his head on her shoulder as they sat on the train.

"I'm hungry," he said as they walked into Caplan's.

"You'll just have to wait," she snapped, suddenly furious

that this wizardly talent was packed into an eleven-year-old who missed his mommy—that, last night—and would consider dashing his talents to bits in comic books.

Henry Caplan's office was all white, severe angles right down to the square crystal jar of clear mints on his desk. It looked like an operating room out of *House Beautiful*. Henry Caplan was all severe angles too, tall and thin and bony and pale, as if the room had thought him up and not the reverse. He had an indefinable European accent that could have been fake and wore a faint amount of cologne that was no less sickening for its discretion. Culture seemed to have refined itself inside him past some horizon point you weren't quite certain should have been passed. You suspected he would discuss famine and Foucault and feminine wiles in the same dulcet decibels that whirred everything into a bland, sophisticated consistency. You wondered how great the distinction was for him between a brilliant painting and a brilliantly prepared meal. He stunned you with charm, the way spiders stunned their meals. When informed that Kevin was Mr. Demerest, he clapped once, loudly, startling in that pristine antechamber to art, and a smile crossed his face that, strangely, reminded Sandy of nothing so much as a cloud suddenly dimming the afternoon sun. She wasn't sure what terms they'd agreed to by the time they'd left, but a one-man show was slated for next year, and she felt, when they were back in the purplish light of a New York dusk, that she'd just come from an interview with Death or one of His sylvan-tongued, sharp-cheeked lawyers to ascertain her suitability for the beyond.

Kevin was still hungry.

■   ■   ■

Kyle and Suzy lived in one large room. A Crock-Pot and a hot plate were the kitchen. The shower was down the hall. Suzy had stopped stirring and now simply stared into the beef stroganoff. Kyle had been tuning his guitar for . . . Daryl didn't know how long. Kyle would fiddle with the knobs, strum, fiddle with the knobs, strum. . . . The guitar made a surprisingly beautiful noise, given how beat up it looked. Daryl couldn't tell if Kyle was drunk or not, though Suzy said he always was. They were all drinking watery beers from flimsy cans a child could have crushed.

Daryl hadn't wanted to come but Kyle had badgered him. The air looked transparent but it was murky with longing and remorse, like a small aquarium choked and opaque with algae. Daryl concentrated on his fingernails, on a cigarette burn in the rug, on the light bulb reflected in the window. He couldn't look at either one of them. Everything seemed poised on some terrible verge.

"I have to go," Daryl said, his voice as cobwebbed as the corners of the room.

"Huh?" Kyle said.

Daryl cleared his throat. "I should be going."

"You just got here."

"I've been here a while."

"Don't you wanna eat?"

"I really got to go."

"Ooohhh . . . I get it."

Fear fluttered through Daryl like a swarm of humming-birds. "Huh?" he said, his voice dried to a wisp.

"Huh? What do you think? It hasn't been that long ago. Saturday night. Handsome devil like you. It runs in the family, you know. What's her name?"

"Who?"

"Your hot date."

"Dad, I don't have any hot dates. Girls aren't interested in a guy like me. I'm fucking green in case you haven't noticed. And if I'm ever lucky enough to get one—and what if she's, like, great—then I have to have her. No matter who she is. Do you understand that?"

"Well . . . sure."

"No, you don't. You don't. You can't."

"Hey, I'm sorry. I shouldn't have brought it up. Sticking my big beak where it don't belong."

"Fuck it. It doesn't matter. I'm moving at the end of the month anyway."

"The end of the month?" Suzy said, remembering what the wooden spoon in her hand was for, and stirring.

"Yeah," Daryl said, "the end of the month. And that's final. No more dicking around. I can't take it anymore. I can't."

"Son, I . . ." Kyle started, but Daryl held up his hand.

"Please, Dad. Don't. Just don't." He picked up his jacket. "I'll try to stop by or something before I go."

"Yeah, do that. If you really got to go. We'll have a going-away beer. Toast your new life. Whatever. Something like that. Promise you will?"

Daryl didn't answer. He was gone.

■　　■　　■

Melissa had never thought of birds as talking to one another, but now, as she listened to their chirps and whistles, she felt she could follow the tenor of conversation, if not its content.

She said, "I don't think I'm getting off."

They had dropped the acid about an hour before. She hadn't tripped since high school. Neil had never done it and it was his curiosity that had propelled them.

"Am I glowing?" he asked.

Now that he mentioned it, he kind of was.

"I can't tell," she said, "but I think so."

"You're kind of glowing too."

She looked at her hand. It wasn't glowing, but it was strange. When you thought about them, hard, really thought, all that they did for you, steer and brush your teeth and rub

217

your girlfriend's clitoris. . . . "Aren't hands astonishing?" she said.

"I guess you could look at them that way," he said, holding his own up to the sun for a better view. "It certainly is weird the way the blood is blue when you see it through your skin."

"Let's not talk about blood." Melissa knew trips developed themes and she didn't want this one's to be blood.

"Do you smell something?" he asked.

She did. She smelled everything and it all smelled wonderful. She was glad they had decided to start their trip by the river.

"Everything works," she said.

Neil leaned over the rock they sat on and his reflection rippled across the water. He spit.

"Why'd you do that?" she asked.

"I'm mixing my water with the world's water although my water is already the world's water because I am of the world and the world is of me."

Melissa thought: I must remember that. Her body drank in the heat and light of the sun and filled her with power. She stood up, stretching her arms, undulating, as if she were a breeze blown, pond frond. Breeze blown. Pond frond. She was a poet. "Do this," she said, still undulating.

"Why?" he asked.

Neil was always questioning. He was always trying to apprehend the world with words when words were paltry little baubles when you stacked them against the reality of the rock beneath her bare feet. She didn't answer. She wouldn't deign to use words. She was free.

"I'd like to suck some ugly old man off," he said.

"Why?" she said before she caught herself. He had tricked her back into the world of words.

"Because it would be a perfectly generous act. I wouldn't even want to have a hard-on while I did it. I wouldn't even want the thrill of degradation. I'd like it to be a perfectly mechanical action on my part, devoid of feeling, even the pleasure of nobility."

Neil was a saint. His sexual history was suddenly illuminated for her. He was trying to apprehend the world by fucking as much of it as he could. Orgasms were the tenets of his philosophy. Sweat and come and groans were its rhetoric. She was the one locked in by words.

"I want to sleep with my grandmother," she said, an act even more generous than Neil's because her grandmother was dead.

Neil laughed. He was right to laugh. It was all too ridiculous. Life was a joke. Death was the punchline. Sex was a series of really great one-liners. God was a comedian. Why hadn't she realized this before? She laughed too. Even the river was hilarious.

Six hours later Melissa sat in their apartment listening to Joni Mitchell to take the edge off coming down. Water had been the trip's theme. It had rained. Neil lay on the couch with his hands behind his head, staring at the ceiling. She didn't want to know what he was thinking. She pushed the pan of Spaghetti-O's to the other side of the table. At the time little circles of pasta in toxic-looking sauce had seemed like the funniest and, at the same time, most appetizing food in the world. Now it seemed the tiniest bit frightening.

Neil said, "I'm not sure that enlightenment should come in a pill form."

Melissa said, "I wish Veronica would get here with the Valium."

■   ■   ■

That last bite on Joan's forearm had done it. She climbed down the ladder from the second-story sliding glass doors onto the lawn. The upstairs deck had been dismantled. Sinkage had rendered it wobbly and perilous. Brenda followed her. Then Kevin. Then Daryl. They had scrubbed themselves with lemons, which still repelled the son of a bitches, and who were, this year, larger than your average mouse.

Joan had the equipment in a truck she'd borrowed from the store: canisters of poison, surgical masks to protect their lungs, bottles to spray with, a chain saw. She took the front yard, Brenda the back so she wouldn't be seen. Kevin was responsible for uprooting the flower beds, a task Joan couldn't bring herself to do; and Daryl was to mow down every tree, each hedge. They were going to burn the limbs and leaves and bark into ash. The destruction had to be total. Joan had secured a county permit because she expected a big, billowing blaze. She had enlisted her children in this apocalyptic strategy to win the Bug War, not because the annihilation of her yard was beyond her, not to a woman fueled by the high octane of vengeance, but because she hoped the fire's gale would be cathartic. They had all been scarred in one way or another by the guerilla tactics of the insects: Kevin on his calf; green Daryl, who they'd mistaken as the safe harbor of an ambulatory tree—that had stung him more than their stingers; Brenda's memory, bitterly preserved in the school's yearbook, of a blazing red bite on her cheek that, skilled a cosmetician as she was, could not be concealed from the photographer and his cool, unforgiving camera. "A family that sprays together, stays together," Joan said. Brenda brought marshmallows.

Joan couldn't kill the bastards. They were hearty and numberless and had the survival instinct embedded in their damnable bug genes. But she had poison and fire and a brain. If they couldn't be murdered out of her life, their food could. By next weekend her yard would be a wasteland, a desert, a dead sheet of soil where no plant would ever grow again. On her little acre photosynthesis would become legend, myth, tale. The greedy little shits would either make reservations at another of nature's restaurants, or they would starve into husks. Like all victories, it was bittersweet. There were her rose bushes, those casualties, that truly understood her. She wished these three would switch subjects, to their sex lives, their favorite fabric. Did their hairdressers understand them? Truly? She wished they would realize that footnotes in Chaucer weren't funny. She wished Professor Levine wouldn't laugh the way Ethel Merman sang. She wished there was such a thing as a personality transplant. She wished brown rice wasn't toxic to a lesbian's sense of humor—there should be warning labels, a red X over the laughing face of a short-haired woman. She wished Holly Near were Joni Mitchell. She wished Holly Near didn't think she was Joni Mitchell. She wished Joni Mitchell would return to being Joni Mitchell. She wished she liked Proust more. She wished she had never named her cat Sappho. She wished she could phone Virginia Woolf for advice. She wished men could be made to wear cheap mascara once in their lives. She wished Veronica hadn't burnt her agile tongue on hot coffee this morning. She wished she hadn't seen Neil emerge from the bathroom, followed by another man wrestling with his zipper.

Neil came over, grinning, the cat and the canary. She slapped him. She called him an idiot. She cried. She hated to cry. She hated him for making her. She hated him. The medievalists seemed to be searching for parallels of the incident in *The Canterbury Tales* and coming up short. She hated them too.

■　　■　　■

Daryl hadn't been invited to the wedding. He made Mike's fiancé uncomfortable. Through the window, he could see about sixty dressed-up people scattered across the pews. The place looked more like a recreation hall than a place of worship. Another car pulled up and he ducked behind the bushes. It was Mike and his best man, who was also his brother. Mike checked his bow tie in the car's side mirror and said, "I don't know if we should have smoked that joint, she had once coaxed tenderly into bloom, cherishing their regal scent, their velvet petals, their thoughtless extravagance. Now they were enemy supplies, but she could not bear to watch when Daryl cut through them with one great, brutal, buzzing slice.

■ ■ ■

"Mom?" Kevin said.

"Hmmm?" she said, hunched over more legal documents. There'd been another postponement.

"Remember Mr. Carstairs?"

"Mm-hm."

"Well, he's sitting across the street in his Mercedes."

"Oh Kevin, I'm not in the mood for another one of your stories. The house lost another inch this week. At this rate we'll be half-sunk by next year."

"At least we'll be able to come in the second-floor windows from the yard."

"I know. Brenda almost fell off the ladder this week."

"If she wouldn't wear those queero heels all the time, maybe she wouldn't be such a super sucko klutz."

"Maybe," Joan said, disinterestedly.

Crickets were whirring when Kevin opened the front door. Mr. Carstairs's window slid down with an ease that implied electricity. The burnt smell still hovered around the yard but the bugs had fled. Joan had won. Kevin hopped on a stump, the remains of an old oak. He liked the pattern Daryl's saw had revealed. It was wriggling its way into his drawings. Mr. Carstairs lit a cigarette and his face was suddenly illuminated, like a vision, by the lighter's flame.

"What do you want?" Kevin asked from his stump. He felt like a statue on this natural pedestal unnaturally cut into existence.

"Nothing," Mr. Carstairs said, the ember near his mouth glowing hot orange. "Just to see how you were."

"Good," he said.

"Good."

"Well, bye."

"Still drawing?"

"None of your beeswax."

"You weren't that talented to begin with."

"Henry Caplan says I am."

"Henry Caplan? The dealer?"

"Yeah." Kevin wondered if Carstairs should know about Caplan. "He saw something or something," he said, trying to cover.

"Caplan's taste is not infallible."

Kevin had to get away before Mr. Carstairs tricked more out of him. "I'm going in now to tell my mom to call the police or something," he said.

"That won't be necessary," Mr. Carstairs said, starting his car. The headlights flashed on, their light seeming to stun whatever they coated into existence. "It was nice chatting with you again."

"No it wasn't."

"Have it your way," Carstairs said, laughing and tossing his cigarette onto the bald yard. It smoldered like a warning. Kevin jumped it from his wooden perch, smashing the small light into the dark crowding it.

■　　■　　■

Daryl and Suzy sat in Zeke Barnum's trailer. P.T. was an ancestral third cousin on his father's side. The couch they were sunk in mimicked the dilapidation of Zeke's traveling carnival. Zeke sat across from them in an intricately carved chair that didn't quite fit as it had been designed to enthrone a Chinese child emperor. Or so he claimed. He sipped Scotch from a plastic Thermos cup and smoked Dutch cigarettes that were as brown as pumpernickel, though not as sweet smelling. He was ordinary-looking in his sweatsuit with his one rope of grayed hair thrown over his bald pate, but his eyes were extraordinary: black and concentrated, burned into his head. He kept crossing and recrossing his legs.

"I'd hoped you'd be greener," he said.

"He looks pretty damn green to me," Suzy said.

"There are," Zeke said, "ways, of course, to enhance the pallor, but the texture seems just about perfect. Do you mind if I touch?"

"I sure do," Daryl said.

"Never mind," he said.

"So do we have a deal or not?" Suzy said.

"Oh, of course, of course."

"And what about Suzy?" Daryl asked.

"Suzy will be the new Madame Zarathustra, poetess of palmistry, priestess of prophecy, predictor of predicaments."

"How do I do that?"

"You swathe yourself in scarves, bathe yourself in rosy light, peer from behind a haze of incense, and tell people what they want to hear."

"It beats waiting tables."

"The last Madame Zarathustra, alas, wouldn't agree with you. I lost her several towns back to some gas station attendant. Poor man, he has no idea what he's getting himself into. She'd started to believe in herself."

"Don't you worry about me," Suzy said, "I got a head on my shoulders."

"When do we leave?" Daryl asked.

"Tonight," Zeke said. "There's been some unfortunate business with your town fathers I won't trouble you with."

"That suits me fine," Daryl said.

"I'm packed," Suzy said.

"Well then," Zeke said, "we're off." He toasted them with his Thermos cup.

They nodded back.

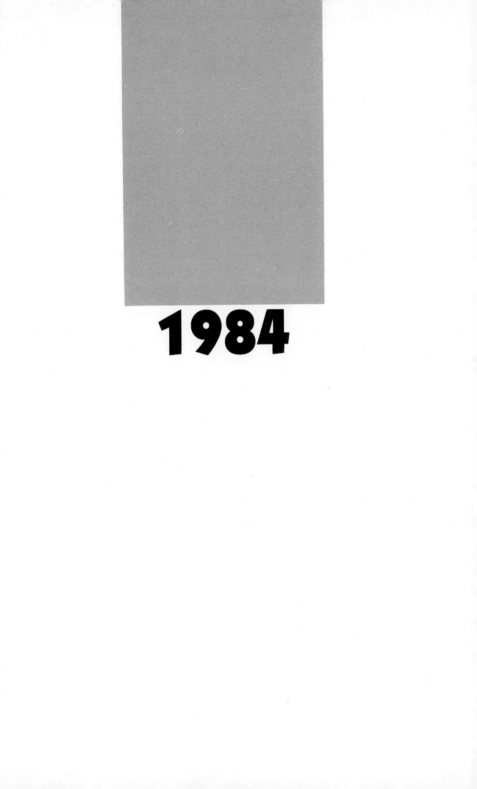

1984

Brenda was glad Joan had won her case, though for the moment that meant nothing in terms of money, moving, or any other matter, because the county had appealed to the State Supreme Court. The entire first floor of their house was now a basement. They did enter through the former second-story, current first-story, windows, just as Kevin had predicted. He, of course, adored the new means of entry and had entitled the show coming up in New York "Windows Are Doors." Brenda entered through the back so as not to be seen stooping to the undignified posture of heaving herself over the sill and dropping to the floor. Books, purses, or groceries had to be left outside, and if you were alone, you dragged a chair over for the elevation needed to reach them in. Worse, in Brenda's eyes, was that she felt watched, even from the back. The yard was so naked it felt like a stage planned for her humiliation. Cars drove slowly past, day and night, checking out the local freak of nature. The soil was hard, bleached, and sandy. When you kicked at it, and she had in rage and frustration, it was almost impossible to believe this sturdy, silent ground couldn't do something as simple as supporting a house. Here and there sat stumps, but the rest of the yard was clean of life. Their yard was a favored playground of neighborhood children who called the blank acre the Moon. When the new Republicans she met with weekly asked Brenda where she lived, she replied that she was an orphan, that her family had been slaughtered by hippies, which was why she favored the death penalty. It was not an answer to their question, but it shut them up and the sympathy it elicited proved useful in her machinations to hoist Louis further up the party ladder.

■　　■　　■

As Joan hurried to Mr. Bowers's office, a paper cup of coffee in one hand, the latest reports in the other, she bumped into Bob Kratz, staining her new jacket, dampening her documents. Fortunately, she had an excellent memory. Bob had been relocated, a polite word for demoted, to a remote area of the company where he couldn't do any harm, any good, any anything. She wasn't sure what he did but read the sports page. His hands were always blackened with newspaper ink.

"Sorry, Bob," she said. "I'm in a bit of a rush."

"That's quite all right, Mrs. Demerest. . . ."

"Ms., Bob. Ms. Demerest. It's a new age and about time you joined us in it."

"Mizzzz . . ." he said, buzzing like a child imitating a bee.

"You keep at it, Bob, and I'm sure you'll have that little word down in no time."

He stepped past her, whistling "Goldfinger." She glanced at her disguised finger and made a note to crush him like a gnat before the month was out. She wished she knew where Daryl was.

She entered Mr. Bowers's office, rubbing at the dark, wet spot on her suit. His pinky was going full speed, a bad sign. One of the Turkish cigars he'd been affecting recently lay smoking in the ashtray. She gulped down the rest of her coffee. She didn't trust people who could live without caffeine.

"Sorry I'm late," she said.

"Nonsense," he said. "If I had one other employee with your energy and determination, I could take over the world."

"I do my job," she said, uncomfortably. She preferred flattery when it took the form of raises, company cars, weekends at Mr. Bowers's river home.

"You certainly do."

Clearing her throat, she said, "I have some papers here concerning the new development and—"

"Joan, there's been a little snag over this project."

"That's not possible."

"It has nothing to do with you and everything to do with local politics."

"What do you mean?"

"Just this. Every one of the contractors, except Slim Mahon, who we both know is small potatoes, is threatening to stop using our services unless you drop your lawsuit."

"I don't believe that."

"Believe it or burn, as our Christian friends say."

"What does my personal life have to do with my professional life?"

"Nothing. The men don't want to pull out. They respect you. You shoot straight but know when to bend the rules."

"You're damn right I do."

"But these men have families to support. They're not playing around. This is their life. It puts bread on the table, shoes on the kid, an occasional diamond on the wife."

"I know that better than anyone, except I don't have a wife I feel obliged to throw jewelry at because I feel guilty about some sleazy affair."

"Your mistress, or mister as the case may be, is your lawsuit, and it's more consuming than any sleazy affair. How much money have you thrown at it?"

"Too much."

"Well, I don't want you to waste any more."

"It wasn't a waste. I won, and I'll win again. They don't have a leg to stand on."

"Unfortunately, when you knock one leg out, it grows another. Nature of the beast."

"What are you getting at?"

"The city has made it quite clear to our boys that if they have anything more to do with our little enterprise, they'll make their lives hell. They can do it. It can take a long time to get a permit if conditions aren't right. There are little violations that might not be overlooked."

"Cowards."

"Bread, Joan. Shoes. Sleazy affairs. Thus the world turns."

"Fuck the world."

"Drop this thing. You've made your point. They're willing to admit they haven't handled this in the best possible way."

"Those bureaucrats have a genius for understatement."

"If it's the house you're worried about, I'll build you a goddamned house."

"It's not just the house. I mean it is the house, my house, and the way they handled it is just plain wrong. What if I'd never developed the confidence—"

"And the money."

"And the money. I would have been buried alive. I want justice. I want a court of law to say I'm right and they're wrong and I want them to pay through the nose for it. It's the only thing they understand, pocketbook logic."

"I'm a businessman, Joan."

"I think I know what that means."

"We all have pocketbooks, and without a job, yours won't be near full enough to slay the dragon."

"You wait."

"There's no reason to make this decision immediately."

"How long?"

"A month."

"I've already made up my mind."

"Don't tell me now. Do it in a month."

"You know what I'm going to say."

"Pragmatism wins out over passion every time."

"You're a smug bastard."

"I'm an old bastard. That's different."

■   ■   ■

Melissa was officially educated. She had the paper to prove it, enclosed in a brown plastic, leather-looking case, written in a highfalutin script, all curlicues and show. She had her Phi Beta Kappa key, resting in a small, velvet-covered box between cuff links, the last Christmas gift she'd bought her father before she'd lost track of him.

She'd bought the shiny blue cap and insubstantial blue gown for nineteen ninety-five. She'd listened to the commencement speaker, a writer who'd had a flurry of success in the sixties through the advent of a book on a crisis that turned out not to be one. He had subsided into an academic career in Connecticut. He'd exhorted them as a good commincemeat speaker should, but his urging had provoked in Melissa a faint despair. When he was through she'd felt too tired and clumsy and frivolous to change a light bulb, much less the world. If she was the bright, young hope of the planet, the whole shebang was headed for the tubes. Which might not be a bad thing, she thought, as her gaze drifted idly over the families stacked in bleachers, Joan and Brenda and Kevin among them. When you thought about Robert Goulet and Vietnam and spray cheese and EST and Robert Goulet and missile silos and room deodorizers and red dye number three and Robert Goulet, it was easy to think that the gift of consciousness had perhaps been intended for another species, had perhaps inadvertently been bestowed on us, the way letters sometimes wound up at the wrong address because the mailman misread a "B" as an "E." She knew there were such things as Leontyne Price and the careless beauty of Veronica's face wiped clean of worry by sleep and the scent of mown grass and really hot North Carolina barbecue and the memory of her childish cheek resting against her mother's safe, alive neck. There was a sumptuousness not to be forgotten, but perhaps also not to be forgiven. Beauty seemed to require broken backs. Pyramids implied slaves.

Melissa shook the dean's hand. She hugged her family. She hugged Veronica. Neil wasn't there, though he should have been to pick up the Wilson Award for Outstanding Literary Criticism, which included a healthy scholarship. Neil was going to Cornell for grad school. He was going to be famous. Melissa didn't know what she was going to be except Veronica's lover. She hadn't applied to graduate school. She'd recently read Barth's "The Literature of Exhaustion" and had thought, It's certainly exhausted me. She wasn't sure she wanted to be a scholar. Was her calling truly to convene committees, hop the tenure track, mix it up at the MLA? Did she want to forage through a phalanx of footnotes and summon the dead, influential aunts of major poets from their graves for insights into sonnet sequences? She often thought that scholarship was the revenge of the intelligent upon the gifted. Semioticians, deconstructionists: they seemed like cults who had lost the trick of the ritual; their theories hot air balloons they drifted higher and higher until the text or antitext or whatever the hell you wanted to call it was a dot on the earth, a blip on the literary scanner. What seemed to matter was the volume of the balloons, the intricacy of their stitching, the audacity of their design. Melissa had wanted to study books because she had loved them. They had saved her life. Now she felt like someone who had spied a beautiful deer, shot it, then gouged it open, as if the still-warm guts and her own bloody hands were beauty's explication. When she'd expressed this to Neil he'd called her a sentimental turd.

She was taking a year off to contemplate. She wanted to pierce ears or sell oatmeal or pump gas, any profession whose rhetoric didn't include allusions to signifieds and signifiers and psycholinguistics. She wanted to be as mute and functional and passive as a coffee table. She knew we lived and died by language but for the moment she didn't care if we lived and died by Spaghetti-O's. She needed a nap, a long one, nine months or so. She wished resurrection wasn't the province of deities.

■ ■ ■

Louis said he'd seen her father downtown milling around with some other bums near the church where they gave out soup.

"What do you mean, other bums?" she'd said.

"I mean I know he's your father and all, but he did look like one."

"You take that back."

"Go see for yourself."

It was easy taking the afternoon off. Brenda was Assistant to the Chairman of the Young Republicans Club. Read secretary. The job description had until she'd changed it. It was one of two paying jobs in the Club, and as Chairman wasn't actually within her grasp—yet—she'd settled for it. The money wasn't great but she had access to everything. That was what the fools who condescended to her didn't realize. But they would after she'd risen to power in the guise of Louis. Every last one of them. She had their names filed on index cards under "C." For Communists.

She slowed down to get a better look at the bums rummaging through garbage cans in alleys. She parked illegally at bus stops to check out unconscious men on the benches. Men with shopping carts piled with cans. Men with signs proclaiming the end of the world. Men bugging passersby for quarters. How many were there and what was wrong with them?

The only thing worse than the men were the women in their shapeless clothes, with their battered hands and filthy hair. She didn't even want to think how they smelled. Men—you could almost understand it. There was something careless about the best-groomed of them. But a woman. It was unforgivable. Brenda seethed. She fumed. She wanted something very much like revenge. Her life hadn't exactly been a piece of cake. They were refusing to participate. It was willful. It was deliberate. It should be punished.

She found Kyle in the park, washing his face in a fountain of bronze angels trickling water from their trumpets.

"Daddy," she called.

He didn't respond. He rolled down his sleeves. She guessed he didn't think of himself as Daddy anymore. She wondered what he did think of himself as.

"Kyle," she tried.

That got him. He turned around and squinted at the car. He smiled. But not really. He combed his hair back with his fingers. "Brenda," he said.

"Come here."

It was painful to watch him walk over, trying to recover his dignity with pats at the dust on his pants and tugs at the buttonless jacket that didn't fit anyway. She hadn't seen him since the Easter before last. She'd made baskets for everyone, even him, though he couldn't even remember birthdays. He'd been living in a room bright with Sunday morning. Suzy had been at church. Kyle, unshowered, had been drinking a beer and watching a show about bass fishing. Brenda could see everything he'd become seeded in the memory, in the TV's broken antenna, in the tattered bedspreads hanging listlessly over the windows, in the undumped grocery bags of garbage slumped around the room.

"Hi there," Kyle said, leaning into the car's open window.

Up close, he looked better than she'd expected. He was clean-shaven and didn't smell any worse than your average man on Saturday night: beer, cigarettes, bad cologne.

"What are you doing?" she asked.

"Getting cleaned up. I heard about a job sweeping up nights in a restaurant near here."

"You'll never get a job looking like that."

"Think so?"

"Of course not. What are you doing?"

"I told you."

"I mean WHAT ARE YOU DOING?"

"Not much."

"I can see that."

"Sorry."

"Oh, don't bother apologizing. I just wanted to see for myself."

"How are you?"

"Great . . . just great . . . just terrible, that's how. If anyone ever asks you if you're my father, just say no."

"This is temporary. I've had a little bad luck, lost a couple of jobs. . . . I really don't know what happened."

She got the wallet out of her purse. A five. Some ones. A few quarters. "Here," she said.

"I will not take charity from my own daughter."

"Fine. Starve. See if I care." She threw the money on the ground and started the car. He backed away from the window. "I don't see why I couldn't have been from a nice family," she said. "I really don't."

As she sat at the park's entrance, waiting to turn, she saw the phantom of her father in the side mirror, hurrying after one of the bills skimming over the lawn. There was a sale at her favorite boutique. A new silk blouse might cheer her up. People were wrong. You could buy happiness. If you were a smart shopper.

■   ■   ■

Bored, Daryl the Snake Boy lay in his pit, a sturdy box about three feet by ten. Children had to be lifted to view him. The dozen or so drugged snakes who were his companions occasionally lifted their tranquilized heads or attempted a few pathetic slithers or wagged their relaxed tails. Mice in every town soon learned to taunt the lifeless reptiles, brazenly lifting up on their hind legs within striking distance of their natural enemies. Daryl's affection for his cellmates did not transcend his fear, so their food was sprinkled with sedative.

Mostly, Daryl napped. When Zeke roused him, Daryl would dutifully stand with a few of his friends dangling—limp, green jewelry—around his neck, from his arms. They would not stay wrapped to his thighs but slid drowsily down to his ankles.

Daryl was made to wear a tight green leotard that outlined all too well the snake between his legs. He had asked for a jock strap or a leaf to shield his cock from freak-hungry eyes but Zeke refused. He didn't want the myth of Daryl's origins dimmed: his mother was a French noblewoman who, separated from her safari, had been impregnated by a boa constrictor, which had strangled the hapless woman shortly after Daryl's birth, to raise the child as his own. Daryl was supposed to wriggle and speak French-inflected gibberish—and no more pig Latin, please—every quarter hour or so. Daryl dozed. Zeke had banned all magazines and newspapers from the snake pit because he felt these homely intrusions from daily life blew fantasy's fuses.

Suzy stopped by on her breaks from prophesying the futures of telephone operators and short-order cooks. Zeke had tried to exoticize her but Suzy's looks resisted artifice. The scarves and makeup and beads, the blowzy layers of cloth, the odor of incense that swarmed around her like an invisible cloud of gnats—it was like trying to spread rhinestones across toast. Zeke claimed it might help if she wouldn't look so bored.

Tonight she seemed nervous. Daryl stood up, several snakes falling from him. They were forbidden to kiss publicly. It emphasized Daryl's human side and was bad for business. Nothing escaped Zeke's scrutiny for its effect on business: clowns' laughs; tattoos, forbidden to games runners as sinister; where people should smell cotton candy and when that scent should fade to popcorn (which was measured to the kernel). Aisles were constructed to encourage spending. He liked the customer to feel lost. He called it the Helpless Factor.

"Hi, babe," Daryl said.

"See that woman?" Suzy said, discreetly tipping her cigarette towards a blonde near the three-headed goat.

"What about her?"

"She's going to die."

"She got cancer or something?"

"I don't know, but I was reading her palm, giving her that old man and money shit, and suddenly—it was like somebody'd shoved a picture in my head—I saw her dead as a damn doornail."

"You're starting to believe your own press."

"This wasn't no little feeling. I'm telling you, that woman's a goner."

It was hard to look at the woman after that, to know she was going to die, though when he thought about it further, the same was true no matter who you looked at.

"So you're the little genius?" a woman said. She was wearing a tight pink mini-dress with bullets dangling from the nipples. She could have been twenty or she could have been sixty. Kevin couldn't tell.

Sandy was standing in a little group, pointing out the intricacies of *Portrait of My Brother Daryl #4*. Henry, in a white suit, kept dabbing at his nose with a bright red handkerchief. He had a slight cold. There was nothing to eat and Kevin was bored. He didn't even answer the woman.

He wandered off to the office, thinking there must be something to do. Henry's cologne could still be detected here too. It was everywhere you sniffed, strung throughout the building like barbed wire. Kevin unwrapped a piece of hard red candy and popped it in his mouth. Henry was gradually emerging from his All-White Period and entering the Age of Red Accents. His shoes were red and so were the windowsills. It was not cheerful. If the all white had been clinical, the reds were the dark bloody aftermath of unsuccessful surgery.

Kevin sat down in the swivel chair and spun around. He was too old for this sort of childishness, but it was fun. He pushed himself around the desk several times and out of the door. He made several runs down the hall, the casters rolling silently over the red carpet. The fifth time he went too far and found himself rattling over the gallery's bare, hardwood floors and into the woman in the pink mini-dress. Her bullets jiggled.

"Kevin," Henry said, pushing through the crowd, "I just had the floors redone."

"Don't be such an old fart, Henry," the woman said. She positioned herself behind Kevin and pushed him around the gallery several times before exiting through the red-rimmed door. Kevin felt like he was sliding through Someone's Lips. Out on the sidewalk, they picked up speed. The wheels clattered alarmingly over the concrete and Kevin clutched the sides of the chair as they bumped over the cobblestones of an alley, as they almost collided with several evening strollers, as he yelled, "Faster," and she complied, laughing, her bullets flicking at his head. She was quite breathless when they returned and it took four blasts of asthma spray to return her to a functioning, breathing, collecting state. She bought several seminal Demerests. Kevin's prices doubled the next day, and tripled after the respectful *Times* review that Friday.

What he didn't tell anyone was that the drawing didn't want to come out of him as much, that it dribbled when it did come, that he thought it was going away.

■   ■   ■

Neil had a cold and he was being an impossible baby about it. He had Melissa reading *People* magazine aloud to him. He had her pulling the covers back down over his cold toes. He had her smearing Vicks Vaporub across his chest, as if one of his symptoms were paralysis of the arms. She ran to the drugstore two and three times a day for candy bars, more ginger ale, new magazines, little presents. "Surprise me," he'd say. Currently, she was in the kitchen brewing a new pot of tea, as he claimed the last one, made all of two hours ago, had gone stale. The phone rang.

"Hello," she said, angrily.

"How did you know it was me?" Louis asked.

"I'm hanging up."

"No, wait, something serious has happened."

"You're not going to tell me you have cancer again?"

"I already tried that. I'm not stupid."

"That is definitely a matter for debate. Out with it. My kettle's boiling."

"My kettle's always boiling for you."

"If I could figure out which would help you more, cutting off your head or your dick, I'd probably do it."

"You can have my head."

"Is that your serious news?"

"I'm going to tell your family you're a lesbian if you don't sleep with me."

"Put Brenda on the phone."

"Huh?"

"I'll spare you the one atom of conscience you have left and relieve you of your revelation."

"You mean you're going to tell her?"

"Bingo, Bozo. You take home the teddy."

"What are you going to go and do that for?"

"To halt these ridiculous exchanges."

"I was only kidding."

"No, I've been meaning to do this for years."

"I'm not with her."

"Liar."

"Honest."

"Louis, Brenda hasn't left you alone since she caught that majorette diddling your baton."

"You're going to tell her, honest?"

"Put her on."

"O.K.," he said, a shrug in his voice. "Brenda? It's your sister." To Melissa, he said, "It's your funeral."

Melissa heard Brenda say, "I didn't hear the phone ring."

Louis said, "Yeah, weird."

"Hello?" Brenda said.

"How are you?" Melissa asked.

"Fine, and you?"

"I'm a lesbian."

Silence. Then, "You realize, of course, that this means I'll never get to be First Lady. Thanks a lot, Melissa." Then tears.

"You're a maniac," Melissa said, and hung up.

Neil moaned unconvincingly from the bedroom. Its falsity arose from the circumstances under which he'd previously practiced this human noise, ones of pleasure, not pain, though for him those sensations had on occasion been mingled.

"Coming," Melissa shouted.

The cough in his lungs was only a cold; the rash on his skin was just that; the spots in his mouth weren't thrush. Melissa's mantra.

■   ■   ■

Joan wondered how long it had been since she'd been in a bar with Clarissa. They sometimes met for lunch in Joan's office or ate cheeseburgers in the McDonald's parking lot, and occasionally Joan's expense account treated them to veal cutlets and Chianti at the Italian place near Bowers Hardware. They never met at night. Joan didn't have the time or the taste for bars. Even at Happy Hour, it all felt desperate: the laughter too loud, the cologne too heavy, the smoke too thick, the light too dim, the lust too raw.

"Joan Demerest," Clarissa said, flicking a kernel of pretzel salt from the table, "I do believe you have forgotten how to have fun."

"I have fun."

"Oh yeah? Doing what?"

"I don't know. I watch TV sometimes."

"Sounds like a panic."

Joan bit a pretzel to buy time. "I think I have a lot of problems."

"Well, let's get to solving them so you can let your hair down."

"I don't think I like men."

"You mean you think you're funny?"

"No, but Melissa is."

"Your Melissa?"

"My Melissa."

"I hate to admit it"—Clarissa sipped her gin and tonic—"but she's probably better off. My problem is I like them too much."

"I don't trust them."

"What's to trust? You have your fun, play your cards close to your breast, then move on down the line."

"It doesn't seem worth it."

"It is and it isn't. I mean it is when you're getting to

know them and still think they might be decent, and it's not once you do know them and realize there's not a prayer they're even halfway decent. It can take a night or it can take a year. Men weren't made to last."

"I don't know how you do it."

"I'm a romantic," Clarissa said, batting her eyes.

"Another round?" their waitress interrupted.

"Yes," Clarissa said before Joan could object.

"Do you ever worry you've been a bad mother?" Joan asked.

"The way I see it, mothers are always getting the rap. I wasn't a perfect mother and they weren't perfect children."

"Maybe they'd have been better if we'd been better."

"I did the best I could with what I had, and if that wasn't enough, tough luck. It's a big, bad world out there and they're going to have to get over it."

The waitress set their drinks down.

"My house is still sinking," Joan said. "How do you prepare for a thing like that?"

"How do you prepare for anything? You're there. It happens. You make it up as you go along. End of story."

"You know what?"

"What?" Clarissa said, biting into her lime.

"I've missed this."

"Well, I'd call that a breakthrough," Clarissa said, lifting her glass.

"To girl talk," Joan said, lifting hers.

They clinked.

■　　■　　■

Daryl honey,

I can't go on like this anymore. I don't want to see these things anymore but they won't stop and I can't make them. I been thinking about supernaturals a lot and I think this may be a punishment from God for what me and you did to your father. It just won't right itself and I can see that now even though you can't. I thought our being in love made it right but it didn't. You can't do things like this. I should have knowed better. I guess God figured you was already punished enough by being green plus you being so young and all, it's really probably all my fault. I can't stand looking at people and knowing what's going to happen to them because it's usually so bad. They lose their houses and their babies and their lives. Life is just all the time losing something. That's all I learned from this terrible gift. I run off with the dwarf man cause I feel nothing for him and maybe God will see this as such a kindness that He will forgive me and take away this sight into the inside of people that I do not want to see. It's all I know how to do. Don't look for me. Somebody else will love you in spite of your being green. I know I did. Pray for me.

Suzy

■　　■　　■

One of the men was snoring, not that Kyle ever slept long or well. Plus, it was damn hot. He would have shucked off his underwear but sometimes there were queers in these places. They usually wouldn't touch you but sometimes they looked at you in that way and he didn't like to think they'd be doing it in his sleep when he couldn't protect himself. Day before yesterday, he'd let a kid who looked about fourteen, but had to be at least sixteen because he drove, blow him in the men's room at the park, but that had been for money, ten dollars, because he'd needed a bottle bad that day. He'd enjoyed it as little as possible. You actually couldn't help but feel the shuddery, inevitable pleasure of being brought to orgasm. All you could control was what you felt afterwards, which in his case was disgust for himself and the boy, whose knees were piss dampened from the pocked, tiled floor. Kyle had begged and stolen and sold his blood and now he'd had his dick sucked for a lousy ten by a kid cruising the park in his old man's Torino. Kyle had stood there, his arms hanging uselessly at his sides, slapping the kid's hand away when it tried to crawl under his T-shirt, watching, not because he wanted to, but because it was better than looking at the scratched-out white patches on the stall's serious green walls where phone numbers and drawings and poems had been scrawled. If that hadn't made him want to sail straight, fly right, sober up, he figured nothing would. He had done something he hadn't even known people did until it was happening and he felt the experience was a border he'd crossed that he hadn't known was there, into a shadowland whose language he willfully only half understood, because to become fluent was to affect the change to citizen, who lived there, from stranger, for whom departure was still a possibility. His guitar had been stolen last week and he'd cried as if he'd been told he had three or four months to live and had been shown incontrovertible truth, along with the diagnosis, that there was no afterlife, only nothingness, which you wouldn't even feel.

Grief.

■　　■　　■

Kevin made only ten thousand despite Henry's promises that he'd make ten times that. He kept it in the bank. He had a small blue savings account book with his name embossed across it in gold leaf. The numbers inside, representing the fat wad of cash stashed in the vault, were typed in a column in official-looking blue ink. He liked to think of the money as all ones. He liked to imagine himself sitting atop a stack of it. He looked in the book at least once a day, scarcely believing those blue numbers were an actual representation of a thing in the world, money, which was actually a representation of something else—his ability to buy. If you looked at the world from a certain angle, there were no objects, only symbols colliding. He had no desire to spend his small fortune. The fact that it was was enough.

He didn't know what had happened, but he couldn't draw. Had his talent fled at first sign of profit? Was it Daryl's absence? He looked at the blank page, and where once there had been a puzzle to figure out, now it was a blank page, nothing more, of no more interest than an end table. He'd start, but after a few listless, lazy lines he'd abandon it and wander off to watch TV or look with Daryl's old binoculars for pretty Mrs. Calhoun. He'd discovered sex. Mrs. Calhoun in her bra gave him a hard-on, which he rubbed against the windowsill while he spied. The girls at school didn't interest him. They were silly and flat and weren't interested in him either.

He didn't mind that he couldn't draw. He had never burned to do it. It had happened to him like tripping over a shoe his mother had kicked off onto the upstairs rug where she planned her strategy against the city.

They didn't know where Daryl was: not a peep, not a postcard, not a phone call. Kevin had interviewed a private detective to find his brother. The disappointing fellow didn't wear a trench coat and his right eye wandered disturbingly in its socket as if it was looking for a way out, better digs, a fresher face or a finer mind to look from.

Melissa lived her homo life with her homo friends. Joan wasn't speaking to her since Brenda's call. Brenda had not invited her sister to the high school graduation ceremony.

His father was as gone as Daryl, but Kevin didn't care as much. Kyle had always seemed like a stand-in father, someone to take up a father's space until the real one arrived. He felt funny about not missing him more, a recent and uncomfortable development in his feelings. But it was hard to miss what you'd never had.

Kevin looked at the collage of his work he'd assembled in the backyard. It probably represented about fifty thousand more dollars. He didn't know if he could do it until he lit the match. It burned down to his fingers and he lit a second. Surprising himself, he dropped it onto the pyre he'd constructed. Canvas curled and browned. Stretchers cracked. The blackened skeleton of an early drawing drifted lazily into the sky as if flight were commonplace and needed only to be wanted to be attained. He resisted snatching a sucker painting he'd especially liked from its approaching incineration.

He could do it.

He had done it.

It was over.

■　　■　　■

Mr. Bowers was expanding into real estate speculation and had Joan out scouting prospective properties. She had never been this far downtown, but there was a building Mr. Bowers wanted checked out before they went into negotiations with the contractors. If the place was in sad enough shape they could up the ante a little, maybe offer to invest, perhaps steal the whole project.

It had never occurred to Joan to do her job at anything less than full speed in spite of the ultimatum, and things were booming. She supposed Mr. Bowers had told them she was going to back off because no one had pulled out. Her deadline had been extended to her court date.

Wise Mr. Bowers knew what he was doing. He must have sensed her weakening. After the first white heat of her anger had passed, she'd begun to consider his arguments. There was no denying their cool rationality, their purse-strings logic. Most compellingly, and Joan thought this was a low blow, something too obvious to bear mentioning, there was Kevin, a child she still had to raise. Wouldn't he be better off in a house whose windows he didn't have to climb

through to enter? Of course. She must have been neglecting
him, what with her job and the lawsuit. Hadn't she missed
his opening? Well, yes. What kind of life would they eke
out on unemployment checks? Not much of one. All of
Joan's instincts but one, her rage for justice, wilted before
the inarguable laws of common sense. But that one was like
a trick match: no matter how hard or how many times you
blew it out, it renewed itself—a small, quiet, persistent
flame.

Looking around, she supposed it was just as well that she
never ventured this far downtown. The unsettling stillness
of abandonment was everywhere. She passed several reeking
bums too bleary to raise their heads at the sound of her heels
clicking down the sidewalk. She had the bizarre impulse to
check her lipstick, as if the least signal of disorder in her
appearance would send her tumbling down the chute that
led here. She wasn't afraid. These men had been K.O.ed
by life and she was never without her little aerosol can of
mace since the maniac, the one she spent her life trying not
to remember, but whose memory would suddenly flash up
at unexpected moments—in court, at a board meeting, as
she was drifting off to sleep—like the sudden silver of a fish
gliding to the surface of a deep, dark water.

The building was a mess. Rats scurried as she opened the
unlocked door. She made a note to take care of that. Several
makeshift beds were scattered across the floor and it
smelled, not of piss, but something stronger, like the body's
despair at its ruin. She rummaged for a Certs. The odor had
violated her mouth and seemed determined to stay there. She
was almost to the point of gagging when a hand touched her
shoulder. Her stomach double flipped. Her heart paused.

"Joan," the hand said. The voice was familiar, but a skel-
etal approximation of the original, so she couldn't fit it to a
face. She found her mace and, freeing herself, turned
around.

Kyle. Or a version of Kyle she would never have guessed

was inside him. But now that she saw it, it seemed as inevitable as the time that had scarred him into being. He looked better than most of them. In fact, he looked like little more than a tired old man in his mid-fifties who'd never amounted to much of anything. The last part of the observation seemed true enough, but the other, his apparent age, was the trompe l'oeil of poverty and sadness and perhaps illness. Kyle was forty-six. His birthday was June third. Joan couldn't remember his sign because she didn't go in for hocus pocus, but she could remember his favorite song, "Wings of a Dove"; his favorite shirt, that disreputable tee with the hole in the underarm; his favorite cologne, Aqua Velva, blue mint; his favorite food, Cheerios; his favored sexual positions—he'd been quite the acrobat now that she thought about it. The figment before her was way past favorite anythings. The whole idea of likes and dislikes suddenly seemed like an improbable luxury.

"Kyle," she said.

"Yep," he said, slapping at some dirt on his pants.

"Do you need anything?" she asked, feeling as platitudinous as a greeting card.

He rubbed his chin as if he were thinking deep thoughts. It was a joke but Joan wasn't laughing.

"As a matter of fact, I could use a guitar."

"A guitar?" She would not have been more surprised if he'd said, "Early African art," which she'd just seen a show about.

"Yeah. Mine got stolen."

"That's too bad." The words seemed so pat she felt she was reading them from index cards.

"I was pretty upset about it myself."

"I can imagine." Actually, she couldn't. There was so much else for him to be upset about. His life, for example.

"You look very fancy," he said.

"Thank you."

"Very fancy." He could have been mocking her but he wasn't.

"Is there anyplace I can have this guitar sent?"

"Not really. Maybe I could come by and pick it up."

"I don't think that's a good idea."

"Oh. Well, I have a little place hidden over here where you could leave it if you want."

"I could do that."

"Let me show you."

He led her to a space behind a wall that only the enforced diligence of the dispossessed could have discovered. They stepped over fallen light fixtures dusted with plaster. He invited her in but she declined. The smell was overpoweringly one of death, but more of the spirit than the body. She noticed an old cassette tape, several sex magazines, a carton of eggs, a set of matching towels, and an empty bottle of Aqua Velva, blue mint.

"Very clever," she said.

"I think so," he said.

Joan heard another rat. "I think I'm going to lose the house," she said. She wanted to cry but it seemed frivolous. Still, her losses marched through her like some lost, drunken, endless, exhausted army. She had to get out of here.

"That's too bad," he said.

"Yes," she said, "I suppose it is."

■   ■   ■

It hadn't been a cold and they had known it—Melissa, Veronica, Neil—but the diagnosis had shocked them just the same. Veronica had been the one to insist that Neil be taken to the hospital that Saturday night, and Melissa had resisted because Neil had resisted because they wanted one more day without that horrible acronym barging into their lives and setting up shop as if it now owned everything about them. They did not want their lives redefined by the absolute and unreasonable terms of death. They did not want it named because once it had letters and could be used in sentences whose other words were drastically altered by its simple, glowering presence, all return passage was canceled to the time before it was said, which became, irrevocably, the Age of the Possible.

But Veronica insisted. They helped him, one of his arms on each of their shoulders, to the car. He made Melissa go back for Virginia Woolf's letters, which he'd been reading, and a pair of underwear, which he wasn't wearing. He asked them to turn on the radio, which Veronica did. Then he asked them to turn it off, which Veronica also did. The lights glowed green on the dashboard and when Melissa found herself thinking how beautiful it was, that delicate, verdant light, she wondered abstractly, as if it had no bearing on herself, if she'd lost her mind. She wanted to open the window. She was suffocating. When they pulled up by the emergency room door she wondered if she could move, and when she could she was surprised but unimpressed.

She would never forget how bright the waiting room was. She remembered asking Veronica if she thought they could dim the lights, and Veronica, instead of saying yes or no or maybe or some other sensible answer, said, "Melissa, Neil's going to need you. Remember that."

After several centuries of waiting, a doctor who looked, gratuitously Melissa thought, like a movie star came out. He said the word. He said it twice. He said it tentatively but still it had been spoken. It had a terrible magic. It changed everything.

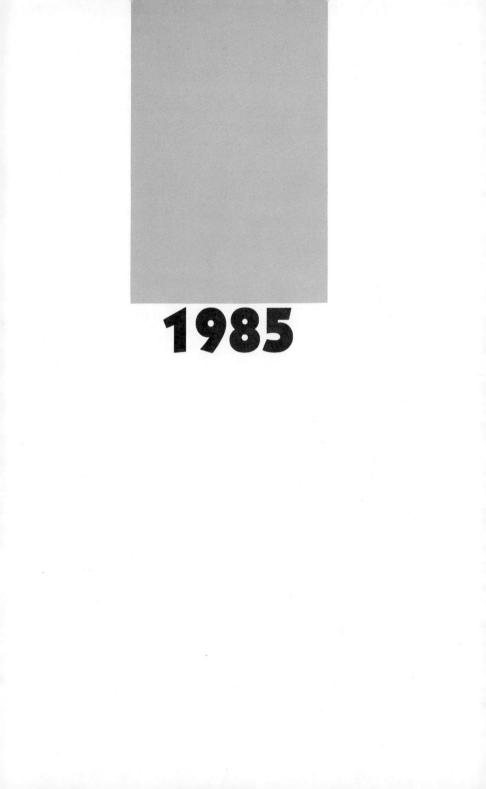

1985

Dearest Melissa,

I was listening to the Ella in Berlin album the other night and slowly began to realize that I wasn't listening, that I wasn't enjoying, that I was past enjoyment. The eye thing has made reading, my one true love, a tedious and unrewarding chore. It's as if a beautiful lover has turned increasingly truculent, isn't worth the effort any longer; and his beauty, despite its presence, seems more like a memory than a thing it is possible, or even desirable, to attain. It's not that I don't like your melodious reading voice. Oh I do (though I do wish you would stop that annoying habit of trailing off at the end of long paragraphs as if a sudden fit of narcolepsy had derailed you), but more and more I wander my past as if it were a lovely maze too intricate ever to emerge from. Also, I am sick of medicine, the smell of medicine, its medicinal taste—I will never scoff at healing concoctions made to taste like cherry or lemon again—the dull routine of its ingestion. I'm sick of that hectoring beep's interruption of what's left of my life. The worst are the four a.m. doses when you and Veronica are asleep (everyone, it feels, is asleep). There's no one there to joke with, my last line of defense. I am alone and I don't find my own wisecracks funny enough to be very soothing, though some of my best zingers come to me then, which I later pretend to have thought up on the spot. I don't think you ever realized how planned my life really was. I loved me in your eyes. You attributed a spontaneity, an infallibility, a generosity in me that had never existed until you created it (the infallibility never showed up—even your wizardry couldn't conjure it). I was my best self with you. I once dallied with the notion of a sex change to become your lover, but decided it was too, too perverse, even for me. Besides, sex fucks everything up—at least it did for me—and you would have undoubtedly left me for some brainy tart with real tits and I would have been bereft, a rebel without a cause, a lesbian without a clit. Then Veronica came along, dispatching the idea completely. She is, you know, better than both of us put together. We could even throw most of our friends into the mix (though they have proven most loyal except for Kurt, which I understand—I am his worst fear realized—try to forgive him) and she would still outshine us. Do you know what her greatest grace is? It's not wisdom or kindness especially, though she has both of those; it is her sensibleness. She looks at a situation, figures out exactly what needs to be done and, here's the rub, she does it. It's not that she isn't afraid like the rest of us mere mortals—my dear, she is—but because she has some chromosome the rest of us lack, she ploughs ahead anyway. It's too tragic that she's a lesbian. Since procreation isn't her thing, our chances for evolving are considerably dimmer than at the moment of her birth. Of course, it's easy for me to idealize her because I haven't woken up to her bad breath.

Melissa, and you must listen to this very carefully, do not poison yourself with despair. You already suspect that the world is a steaming pile of shit and indeed, most of it is. But God—yes, of course, I believe, or perhaps should say hope—arms us with shovels and yours are anger and intelligence. Anger is not despair and it is imperative that you not confuse the two. Anger calls us to arms. You have seen how I have been treated—the fear, the bigotry, the blinding hatred—but it is not a parable whose moral lesson is to retreat to your darkened room scowling at the world's ignorance. People do change, and they don't do so willingly or by accident, but because others force them. The retreat I spoke of is self-pity and arrogance, both of which the two of us possess in abundance. Don't give in.

So why am I giving up, you're angrily asking yourself (good—anger). It's simple, dear. I'm tired and have a right to be tired. This body is mine to dispose of as I wish. You have seen me. I have been an impossible bitch, which I don't apologize for. Suffering does not ennoble us or save us from ourselves (as that twisted genius Flannery O'Connor or any other Christian would have us believe). It simply degrades us. I am sick of the humiliation, the endless dying.

This is also important: I do not regret my life. In ancient Egypt fourteen-year-olds were considered old-timers. In India they drop like flies. I've had a good, if short, run, which is not to say I'm not enraged. I am. Deeply. But during the past few days I've also been assailed by an odd and unexpected serenity that I do not question. Life is good, and my suicide—yes, it's one of those notes, I'm afraid—injects a note of choice into the process that I need to wrest victory from the jaws of oblivion. Ever since I decided, I've been restored to myself, though I don't kid myself either— the slight break in my long illness has helped.

I have taken care of as much as I could so as not to burden you. Unfortunately, my mother will have to be called, but get sensible Veronica to do it. You would undoubtedly start screaming at the hapless woman, who, though a bitch, finally can't help who she is anymore than we can. Let her conscience, if she still has one, be her guide. On second thought, maybe you should call. If there's a hell, it will be decorated like her living room. Try to be nice to her at the funeral. I sometimes think bad taste is sufficient enough punishment for anyone.

I won't go trotting down memory lane, partially because Mother has tired herself with all this dispensing of wisdom, but mostly because we know where we have been and have our own precise or clouded versions of it tucked inside ourselves. We have loved one another and that has been a great thing.

Neil

■　　■　　■

It was finally over. Joan's lawyer had warned her to prepare for the worst and she had, rehearsing the judge's decision while she was driving, while she touched up her lipstick, as she had packed up her office. As usual, the actual event was dim—tedious and overlong—when compared to the blazes her imagination had ignited. She'd been too sad and tired to be carried from the courtroom raging about justice, or to spit in Belmont's face, or to mutter more than a mere "Hmph." Her lawyer had taken her hand and said, "I'm sorry, Joan. I really am. Can I take you to lunch?" Lunch. It seemed ludicrous. She shook her head no.

She couldn't bring herself to go home and she couldn't go to work because she didn't have a job. Clarissa's? Her children? No. And no. They would try to comfort her and it would not be comforting.

She drove. She kept the windows up to muffle the noise of the big, busy world. She kept the radio off. She didn't want to be sung at. She didn't want to know the time or the temperature or the traffic conditions. She averted her eyes from clocks on bank signs. She kept catching glimpses of her eyes in the rearview mirror, and each time was startled that she still looked like herself. Some essential piece of her—was it her will?—had swirled down the drain of the legal system.

She drove. The blue sky went amber, and that bled into a drama of reds and oranges, and that faded into the shifting grays of dusk. She stopped for a box of doughnuts. It had taken her years not to taste the drudgery of her first job in their sugar. She wondered if Jenny, her old adversary, was dead.

The boy behind the counter was sullen and pock-marked and his skin was yellowy under the fluorescent lights. His collar was smudged with chocolate. The barely filled coffee-pots looked like they'd been there since this morning. The doughnuts blurred under the dingy glass counter. There were no Jennys here. A veteran, Joan could tell the glazeds were freshest. Their icing was still moist and transparent in patches. She ordered a dozen.

The boy folded the flat cardboard into a familiar box. She had never mastered that. Her boxes had been ill-constructed, and more than once a customer had returned, holding up the box like a magician's trick, the flaps of its bottom undone, the doughnuts gone.

The boy put on the familiar plastic glove. Joan had always been careful to choose the best, but he simply picked the first ones his flimsily gloved hand reached. She couldn't blame him. It was hard to get excited about doughnuts.

"I used to work in a place like this," she said.

"Must have been a long time ago," he said.

"Not that long ago."

"I'm not going to be here much longer."

"Another job?"

"I'm moving to California."

"Congratulations."

"I'm going to be an M.C."

"How do you do that?"

"You sound just like my mother."

"I'm not anybody's mother," Joan said. She was sick of being typecast.

"Hey," the boy said, his face cracking into a wide, crazy smile. He had nice teeth. Perfect, too perfect: caps. "This bakery is filled with hundreds of doughnuts," he said, strained, exuberant, "valued at more than one hundred thousand dollars." Then the smile wilted into a sullen wrinkle and he said, "What do you think?"

Stick to doughnuts, Joan wanted to say. "I think you've got something." Like delusions. Like a mouthful of expensive dental work.

"You really think so?"

"You have a great smile."

"I'm getting my face sanded next week."

"Good luck," she said.

In the car she kept thinking, It's not me, but she only half-believed it. She tried repeating, You're Joan, but so many of the borders she had previously used to define herself had been overrun or abandoned, or had shifted to somewhere she couldn't find, that the word seemed to describe a place like Persia, which only existed on ancient maps and could not help you navigate the way home.

"Help," she whispered over her bitten doughnut, glaze moustaching her lip.

■　　■　　■

Louis was rattling around the bathroom. Brenda would attend to the details when he emerged. She knew the groom wasn't supposed to see the bride, but with Louis, hairs were always out of place, ties insufficiently knotted, shoes sloppily laced. She couldn't leave his appearance to the wilds of his inattention. Not today.

She unscrewed another of the light bulbs glowing around the vanity. There. That was perfect. The wedding was going to be held in the park and now she realized that the location was a mistake. The sun didn't have a dimmer switch. She thought that's why the hippies, those dinosaurs, had gone wrong. They had mistaken nature for their friend. Without blow dryers and politics, Brenda was convinced that nature would eat you unhesitatingly. Nature was about fucking and eating. Politics was about legislating who fucked whom where and under what circumstances. Nature was about berries. Politics was about luncheons. Politics was simply enforced good manners. People, as a rule and a group, didn't want to behave. Politics was the mother no one really liked. Brenda understood this with ferocity. Louis never would, but his ignorance was what made him a good politician. He understood politics at a crucial but superficial level, that of a popularity contest. Brenda knew politics was ultimately about bombs.

She smudged a dab more perfume behind her ears and sniffed: perfect.

"Louis?" she said. "It's almost time. Let Mommy see you."

No answer.

"Louis?"

She shut off her vanity and went to the bathroom. It was locked.

"Louis? Honey? This is not funny. We have to be there at three, sharp."

She picked the lock with a bobby pin. The window was open. A rope of sheets tied to the toilet hung over its ledge. There was a note taped to the mirror:

Sorry, Babe,

Just can't cope. I'm too young or something. You're a great gal but I want something else I don't know how to say. Don't be too mad. Got to run because I think I hear you coming. Take care, you hear? I loved you. I think.

Louis

■   ■   ■

Sandy hadn't been this unhappy since the time she'd realized she hadn't completed a painting or drawing in years. It wasn't just Kevin's sudden inability to draw, which she'd become convinced of on the basis of a couple of quick sketches he'd tossed off and just as quickly destroyed. They'd been the gifted renderings of a promising thirteen-year-old, nothing more. The assured poise of genius was absent. She was still bewildered. His talent was like a long illness from which he'd miraculously recovered. It only confirmed for her the essential mystery of art, which she'd been distracted from by the bogus, glittering trappings of high finance and high profile that had come to drape it recently like pythons of cheap tinsel. She supposed Kevin's loss was tragic, but she only felt the abstract compassion of a newspaper reader who discovers some disaster in a small village on the other side of the world tucked away at the bottom of page fourteen. She guessed if he seemed more affected she would have been. She had her dozen or so Demerests. In about five years they'd be worth a hundred thousand or more. She could probably retire, selling off one every so often to save herself from work, though what she might be saving herself for was mysterious to her.

Recently, she'd begun an affair with another teacher, Frank, who was lively, a bit of a cynic, didn't expect much, made wonderful Indian meals, and had the long, muscular legs of a dancer. She supposed she should marry him (he had asked) but there was something—maybe his low expectations, the one aspect without which she would never have embarked upon this—that finally made him not enough; and that would be settling. God knows she had settled and settled, but marrying a man she didn't love would have seemed like the final settlement, a fort whose gate she might not have the strength to break down once it was locked. At age thirty-five, she'd finally realized that there were decisions from which you didn't recover.

Someone knocked. Frank and her friends knew not to stop by without calling, but tonight she was grateful for the interruption. The fact that she could get up from the chair was proof that she hadn't slid so far down into The Pit, her pet name for depression, that she couldn't crawl back. It was Kevin. She hadn't seen him since he'd started junior high school and the change was remarkable. He was still a boy but he wasn't a little boy. He was a boy with hormones pushing peach fuzz over his lip and muscles tightening the skin of his arms.

"When did you grow up?" she asked, not asking him in.

"Yesterday," he said, walking past her and stretching out on a chair he'd once hopped backwards to achieve.

"Won't you come in?" she asked.

"I don't want to joke around, Sandy. I have a serious favor to ask you."

"This sounds like it calls for more wine," she said, shutting the door and making her way back to the bottle of zinfandel she'd almost polished off.

"I want you to teach me about sex," he said.

She filled her glass and said, "Something about birds and bees. I've never quite understood it myself."

"No, I mean I want you to show me."

"Sorry, my diagrams are all terribly smudged from overuse and mishandling."

"No, I mean show me how."

She got it. "You can't be serious." He didn't answer. "I'm old enough to be your mother." Some situations, she reflected, were so ludicrous that they required clichés to defuse them.

"I'm almost fourteen."

"I'm twice that with years to spare."

"You're a good teacher."

She laughed.

"Pretty please," he said.

Later, she realized that was the moment when she'd decided what the hell, though they'd argued for another hour and she'd uncorked another bottle. She thought it'd be good for him to learn persistence in these matters, the glamour of longing, the sweetness of possible failure, the thrill of the hunt: finesse. She supposed she was a good, or at least thorough, teacher. Pretty please. The innocence of it. The sex itself had been more like a toy of sex, herself as manual, lecturing on eagerness, her body a map of pleasure full of the usual false shortcuts and unexpected dead ends that had to be taken before they could be circumvented. She held his face in her hands and forced his eyes open so she could watch the astonishment of his first orgasm, his bewilderment at the pleasure of his body.

She'd once taken part in a drunken, impromptu orgy. She'd had her married man, that tired rite of passage. There was the brief lesbian fling in college and the tentative slaps with the sculptor finally too tender to be much of a sadist. There'd been the married couple in New Jersey, plucked from the personals for the kick of it. That was the only one she regretted, more because their idea of a three-way had been as unimaginative as their taste in furniture. She'd felt more like they were playing a tame version of musical chairs, herself as chair, than abandoning themselves to revels. There'd been the awkward chitchat before, the inevitable Polaroids, and the long train ride home. She remembered it in the badly lit, inadequately detailed sets of pornography.

Now she was, there was no getting around it, a child molester. She hoped she wouldn't develop a taste for this sort of thing, lurking around junior varsity football games, coming to a bad end in New Orleans. No, she didn't have the stamina for degradation. Like Kevin's orgasm, and most men's when she thought about it, this was a one-shot deal. It rounded out her sexuality nicely. This was her last field trip to the edge.

She looked at his sleeping shoulder, at the tones the moonlight had discovered on his skin. She crept over to the closet and pulled out an old sketch pad, fumbled through a drawer for some charcoal she thought she remembered. She eased back beside him. The light was gone. She'd have to do it from memory.

■　　■　　■

This was a nice complex with a clubhouse and a pool. It wasn't sinking. The grass stayed clipped for several weeks after the maintenance men cut it and the hedges were kept manicured into perfect green globes. It was nature, but it was nature that had been given a good scrubbing behind the ears, some henna to highlight its essence, a nip, a tuck, accessories. After all, nothing was born perfect. This was as true for trees as it was for tresses. There was something unkempt about even the prettiest trees one saw in most parks. Brenda loved the sidewalks crisscrossing between the buildings and the crisply painted parking spaces. The pink glow of the street lamps made her feel safe at night.

She turned the radio down another notch. She didn't care for music unless it was almost not there, something piped into malls, something to shop by. She rearranged the accent pillows on the couch. She still wasn't sure about white. She'd bleached them again today and already they looked dingy. She lit the bayberry incense Melissa had given her as a housewarming present. Melissa, the incorrigible radical, would give incense instead of something sensible like a lovely crystal paperweight. Brenda liked the dense fragrance well enough—it didn't have the acrid edge of deodorizer— but there were hints of frenzy and nudity in its smoke and it made her uneasy.

She was lowering the heat under the steak Francesca when the doorbell pealed. That would be Joan. Kevin had called to say that he was worried about their mother. She sat around in a robe watching TV all day. During commercials she lit matches, stared until they almost burned her fingertips, then tossed them into the fireplace. Brenda hoped her own example would inspire her mother. Brenda had survived desertion and humiliation and a family that seemed designed to rob her of greatness. She'd more than survived. She was Chairman of the Young Republicans Club. Naturally, she was sorry about the scandal swarming around her predecessor's departure, but was it her fault that he'd been a shoplifter as a child, had engaged in homosexual dalliances as an adolescent, and was practically a drug addict now? No. She'd simply let the facts speak for themselves. Some people were role models. Others were not.

"Mother," Brenda said, flinging open the door, "you look wonderful."

"No, I don't." .

No, she didn't. She didn't even look presentable. Her hair was pulled back into a rubber band and her lipstick—her one stab at a public self—was garish against her pale skin. And that dress. Brenda tried not to shudder. It wouldn't be upbeat.

"It's nothing a little eyeliner can't fix," Brenda said, patting Joan's shoulder. "You're still a very attractive woman when you want to be."

"What's for supper?" Joan asked.

"A surprise. Would you like some bottled water?"

"I brought my own," Joan said, pulling a pint of bourbon from her coat pocket.

"I really don't think you should be drinking in your state of mind."

"Thanks for the advice," Joan said, unscrewing the cap.

"Speaking of Daddy, how does he like living with Daryl?"

Joan set the bottle aside, untouched. "I wouldn't know."

"I wish Daryl would take that sign out of his front yard."

"It's a living."

"Lizard Boys have a limited appeal. There's no return market. Once you've paid your buck to see them, kaput."

"There are a lot of suckers out there."

"You have a point," Brenda said, thinking warmly of her future constituents. She was going to start with City Council. Next year. She was already nosing around for a husband, a tiresome necessity. Voters didn't trust single women. She'd met a lawyer at a recent benefit for some ghastly childhood disease she couldn't remember the name of. He was thirty-five, which she hoped would enhance her eighteen years by at least five in the public's mind. Aging by association.

"What are you thinking about?" Joan asked.

"My next husband."

"Your wedding dress is still warm."

Brenda was tired of being called ruthless when she was merely realistic, calculating when she was clear-sighted, paranoid when she was prudent. Her own mother. Hadn't she made dinner? Hadn't she forgiven Joan for that stupid, sinking house that had wrecked her adolescence? She was sick of always having to be the strong, normal, optimistic one.

"I'm not as heartless as you people would like to think," she said tearfully.

"I'm sorry," Joan said.

"I love," she said, two large tears squeezing from the corners of her eyes, "in my own efficient way."

Joan stood and pressed her daughter's head against her stomach. For once, Brenda was grateful for polyester. It was, at least, cool against her hot cheek.

"Yes," Joan said, "I suppose you do."

Friday night, Melissa and Veronica were going to eat hot dogs in Times Square to save money, and then they were venturing down to SoHo to the Performing Garage to check out Richard Foreman. They were going to smear on lipstick and wear rhinestone drop earrings and visit a piano bar Neil had frequented that featured, as he said, "the last grumpy goddess of dissolution" at the keyboard. They were going to drink martinis straight up in chilled stemmed glasses and try to palm themselves off as the latest word in lesbian chic. Saturday morning, they were going to the Metropolitan to ogle paintings until their corneas throbbed, and that afternoon, after a hurried slice of pizza, they were going down to West Broadway near Houston to see if Neil's tales of cheap, black forties dresses were fact or fiction. They were going to buy a good bottle of champagne and pour it over one another in their Chelsea Hotel bathtub and lick each other raw. After a nap, they were going to Chinatown for a cheap meal and then they were off to torture themselves with a Marguerite Duras double feature, which they would actually be disappointed to understand or enjoy. Then they were going dancing. Neil had told them to forget the lesbian bars, which were in the spirit, if not the state, of Iowa; so they were going to attempt the Palladium if they could get past the fashion police at the door, armored as they would be in their ultra-chic, everything-old-is-new-again black dresses. They were going to slick back their hair, wear sunglasses and tattered fishnet hose to beat the odds. They planned to spend Sunday morning hung over at Tavern on the Green, though Neil had said it was only a feast for the eyes, not the stomach, and the only thing worse than their eggs Benedict were their Bloody Marys. Still, one couldn't always trust Neil, who had a healthy suspicion that anything popular had to be bad, and he was not, as he himself had pointed out, infallible. Before they left, they were going to Battery Park to view "that Bitch in the Harbor," as Neil had called her, and whom he proudly claimed never to have seen except in postcards, averting his eyes the one time he'd had occasion to be on the Staten Island ferry—the occasion being an Italian typesetter who lived on that maligned isle. They were going to buy Lady Liberty hats. They were going to wear them home.

But first they were going to Henry Caplan's. Melissa had the painting wrapped in brown paper wrapped in plastic again. She had been terrified until they were actually sitting on the stark white chairs outside Henry's office. She wouldn't let Veronica refer to the painting, though that's obviously what it was unless, as Veronica said, Melissa was carrying around an awfully large, thick credit card. On the train up, Melissa had thought everyone was staring at the painting, including a man in sunglasses who turned out to be blind. She'd sprayed the package with perfume to disguise the smell of paint. She'd eaten a sandwich off of it so others would think it an item of no more value than a TV tray. In fact, the only thing she didn't do was nurse the painting so strangers would think it was her infant. The other passengers were afraid of her.

Henry Caplan's office was this throbbing red. Melissa felt like she was in someone's sore throat.

"Well, well," he said, clapping his hands, "what have we here?"

Melissa unveiled her portrait of Daryl.

"Aaah . . ." he said, "an early Demerest."

"Wrong," Melissa said, her confidence returning, "peak Demerest."

"Perhaps."

Veronica sat mute.

"Well, it's not as if it's the only portrait extant. There must be dozens."

"You have two," Melissa said, reciting Sandy's brief. "Four are dispersed among collectors. Sandy has one. I have one."

"He's so hot I could almost sell the ashes of the others."

"Kevin's already bottled them."

"Such a clever boy."

"How much are you prepared to offer?"

"Five thousand."

Melissa laughed. "I could sell it on a street corner for ten."

"Very well, ten."

"Try a hundred."

"Thousand?"

"You have to ask?"

"I do because it's a fantasy figure, surely?"

"You and I both know this painting will be worth a quarter of a mil in ten years."

"So why not wait?"

"I don't have time to wait."

"Twenty-five thousand or you can take your desperation elsewhere."

"Eighty," Melissa said.

"Fifty and not a penny more."

"Sixty-five."

"This is not a fish market, Miss Demerest."

"Sixty-five."

"Too risky."

"Holly Soloman is right around the corner."

"Seventy."

"Sold to the man in the tonsillitis red office," Melissa said.

"And the reptilian smile," Veronica added.

"Dykes have never taken to me," Henry said.

■   ■   ■

As Brenda watched the cheerleaders, she wondered if she'd made a mistake by not going to college. The black-and-white portable was dusty. Everything was dusty. Men were pigs. She'd taken the garbage out when she got there. She had gagged on it as soon as Daryl had opened the door. There were several empty TV dinner pans lying around encrusted with dried gravy, whipped potatoes, baked apple goo, or bejeweled by a few shriveled peas. Everywhere she looked there was something to sigh over: forgotten socks, cigarette burns, filthy ashtrays, muddy cups of coffee, cracked plaster. Kyle was napping in his room.

"Mother told me Kevin burned up his art," she said. She could never think of anything to talk about with her family except her family.

"I could have killed him," Daryl said.

"Oh well," Brenda said, trying to see the bright side, "he can always make some more."

"Good shot," Daryl said to the TV.

"Did you hear Melissa's friend died?" This was the first time she'd seen Daryl since he'd gotten back and she didn't know what he needed to be updated on.

"No."

"AIDS. I hope Melissa doesn't get it."

"Aw, man, he was robbed," Daryl said, motioning to the tube.

"I think it's very nice what you're doing for Daddy."

"I have my reasons."

"Or reason."

Daryl didn't answer.

"You know what I mean," she said.

"What?"

"Suzy."

"Have you told anybody?" he asked, not looking away from the game.

"No."

"Please don't."

"I hate this family. I really do."

"So what do you keep coming around for?"

"I really don't know anymore. I keep wanting something and I keep hoping the next time I come back it'll be there. Do you know what I mean?"

"I guess I don't expect much. It's easier."

"Well, I do expect much and I'm not apologizing for it."

"Things is what they is."

"Wrong. Things are what you make them be."

"Good luck."

"Look at me," she said, taking out her compact. "I practically had to make myself up from scratch."

"You are something."

"And I'm going to be even more."

"Go for it."

"I have to run. I have a luncheon, a hair appointment, then a cocktail party."

"Makes me tired just thinking about it."

"Tell Daddy I stopped by."

"Sure you don't want me to wake him?"

"That's O.K. I'll try to stop by again real soon."

"Okey-dokey."

If Brenda couldn't see the purpose of something, she lost interest. Means. Ends. She'd discovered that if you concentrated long enough, you could uncover the usefulness of almost anything. When she disliked someone, she reminded herself that everyone was a potential voter and it immediately made anyone except the most hardened Democrats tolerable.

But the polls weren't enough to make her family worthwhile. If anything, they were a political liability. She concentrated fiercely, and by the time she'd found a parking place at La Belle Boite, she had it: her family was what she didn't want to be. They were an object lesson. It wasn't love but then what was? It was hard to even like people once you got to know them. Brenda preferred people in groups: conventions, rallies, voting blocs. Anonymous, malleable, controlled.

■   ■   ■

Kevin looked over at Francine, seventh-grade bombshell, who had already finished her test and was applying lipstick. He wanted her.

He kept the remains of his art in peanut butter jars. The labels ranged from *Really, Really Early Stuff* to *A Bunch of Stuff I Did in a Big Hurry Right Before I Burned Out*. He actually didn't know which period was in which jar—he'd burned it all together—and anyway, he'd had to enrich each one from other sources: grills, fireplaces, former fall-leaf piles. It didn't matter. Sometimes art was like presents: it was the thought that counted. Sandy had tried to arrange for a show of the jars but no one dared cross Caplan and, besides, he had a steady, anonymous source for early De-merests, some of it slight, but all of it recognizably Kevin's, that made the ashes less interesting to collectors. The source, of course, was Raymond Carstairs. He'd called Kevin and said, "I just want to thank you for my CD player, my villa in Provence, my burgeoning collection of antique per-fume bottles, the four-star dinners, and the five-star whores." "You're not welcome," Kevin had said, slamming down the phone.

Sandy wouldn't sleep with him after that first time. She was planning to sell *Suckers #11* when the school year was up and move to an island off the coast of Maine. She was drawing again, elaborately toned charcoals of naked body fragments that you had to stand in front of for a few seconds before you realized what they were. They were simple, but they were beautiful.

He visited Daryl once or twice a week, but there was nothing to say, not to Daryl, not to his father. Nothing. They'd watch basketball games while Kyle picked his guitar and answered the door to let in customers. Then Daryl would go to the box in his bedroom, lie down with his liz-ards, and Kyle, after taking their money and their jackets, would lead the tourists back to gawk. Daryl pretty much stuck to the story Zeke had concocted, changing the boa constrictor to a mutant lizard. Lizards were less dramatic than snakes but Daryl didn't fear them and couldn't afford tranquilizers. He had seven interchangeable pairs of green leotards. Kevin was starting to wonder why he bothered stopping by, but their mutual blood had reasons more potent than Kevin's boredom and sadness and so he returned, like someone hypnotized.

Francine. He wanted to whisper in her ear and nuzzle her neck and try his Sandy-trained tongue out on her clit. He wanted to fuck himself limp. She caught him looking and smiled, but it was the kind of smile you'd give to someone's kid brother. He'd have to change that. Francine was somebody you could start spending ten thousand dollars on. He could afford to start dipping in anyway because he had a scheme for T-shirts that he thought would go over big.

■　　■　　■

Daryl had rescued Kyle. He'd picked him up in a taxi and had said Kyle could stay there until he got on his feet. No demands. No expectations. Kyle had had a lot of time to think since then, and he had decided that it was the selflessness of the act that had finally helped. Daryl loved him no matter what. It was something to be worthy of again.

Kyle tried to remember the life before and couldn't. He could hear Jim, who thought he was Albert Einstein, going on and on about the theory of relativity, which Jim thought had something to do with the inescapability of family, and though Jim hadn't seen his family in years, he made charges against them daily as if the crime of his birth had been committed a short time ago. Kyle could see the shoes taped to his own feet. He could smell the rancid clothes. You never knew you stank until you smelled somebody else. He couldn't remember the cold nights. They were too cold to remember, but even that was a form of memory. He could remember, but he couldn't imagine how he had gotten there, that it was actually himself he was seeing in these scenes. Like a country song, it was the drinking, it was the divorce, but it was also that he'd wanted life, his life, to be something that it was not. He hadn't even known what it was that he'd wanted except that playing the guitar, writing songs, vaguely articulated it. He only knew that he'd wanted more. More what? More anything. More everything. But now he realized he'd been dealt a hand that included character and ability and he either had to bet on a pair of deuces or throw in his cards, cash in his chips, call it quits. What he'd been wasn't an option. He'd been spoiled by picking his guitar on a couch instead of a curb, by a TV you didn't watch through a store window, by shaving cream, by cupboards with food in them, by his bed, his pillow, his *Playboy* under the mattress. Was it enough? No. Would it have to do? Given the alternatives, it would have to. And he was going to have to get a job. There was an ad in today's paper for work in a guitar shop that might not be bad. He was going to stop by tomorrow.

■   ■   ■

Daryl had done his penance. His father might not be O.K. tomorrow or three months from tomorrow or three years from that, but for now he was fine. Occasionally, Kyle had one too many, but he did have a job to start next week and could keep track of the new guys who'd come through the NBA while he was away. That's what it seemed like, that he'd been on a long trip in a place so foreign that he'd had to learn his own country from scratch. A can opener had confused him at first. But he was better, or as good as he was going to get. You couldn't save people, but you could help them up, dust them off, and point them in the right direction. That was good to know. It made fate seem like not such a fact. He still hadn't told his father that it was Suzy he'd run off with. He kept meaning to but he'd get up the nerve, start, then wonder who he was doing it for. Honesty was sometimes cruelty gussied up.

Daryl shut the front door quietly. The black fall sky was pinpricked with stars. It was cold. He zipped up his jacket. A sudden gust of dead leaves blew past him. His father had raked them up today. Once again, he wasn't saying good-bye. In his pack were the green leotards he'd need for money, a book about psychics, and a bag of carrots. Kyle didn't like carrots. Daryl didn't want them to rot.

He stepped onto the road that led to others that led to even more. All the roads in America were connected. You could start at any one and get to any other. Somewhere among the crisscross, Suzy was hiding from God.

■　　■　　■

Melissa thumbed through the Farrah Fawcett notebook she used for jotting down ideas, appointments, errands she had to run. She'd found it at the Goodwill near the storefront she and Veronica were renting. They'd started an AIDS advocacy program with the proceeds from Kevin's painting. Sixty-five thousand dollars, after taxes, had not proved to be a lot of money. Melissa was learning the frustrating art of fund-raising. Without Veronica's know-how from the Rape Crisis Center, her energy, her enthusiasm, Melissa would have knuckled under after the first week. Neil had been right. Veronica was better than everyone, and Melissa could speak as someone who had woken up to her bad breath.

She couldn't help but think about him every day. He was everywhere she turned in her apartment, in the pink Depression glass creamer, in *Anita Bryant's Greatest Hits*, in the twelve versions of the "Messiah," in the autographed glossy of Susan Hayward, in the Lalique figurines, in the leather-bound Woolf. She'd thrown out the world's largest *Blueboy* collection (the older she got, the uglier dicks looked), the leather chaps, the cock rings. She and Veronica had tried out the handcuffs (their sex life had come to that). Veronica, giggling, had allowed herself to be locked to the bedposts. Melissa had been so moved by her girlfriend's trust, that she had burst into tears. These days, she burst a lot. Last night, over a telephone commercial, long distance, the next best thing. She could never forgive that.

"Hello, Melissa," Joan said.

Melissa, absorbed in doodling, hadn't heard her come in. "Hi, Mom."

"So this is it?" she said, looking around.

Melissa looked with her: a metal desk, some wooden chairs, a file cabinet with drawers that stuck, a coffee maker, a bulletin board pinned with a volunteer schedule, announcements, and several Gary Larson cartoons: all of it donated. It had taken them a week to scrub and sweep and spray away the storefront's previous occupant, a hearty colony of mildew.

"I guess it doesn't look like much," Melissa said.

"At least you know what you want to do."

"Want? I don't know about that."

"At least you have something to do."

"It's more like, at least there's something I have to do."

"I don't have anything."

"We can always use volunteers."

"I don't think so, Melissa."

"Too queer for you, huh?"

"Could we please not turn this into a prizefight?"

Melissa was about to retort when she noticed Joan was wearing bedroom slippers. Her heart didn't break, but several thread-sized cracks splintered across it.

"Do your feet hurt? she asked.

"No," Joan said. She glanced down at the accused and said, "Oh. I guess I forgot."

Bobby, the cute college freshman with dimples and a bubble butt, came in. Neil would have loved him.

"Hi, Melis," he said. He shortened everybody's name.

"Hi," she said. "This is my mother."

"You wouldn't catch my mother near a place like this."

Joan crossed her bedroom slippers as if she were trying to

hide them. Bobby went over to the schedule. "Honey," he said, "you know I have class all day Tuesdays."

"I forgot," Melissa said. "Just pencil yourself into another slot."

He unslung the backpack he carried everywhere and dug through.

"I have to go," Joan said.

"Wait," Melissa said.

Bobby had finished writing and was trying to zip his pack back up. It was stuck and after a few more tugs, he gave up. "My birthday is the seventeenth," he said, shaking the unzipped pack at Melissa. "Remember this."

"New clutch for Bobby," she said loudly, scrawling over Farrah Fawcett's face with exaggerated swoops of her arm.

He laughed, making sure the door was shut tightly behind him. The door never wanted to close. You had to make it. Melissa watched him unlock his bike through the large plateglass windows. It was one of those bright white April days.

"He seems nice," Joan said.

"He's a gem," Melissa said.

"Why did you want me to wait?"

"Because someone needs to tell you to get off your ass. Burn the fucking house down and move to Alaska for all I care, but do something. For Christ's sake, you're not dead."

Neil was dead. His darling mother had had him buried by a foaming fundamentalist sixty milligrams of Valium couldn't blot out.

"You're right," Joan said without a stitch of conviction.

"Or you can hang around the house in your robe until you're buried alive."

That Joan felt, like a sliver of glass Melissa had flicked at her heart. She didn't like the idea of spending eternity in her living room. It was drab. She'd constantly be dusting. People barely visited as it was.

Heat whooshed through the vents. It was unseasonably cold. Joan studied her house with an indifference she didn't feel. Kevin was wearing cologne to attract girls, though there were none in the car. The lighter clicked. Joan tamped another cigarette lit. She thought about how often in her life victory had risen from the ashes of destruction. She was capable of violence. Everything seemed wrong. Her daughter was a lesbian, though when you considered the alternative, men, it seemed like a sensible choice. When she saw Brenda, she wondered if she'd made all their childhoods up. Was she to be held responsible for what they'd mutated into? The sheer variety of their adult forms surely argued against her culpability. Daryl had the right idea. Get as far away as possible. Send postcards. Call collect. Keep moving.

Joan guessed they wouldn't see the flames until the place was pretty well incinerated, then smoke began to curl gently from the chimney, conjuring images of hearth and home and happiness and heating. That was all she wanted: proof. She started the engine.

"Where are we going?" Kevin asked.

"You're going to your father's," she said.

"I don't like my father."

"You're not supposed to like your parents."

"I like you."

She pretended to be involved in crossing an intersection.

"I can't take you with me," she said.

Dusk was falling.

"Why not?"

"I don't know where I'm going."

"So?"

"So you have to go to high school, meet girls, smoke in the bathroom."

"I don't smoke."

"Don't start."

A car passed, flashing its headlights. Joan dimmed her brights.

"Let me out here," Kevin said.

"This is nowhere."

"I'm not living with him."

She stopped at a light. She rested her forehead on the steering wheel. When the light changed, she was still sitting. The car behind her beeped. She didn't move. They passed her.

"He gave us the finger," Kevin said.

"You win," she said, straightening up. The light was red again.

"Stop by the bank so I can get my money."

"That won't be necessary."

"We need money."

"No," she said, "Clarissa has an extra bedroom and a fold-out couch. We'll stay with her."

"That's cool."

Sirens approached. Two fire trucks fled past, momentarily dying the inside of the car, Kevin, and Joan red with a flash of emergency light.

"Too late," Joan said.

She took the next exit and floored it when they hit the interstate. She rolled down her window in spite of the cold. There had been a time when she had felt defined. But years tumbled by like fat, blind acrobats. Things changed when you weren't looking. All she knew now was that she was a woman in a car racing the dark. She had a child at her side and a friend to stay with. They were small, homemade dams and seemed shabby against the force of grief, but they would have to do: there was nothing else.